GOING BATTY

A HORROR COMEDY MYSTERY

FREAKY FLORIDA BOOK 5

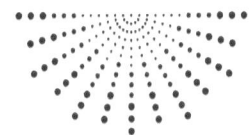

WARD PARKER

MAD MANGROVE MEDIA

CONTENTS

1

VAMPIRE ROMANCE FICTION

"Then the vampire ape-man ravished me on the beach," Gladys read in her New Jersey accent.

Everyone in the room was silent. Missy studied their faces and saw uncomfortable expressions on each.

"The end," Gladys said.

It was the weekly vampire creative writing group at Squid Tower. Missy Mindle, midlife witch and home health nurse for the vampires, moderated. She received a small stipend from the HOA for her efforts, much too small for all the bad prose she had to endure. Folks in retirement often discover writing talent they never knew they had. But usually, they try to develop a talent they didn't have. If they're vampires, they could keep trying for hundreds of years.

"I'm used to hearing your pornography thinly disguised as romance," Sol said, scratching one of his pointy, bat-like ears. "This seems different."

"It's like you're describing a dream," Doris said.

Gladys smiled. "It *was* from a dream. I've been having these recurring dreams about an ancient race of vampire ape-men. They want to enslave all the vampires and supernatural creatures who live in Florida and kill all the humans."

"Sounds more like science fiction to me, except for the ravishing," Bill said. Bill preferred military action stories with lots of guns and explosions.

"The dreams have been haunting me," Gladys said, wiping away a tear. "I wake up in the middle of the day with the sensation that someone was just in my bedroom. There's always a voice in my head saying, 'submit or die.' I figured if I turned my dreams into stories, it would be cathartic."

"Instead, it becomes pornographic," Sol said.

After the session was over, Missy took Gladys aside.

"If you need to talk to someone, I'm always available," Missy said. "I took some psychology classes in nursing school and Acceptance Home Care trained me in counseling for supernaturals. It's healthy to be able to talk to someone and bare your soul. Or whatever it is vampires have."

Gladys touched Missy's arm. "Thank you, honey. I don't know what's come over me. These dreams don't feel natural."

"What do you mean?"

"I don't feel like they're coming from my subconscious. It's like someone else is planting thoughts in my head. That's why it's so disturbing. I feel violated."

The community room emptied of all the other vampires. Missy invited Gladys to sit with her in the folding chairs.

"Have you ever had dreams like these before?" Missy asked.

"Never."

"Have your television or reading habits changed?"

"No. And I'm telling you, it feels like the dreams aren't coming from within me."

What was left unsaid was the question of where they were coming from. In the world of the supernatural, anything was possible. According to her counseling training, vampires dreamed like humans, but being undead, they were especially susceptible to picking up the brain waves or dreams of other undead creatures. Usually, that meant other vampires. In this case, it could mean vampire ape-men. If they even existed.

"It's important that you remember they are only dreams," Missy said. "Even if they're influenced by someone else, they're not real. You're safe in your coffin each morning when you go to sleep."

"I sleep in a bed."

"It doesn't matter. The important fact is that you're safe."

"I wish I could believe you," Gladys said, a haunted look in her ancient eyes.

GLADYS' eyes snapped awake as she lay on her posture-support, memory-foam mattress (she gave up sleeping in coffins decades ago because of back pain). She had gone to sleep right after the creative writing group because of her constant fatigue. It was 3:15 a.m. What had awakened her?

Something was in her bedroom.

She turned on the light. No sign of anyone. There never was anyone in her bedroom, hadn't been for eighty years since her husband passed away of natural causes before she became a vampire. Her human housekeeper was the only creature besides herself that ever set foot in this bedroom. Three times a month on Tuesdays.

Still, she sensed she was not alone.

The sliding glass door to her oceanfront balcony slid open. The blackout curtain clicked as it slid aside, then the vertical blinds clattered.

And in walked a burly man wearing a T-shirt with the logo of a pool-cleaning company. He didn't have much in the way of height but was broad-shouldered, barrel-chested, and primal. He had a broad nose and a low, sloping forehead beneath a peaked hairline of slicked-back hair. His eyes glowed yellow-green under bushy eyebrows.

Gladys was terrified. But the thought of a man in her bedroom was rather appealing. She knew how this would turn out if it followed the typical plot of the romance novels she preferred.

The man smiled. He had big teeth. And even bigger fangs.

A deeper fear spread through Gladys, the kind prey feel when trapped. Ever since she had been turned as a vampire, she had only known the feelings of power and freedom that predators enjoy. Never this sense of helplessness she experienced now. She was a vampire; she did the hunting. She wasn't supposed to be the hunted.

"My name is Thogg," the man said. "I have been watching you for weeks."

"Why me? I'm just a little old vampire from Hackensack. Why are you hunting me?"

"Your stories. They are beautiful."

"My stories? How did you read them? I've never been published anywhere except in the Squid Tower newsletter."

"That's where I read them. But I also hear them in my

dreams. And feel them in my heart. It is finally time. I will have you now."

Gladys involuntarily arched her back, offering her exposed neck. She didn't understand why she did it. She simply had to.

Thogg crossed the bedroom to the side of her bed in a blink of an eye. He loomed over her and bent down, his cold, foul breath washing over her.

The pain of his bite was much worse than what she remembered when she was turned into a vampire so long ago. The slurps and gulps of his feeding were more disgusting than those of the debonair bloodsucker who had turned her.

Was he going to drain her? That was the last thought she had before a blanket of gray covered her mind and she faded away.

MISSY'S CELLPHONE awoke her at noon. She normally kept the hours of her vampire patients and didn't appreciate the real world intruding like this. She fumbled for the phone on her bedside table and accidentally dislodged one of her cats.

The number on the screen was her employer.

"Wha?" she mumbled.

"Missy, this is Maxine from Acceptance Home Care. Our monitoring service notified us that one of your patients sent a distress call."

Missy sat up in bed. "Who?"

"Gladys Finklestein. Apartment nine-oh-eight in Squid Tower."

"Okay, I'll head right over."

Missy began throwing random clothes on. She was a simple

home health nurse who mostly practiced preventive medicine with her vampire, werewolf, and other monster clients. These supernaturals had many self-healing abilities and rarely became ill, but their blood counts and blood pressure still had to be checked. They often had preexisting conditions from before they were turned that she needed to monitor—the typical ailments of seniors—everything from arthritis to hearing loss. Being a vampire made you immortal, but it didn't fix your enlarged prostate.

Her supernatural patients couldn't go to human doctors. Undead vampires could never bluff their way through a medical exam. Unfortunately, they couldn't call an ambulance either. There were companies that provided emergency services for supernaturals, but they only existed in big cities. In Jellyfish Beach, you had to push the button on your monitoring device, talk to an operator, and then depend upon Acceptance Home Health to send a nurse to you.

That would be Missy. And if she couldn't resolve the issue, she would have to call one of the few area doctors who treated supernaturals. You know, the kind who had lost their regular medical licenses.

Missy took a small cooler and her tote bag full of medical supplies, as well as some magick potions and powders, and drove to Squid Tower on the beach. She was rarely here in the daytime. To the typical passerby, Squid Tower was unremarkable among the other residential buildings along this strip of A1A, the ocean road. It was an older, somewhat ugly building compared to the newer, luxury towers. The only thing that made it stand out was the large number of units with hurricane shutters sealing their windows even during the winter tourist season. That and the fact that no residents were ever seen on the grounds during the day. The day gate guard saw her pass and let her through. She parked in the visitor lot and hurried to the elevators.

After she rang Gladys' doorbell, Agnes greeted her. Agnes was the HOA president and informal leader of the vampires. At least ninety years old in body age and with over 1,500 years in existence, the tiny vampire radiated strength and power.

"I let myself in after the service called," Agnes said. "Gladys is weak and barely conscious. She has the wounds of a vampire bite."

"You've got to be kidding," Missy said. "Since when do vampires feed on vampires?"

"Only in times of extreme famine or other desperate situations."

Missy knew that vampire blood was different than human blood. It had additional, unidentifiable antibodies and blood cell counts were lower than in fresh human blood. She wondered how nutritious it would be.

"Well, first things first," Missy said entering Gladys' bedroom. "She needs a transfusion."

Gladys lay on her back in bed, barely conscious, breathing shallowly. Dangerous lines of sunlight slipped in through the vertical blinds.

"Agnes, stay outside the bedroom until I do something about this sunlight. Missy pulled the comforter over Gladys' head and checked the window. She found the blackout curtains and pulled them closed, making the bedroom safely free of daylight.

"All clear," she said.

She pulled a chair up to the bed and wiped the crook of Gladys' arm with an alcohol swab. From her cooler she took a bag of vampire blood, a rare commodity, and set up an IV line.

"Can I help?" Agnes asked.

"Yes, please hold this bag."

Missy then cleaned the wounds on Gladys' neck over her jugular vein. They were large, as if made by the canine teeth of a tiger. She cleaned them with alcohol swabs and irrigated them with saline solution to get rid of any traces of vampire saliva which prevented blood clotting. Next she checked the vital signs. Blood pressure was low, as expected. The pulse rate was six beats per minute, which was good for a vampire.

"I don't know who could have done this," Agnes said.

Missy thought about what Gladys had written of the vampire ape-men. It wasn't her place to divulge her patient's dreams.

As the transfusion kicked in and the wounds were cleaned, the punctures began healing, so quickly, in fact, that Missy could almost see them get smaller in real time. Gladys' eyes fluttered open.

"What happened?" She said in a faint, groggy voice. "Oh no, now I remember."

"Do you know who fed upon you?" Agnes asked.

"No. I didn't recognize him, except from my dreams."

Agnes looked at Missy with a puzzled expression.

"His name was Thogg. He entered my room without being invited," Gladys said. "There was something about him that seemed very old. The oldest vampire I've ever met. Kind of handsome, too, in a crude way, like a ditch-digger. Not really an ape-man like he was in my dreams. And he said he enjoyed my stories."

"How did he read your stories?" Missy asked.

"From our newsletter. I don't know how he got a copy, but

my stories moved him," Gladys said with a sparkle in her eyes. "My words actually moved him."

There wasn't anything else medical that Missy could do, beyond the transfusion and the cleaning of the wounds. She could, however, cast a warding spell to drive off any vampires attempting to enter the condo through the balcony or windows. Assuming they weren't abnormally powerful vampires, that is.

The bag of vampire blood was depleted. She removed the IV line and handed Gladys a second pint from the cooler, this time it was human Type O blood.

"This is for snacking. Please call if you're in any danger," Missy said.

"I should read her stories," Agnes said to Missy when they were safely out of range of Gladys' hearing. Which wasn't until they were in the elevator due to vampires' enhanced auditory abilities.

"No you shouldn't read them," Missy said. "Believe me, you're not missing anything. I think the vampire was manipulating her with his compliments."

"Of course he was. It's what we do with our prey."

"Shouldn't Gladys have known better?"

"Yes. But he found her vulnerable spot. So, on top of your warding spell, I'm activating our neighborhood watch group."

"You mean Bill, Oleg, and the other military wannabes?"

"They're the only vampires who'd enjoy spending their entire night patrolling the property," Agnes said. "And to be fair to Oleg, he did actually serve in the military."

"As a cavalry officer three hundred years ago. It doesn't mean he'd be good at patrolling for vampires."

"Beggars can't be choosers," Agnes said.

The elevator reached Agnes' floor. She thanked Missy and

said goodbye, trudging with her quad cane down the hallway, which was devoid of any natural light, to her condo.

IT WAS SHORTLY before midnight when Missy received the call from Agnes. Gladys never showed up for dinner when the Blood Bus arrived hours earlier, as was her normal routine. Someone went to her condo to check on her. No one answered the door.

Gladys was missing, leaving the door from her bedroom to the balcony wide open.

"Can your magick help us find her?" Agnes asked.

"I'll do what I can," Missy said.

2

FLATTERY WILL GET
YOU EVERYWHERE

W hy was the vampire staring at him—the one with the glowing red eyes standing in the darkness next to that palm tree?

This kind of thing had been a common cause of anxiety for Bernie Burdine when he was first hired as the gate guard on the night shift at Squid Tower. At the time, he was an ordinary human with extraordinarily bad career moves. He didn't even know vampires existed, let alone inhabited the entire high-rise condo building. Once he realized whose security he was guarding, he was regularly freaked out whenever they looked at him like he was dinner. Mr. Schwartz did that all the time.

Once Bernie was turned into a vampire himself, it was no longer a problem. So why was this one stalking him tonight? Had he accidentally clipped this guy's trunk with the gate arm? Those things happen. No big deal. The HOA will pay for it.

Those red eyes still stared at him like the channel marker lights at the ocean inlet. Bernie returned his attention to his tablet and the lyrics he was trying to write. Bernie's true calling was not to be a vampire gate guard. No, it was to be a musician-songwriter. He'd struggled for a lifetime to achieve that. Now, the best he could do was play keyboard two nights a week at Shell Shuckers at the beach. It was mostly the typical beach-bar stuff like Jimmy Buffett, but sometimes he slipped his own songs in.

Whoa, the burning eyes were right outside the gatehouse door. Bernie opened the door a crack.

"Can I help you, sir?"

"I wanted to compliment you on your beautiful music," the vampire said in a deep, commanding voice. He was a stocky guy with bulging muscles. Younger than all the geezer vampires that lived here.

"I wasn't playing any music," Bernie said.

"But many nights you do. Beautiful, heartbreaking songs with such a resonant voice. You wrote them, am I correct?"

"Yes, I did." Bernie couldn't help but smile. "You liked them?"

"I did."

Bernie reached into his backpack and handed the vampire a CD.

"For you, it's free. On the label is my website where you can download my other songs."

"You are very kind," the vampire said. "You and I have more in common than music."

"Are you from Long Island?"

"I'm originally from France. But I can sense we have a similar heritage."

"I'm Jewish," Bernie said. "Grandparents were from Poland. And I have a little Italian mixed in. That's where I get my spiciness."

"I mean a heritage that comes from long before nation-states."

Bernie got that sinking feeling that this guy was a weirdo. Too bad, because he had good taste in music.

"Who is your leader?" the vampire asked.

"You don't know who the president of the United States is?"

"Who is your vampire leader?"

"Agnes Geberich is our HOA president. She's basically our community mother."

"You need a stronger leader. A leader who can protect you."

"Why?" Bernie asked. What was this guy's deal?

"I will explain at another time. For now, I will leave you with this."

The vampire fixed him with his eyes, which began glowing red again. Bernie's brain got all foggy.

This guy's mesmerizing me? he thought. A vampire can't mesmerize another vampire.

But he was wrong. Against his will, he pushed the door open the rest of the way and unbuttoned the collar of his uniform shirt. He tilted his head, offering his exposed neck to the vampire. He didn't mean to. Yes, he wanted to.

The light in the gatehouse went out.

The sharp pain as the abnormally large fangs punctured his skin was intense. An image of a saber-tooth tiger flitted through his foggy brain.

His heart fluttered weakly. Everything turned gray. And he was lowered into his chair, his head resting on the desk.

Thirty minutes later, an elderly vampire couple pulled up in the residents lane of the gate after shopping for sale items at the MegaMart. The gate didn't open. The husband tapped the horn.

The gate remained shut. The gate guard appeared to be asleep at his desk.

The horn blared through the night, disturbing everyone until two vampire pickleball players left the court to find out what all the fuss was.

THIS TIME, when Missy received the call from her employer, she was already at Squid Tower visiting a patient. And, since there was a rogue vampire on the loose, she'd had the foresight to bring her cooler of blood in case she needed to do another transfusion. It sounded like she did.

Bernie was passed out in the gatehouse with his face resting on the desk. A trickle of drool ran down his chin, just like all the times Missy had found him asleep on the job when he was human. Vampires didn't drool much because they produced saliva only when they fed. Leave it to Bernie to be the exception.

"Nothing to see here," Missy said to the small crowd gathered around the booth.

"I'm the one who called the home care company," said a New-York-accented woman in tennis whites. "Harold was blaring his horn like he was stuck in traffic outside the Holland Tunnel."

"How long was I supposed to wait?" Harold said, leaning against his car, which was still behind the gate. "Until the sun comes up and we burn to a crisp in our front seat?"

Schwartz, who had also been playing pickleball, shoved his way through the milling seniors into the gatehouse.

"Try not to be so helpless," he said. "The button for the gate arm is right here below the window. With a moron like Burdine on duty, I had to let myself in all the time while he was in the bathroom. That wasn't a problem once he became a vampire. But really, Harold. If you can't figure out how to let yourself in, maybe you should fry to a crisp."

The gate arm went up. Harold jumped in his car and drove through. Just before he cleared the gate, the arm dropped and clipped the tail end of Harold's car.

"Hey!" he yelled out his window.

"This thing really drops fast," Schwartz said. "Maybe Burdine isn't as much of an idiot as I thought . . . No, he is."

"Folks, he needs medical assistance," Missy said. "Will you clear the area and let me do my job, please?"

"Whoever heard of a vampire preying on another vampire?" the pickleball woman asked.

"Only in the Old Country, during times of great famine," Schwartz said.

Missy tried to ignore the chatter. She had squeezed into the tiny gatehouse and was administering an IV line to pump vampire blood into Bernie.

"Did anyone see the vampire who did this?" Agnes asked. She had joined the crowd.

"I saw a stocky individual running away from the booth as we were pulling up," said Harold's wife. "Couldn't make out his face, though. And then, he just disappeared."

Agnes tapped furiously on her phone and not long afterwards, Bill strolled up. He had an assault rifle strapped to his side, barrel pointing downward.

"What kind of scout are you?" Agnes asked. "Our gate guard was attacked on your watch."

"A diversionary tactic misled me," Bill said, offended. "I think there are more than one of them on the property."

"What happened?"

"I saw an individual on the dune crossover. I thought it may have been a human trespassing from the beach. When I approached him, he disappeared right in front of my eyes. Then a bat flew by overhead. It was as if," he struggled for words, "it was like the man turned into a bat."

"Are you saying he turned into a bat like in a bad vampire movie?" Schwartz asked.

"That was my observation," Bill replied.

"But vampires don't really turn into bats," Agnes said. "And I should know. I've been around a very long time."

"I volunteered to provide security. I'm just telling you what I saw."

"I think that's what happened to the vampire who fed on the gate guard," Harold's wife said. "I swear I saw a bat after the vampire disappeared."

"Your imaginations have gotten the best of you," Agnes said.

"I wouldn't be so sure," Missy said as she tended to Bernie. In her experience, the supernatural always got weirder than she could imagine.

MISSY'S SEARCH for Gladys began with tracer spells, which were crude and relatively simple magick. After Agnes let her into Gladys' condo, Missy knelt on the floor of the living room within a magick circle drawn with chalk, a five-pointed pentagram within it. Missy concentrated on a photo of Gladys found on a side table that depicted her head-to-toe. She summoned energies from the earth and from within her, then recited a short incantation.

She released the tracers: thousands of tiny micro-dots of energy that flew off like insects. The swarm dispersed over the landscape to the north, south and west. No sense sending them east over the ocean.

No, on second thought, Missy directed some of the swarm east as well, on the slimmest of chances her vampire kidnapper took her on a boat. Who knows, maybe they booked her on a cruise ship to the Caribbean.

If the tracer spells found anyone who matched the image in Missy's mind, they would ping her. Then she could perform a more complicated locating spell to pinpoint where Gladys was.

She sensed the tracers spreading out over Jellyfish Beach. And they were silent. They traveled farther, into neighboring cities to the north and south and unincorporated areas to the west.

Still nothing.

If Gladys had been outside hunting with her vampire captor, the tracers would have found her easily. Even if she were inside, in a lighted room, the tracers could spot her. But if she were locked away in a dark room with no windows, then no dice.

Several minutes later, it appeared that no dice was the result. Missy would have to use another search spell. Fortunately, she was in Gladys' condo and had access to her personal belongings.

She broke the magic circle and wandered the condo. Gladys' purse was nowhere to be found. You'd think the mesmerized victim of a vampire wouldn't grab her purse before being spirited away, but you didn't know senior vampires. A long human lifetime of having your purse with you always, plus a hundred years of doing so as a vampire, made the habit permanently ingrained. Plus, the purse held lipstick and credit cards. No modern vampire would leave those behind.

But she did leave behind her cellphone. It lay on the kitchen counter. Like many seniors, Gladys was obviously not inseparable from it, but it would nevertheless hold enough of her spirit essence to be useful.

First, Missy tried to unlock the phone, a very non-magickal way to investigate Gladys' contacts. But again, no luck.

She carried the phone to the magick circle and knelt inside it again. She would attempt a new spell that she had learned from the powerful grimoire she had inherited from her late father. In an addendum of the book were several spells inscribed by the Spanish sorcerer Don Mateo of Grenada, who had fled to the New World to escape the Inquisition. His ghost had been Missy's house guest ever since she found the book.

The spell had no name, but allowed the magician to isolate and amplify a creature's spiritual energy. Then, by infusing it with magick, that spiritual energy would be compelled to rejoin its counterpart—larger deposits of the identical energy. In other words, the spirit energy from Gladys' phone would seek to rejoin its source, the energy residing in Gladys herself. It was a powerful attraction, like a magnet to the opposite pole of another magnet.

It was a more difficult spell, and Missy had to amass much more power than she needed for the tracer spells. She pulled it from the four elements of earth, air, fire (from a candle she lit), and water. Only steps away was the entire Atlantic Ocean, and she drank from its abundant energy.

To help things along, she grasped the power charm she

always carried in her pocket. It was like a catalyst to activate all the energies.

Finally, she recited the words of the spell. She had written them on an index card because she hadn't had time to memorize them. They were in Don Mateo's Renaissance-era Spanish, but the English translation was:

The spark of life within your breast,
The essence of your soul,
Is in this object you loved best:
I seek to make you whole.
Come forth, reveal yourself to me,
And seek the larger part of thee.

The power surged through Missy, from her solar plexus through her heart and out of her fingertips. And suddenly, an orb of light floated in the air before her. It was the embodiment of Gladys' spirit essence harvested from her phone.

"Find her," Missy whispered.

The orb disappeared. Missy waited. And waited. And just as she was about to give up, a vivid image filled her head.

It was a giant yacht moored in a marina behind luxury homes on the Intracoastal Waterway. An almost disgustingly large yacht that probably cost more than the GDP of several countries. The image was so vivid, Missy felt as if she were standing on the dock beside it. The yacht's lights were off, and no one was visible. But she sensed creatures inside. Several vampires. Ancient vampires. Somehow, she could sense their immense ages, much older even than 1,500-year-old Agnes. They were a completely different sort of vampire.

And among them was Gladys. Missy was certain, because her brain pulsed with a painful, high-pitched whine as the orb of Gladys' spirit essence struggled to join with Gladys while it was actually inside Missy's head.

But something more disturbing than the whine grabbed her attention. She felt the prickling in her scalp of being watched. She wasn't here in body, but something inside the yacht sensed her magickal presence.

She felt naked and exposed. Hatred and hunger pressed into her like prying hands, violating her. She gasped in revulsion.

And then she was gone. Now she was lying on Gladys' tile floor within the magick circle once more. The candle had gone out and a wisp of smoke dissipated above it. She shivered and struggled to find the strength to sit up. The spell had taken a lot out of her.

She hadn't seen the name of the yacht on its hull and didn't recognize where it was docked, but a massive boat like that shouldn't be hard to find.

But then what? How could Missy and the vampires of Squid Tower rescue Gladys? Missy's magick couldn't do everything on its own. The vampires needed a plan.

3

NEANDERTHAL-ISH

Generally speaking, vampires aren't into pets. Humans find their beloved pets' lives to be too short, so imagine if you were a vampire with an eternal lifespan. Bonding with creatures whose lives were so fleeting would be unbearable.

But not for Ethel Murray. After she lost her husband in the Spanish-American War, she depended on pets for companionship, as she didn't have children and never remarried. She always had at least one dog—she was partial to yellow labs—and a couple of cats. When she was turned during the Eisenhower administration, she couldn't give up her pets, even though she'd gone through so many over the decades.

She always walked her lab, Lonnie, the moment the last light from the sunset was gone. It wasn't easy for Lonnie to adjust to her nocturnal schedule (unlike the cats who had no problem with it), but Lonnie managed.

Straining at his leash. he pulled Ethel through the swale

between the parking lot and the bike path along the beach road. Ethel was careful to clean up after him, since the vampires were so obsessed with cleanliness. They went on a rampage every time the werewolves next door left poop on the Squid Towers property, whether it be from their dogs or, as some vampires suspected, from the werewolves themselves.

So, clutching her little plastic bag of dog turds, Ethel walked with Lonnie back toward her condo through the entrance gate of Squid Tower.

That was where she saw the abduction.

A bat flittered by, passing right over her. It hovered outside the window of the gatehouse, bumping against the glass like a giant, black moth.

Then, before her eyes, it transformed into a man, who dropped to the ground, landing lightly on his feet. It was a muscular, stocky man, not tall, wearing dark clothing. He entered the gatehouse without knocking.

What was this creature? She knew the lore about vampires turning into bats was nonsense. She couldn't do it and never heard of a vampire who could. Was this some kind of shifter she'd never heard about?

The shifter, or whatever he was, backed out of the gatehouse. The gate guard, that moron Bernie, followed him. Bernie was moving zombie-like, as if he had been mesmerized. Vampires weren't supposed to be able to be mesmerized.

Ethel stopped in her tracks, too frightened to move. Lonnie whimpered and hid behind her legs. Her fangs extended as the threat of violence grew. Ethel had never had to fight a supernatural creature before. Ethel had always had her doubts about Bernie, anyway, since a Caribbean vampire had turned him. As she would whisper to her bridge partners, his maker was not a first-world vampire.

Bernie followed the dark-clad shifter down the driveway to the edge of A1A. A white van pulled up, and the shifter pushed Bernie inside, climbing in after him. The van sped away.

Ethel realized she'd just witnessed an abduction. Since vampires can't call 911, she did the next best thing. She called Agnes.

AFTER AGNES TEXTED HER, Missy showed up at the property-management office on the first floor. Agnes and Henrietta played footage from the security cameras over and over. A stocky man in dark clothes entered the guardhouse and then exited it with Bernie in tow. Bernie followed him as if he were mesmerized. Then they got in a white van on A1A, which drove away.

"Two taken from us," Agnes said. "I believe it's safe to assume that another vampire community is trying to take us over."

"Why would they do that?" Missy asked.

"There's a vampire mafia of sorts in the Miami area that extorts vampire communities to use mob-affiliated services like blood delivery and trash pickup. Sometimes they just demand cash."

Henrietta rolled her motorized scooter backwards away from the video monitors.

"I don't know," she said. "Don't they first make you an offer you can't refuse, before they kidnap your vampires?"

"True," Agnes said.

"Did you see this angle?" Missy pointed to one of the video monitors. "Can you rewind this? Watch carefully. It happens really fast."

Henrietta rolled back to the monitors and navigated a computer mouse. She'd been turned fairly recently and knew technology much better than the 1,500-year-old Agnes. Or Missy, too, she was ashamed to admit.

Henrietta slowed down the frame rate and the pixilated video showed something fluttering against the window of the guardhouse.

"That's a bat," Missy said. When a man suddenly appeared, she said, "There wasn't an edit in the video. That guy transformed from the bat."

"That's impossible," Henrietta said.

Agnes explained that Ethel believed the man was some kind of shifter.

"But why a bat?" Missy asked. "That's vampire lore. Why not fly around as an owl? They can see great in the dark."

"You need to locate that yacht you saw in your spell," Agnes said to Missy. "We have to begin fighting back."

"WHY WERE YOU SPYING ON US?"

Missy's head shot up from her book, her heart pounding. A man was standing in her living room. A vampire, actually, Missy could tell immediately. He matched the description Gladys gave of the vampire that attacked her.

"I wasn't."

"You were spying on us in our yacht," he said in an unidentifiable European accent. "Using magic to do so."

"I was searching for someone who has gone missing."

"Why are you, a human, working with the vampires?"

"I'm a nurse," Missy said. "I give them healthcare."

"I've been around for a hundred and ten thousand years and have never needed healthcare from a human."

"Wait, how many years did you say?" Missy asked.

"A hundred and ten thousand. Give or take a few thousand."

"I've never heard of a vampire that old."

"You have now."

"Why have you abducted our vampires?"

"*Your* vampires?"

"The vampires from Squid Tower," Missy said. "Why? What have they done to you?"

"The one called Gladys. I enjoy her romantic stories."

"How did you get your hands on her stories?"

"She prints them out and leaves them everywhere in that building."

"What about Bernie? Why did you take him?"

"Bernie? Who is this Bernie?"

"The gate guard. Skinny guy, features kind of Neanderthal-like."

The vampire exploded in rage. Too late, Missy realized he kind of looked like a Neanderthal, too.

"No offense," she said, ineffectually.

Missy clutched the amulet she wore around her neck to ward off vampires. In theory, she wasn't supposed to need it. The vampires at Squid Tower were forbidden to attack her, but with their predatory instincts being so strong, it was a good idea to wear the amulet just in case.

She had the feeling the amulet might not be strong enough

to fend off this particular vampire. There was a lot of power in this bloodsucker.

"You know nothing about Neanderthals," the vampire said angrily. "You modern humans use the name disparagingly like we were a bunch of stupid cavemen."

"Didn't you live in caves?"

"It was an ice age. Where else would we live? A wooden hut with a thatched roof?"

"I had no idea vampires existed that long ago," Missy said.

"Vampires have been around longer than modern humans. And don't say Neanderthals weren't modern. We were just as good as the Cro-Magnons. Only not as good at genocide."

Missy decided it was best to change the subject. She was also silently conjuring a protection spell in case he attacked.

"What is your name?" Missy asked.

"I am Thogg, the leader of my clan."

"I'm Missy. Pleased to meet you."

"I know who you are, witch. I am warning you to stay out of our business."

"But what do you want? Why did you abduct Gladys and Bernie?"

"I am growing our clan. I will rule all the vampires in that pitiful community. They're all weak and need a powerful leader. Soon, all of Florida will be under my rule."

"Leave them alone," Missy said. "They're just a bunch of retirees who want to enjoy their Golden Years for eternity."

"They will submit to me or they will die."

"I'll pass along your message."

He glowered at her beneath a pronounced brow ridge over his eyes.

"I'm not stupid," he said. "You don't want them to submit to me."

Missy raised her hands.

"I don't want to be in the middle of this."

"Too late," Thogg said as another vampire entered the room. He looked similar to Thogg, which is to say Neanderthal-ish. But he was a little taller, with lighter hair and a beard. His expression conveyed that he didn't come to make small talk.

Thogg nodded in Missy's direction. His henchman drew a pistol.

"No," Thogg said. "We will drain her. To send a message."

They lunged at her faster than her eye could register. They both hit the bubble of her protection spell simultaneously, almost breaking it. The force of their impact rocked Missy's chair backwards.

"Oh, please," Thogg said. "I've beaten much more powerful witches than you. Back in the Stone Age, there were some scary-powerful shamans."

She didn't doubt him. As civilization and science advanced in the world, magic grew weaker. But Missy knew she needed something stronger to beat these guys. The problem was, her ethos was to do no harm. That really cut down on her ability to kill things.

They hit the bubble again from different angles, pushing deeper into it than before. The protection spell would not stop them much longer.

Her thoughts went to the Red Dragon talisman. It should give her the power to compel the vampires to leave her home. Unfortunately, it was in her bedroom.

The two vampires stopped and stared at her with their arms folded.

"The spell is draining all your strength," Thogg said.

Missy knew he was trying to mesmerize her. She conjured a quick spell to boost her ability to concentrate and ignore Thogg's influence.

Then, desperate to get to her bedroom, she attempted a double-whammy of a spell. It was difficult to pull off in any circumstance, let alone having two vampires about to leap on you.

She checked to make sure the protection spell was holding, then conjured a body double of herself. It was merely an optical illusion, basically making a magick version of a video loop of her sitting in the chair as she was now. Then she cloaked herself with invisibility and slipped out of the protective bubble while Thogg continued to talk to the apparition of her in the chair. She went to her dresser and groped around in the top drawer beneath her underwear until she found the talisman, the metal carving of a dragon small enough to fit in her palm. There were only a few others like it in the world, one of which had been owned by Moses and King Solomon.

The moment she grasped it her body hummed with power.

"Okay, I admit, you tricked me." Thogg was standing in the doorway. "But here you are, outside your silly protection bubble. I can't see you, but I can smell you. I didn't think you'd make it this easy for me."

Missy thrust her fist that held the amulet toward the vampire.

"By the power of the Red Dragon, I command you to leave my house!" she shouted in a voice she hoped was scary.

Thogg just stood there smiling. His henchman came up behind him.

"Begone from my home now, I command you!"

It still didn't work. Did she forget a step?

"What exactly are you trying to do?" the Neanderthal vampire asked her.

"The Red Dragon is supposed to force living souls to obey me."

"Well, there's your problem. We're not living. And, just speaking for myself, not Fred here, but I don't have much of a soul. Sorry."

Okay, I'm doomed, Missy thought.

Then she remembered the Red Dragon greatly amplified her natural power of telekinesis. In other words, she could move stuff with her mind.

She sent her dresser flying out the bedroom door, hitting both Thogg and Fred. It knocked them out of the hallway and into the far wall of the living room, where the dresser exploded into dozens of splintered pieces.

"That was an antique," Missy said sadly.

Thogg got to his feet among the wreckage. He had a pink pair of panties on his head.

"That was more impressive than your other tricks," Thogg said.

Fred got to his feet a little more slowly than his boss had. He had a head wound on his temple that quickly healed, vampire-style. He and his boss moved toward Missy's scent.

She sat down in her chair on top of the apparition of herself. She quickly cast a spell that masked her scent and a second one that imitated it which she attached to the apparition. Fooling human senses were easy with simple magick like this. Vampire senses were a different story.

Then, still cloaked in invisibility, she attempted her gambit. She sent the apparition of herself across the room toward the laundry room and its door to the garage. The apparition was a crude facsimile of herself running, but it caught Fred's eye and he instinctively shot after it. His instinct took over the way a cat is drawn to sudden movement. The sound of the door to the garage opening prompted her to make the apparition dart among the junk in the garage to draw Fred out there.

Thogg, on the other hand, remained where he was. His nostrils flared as he drank in the air. Missy's scent trailed her apparition, but it also lingered in the chair where she sat invisibly despite her attempt to mask it. It was probably old, residual scents she'd left in the chair from before.

Thogg moved closer to her, his head swinging back and forth between the chair and the laundry room. When a clatter came from the garage, he hesitantly moved in that direction.

As soon as he left the room, Missy charged toward the kitchen and unlocked the deadbolt on the back door. Her hands were shaking. She opened the door and stepped out.

To find Thogg and Fred standing in her moonlit backyard. Thogg smiled at her.

She jumped back inside and slammed the door. She didn't know what to do now. She ran back to the living room toward the front door.

Thogg and Fred came inside, Thogg blocking the front door.

Her heart was pounding. She was out of ideas, probably because her brain was fried from panic and adrenaline. As her invisibility wore off, she cast another protection spell. It was the only thing she could think to do. All it would do is buy her some time before the inevitable bloody end of her.

Thogg nodded toward Fred. His henchman walked across

the wooden shards of her dresser until he reached the bubble. He pressed his hand against it and smiled.

"I've been giving it some thought," Thogg said from his spot by the front door, "and I believe I know a way to defeat your spell."

He uttered something in an incomprehensible language to Fred, who smiled and flattened his hand, pushing it into the bubble with his eyes closed.

Missy recoiled with fear. She had the urge to lash out any way she could.

Her destroyed dresser caught her eye. She grasped the Red Dragon talisman in her pocket and felt the jolt of power. And then she used her telekinesis.

A three-foot-long shard of wood with a splintered end launched from the floor and impaled Fred in the back. The pointy end burst through the front of his shirt.

Blood poured from the wound for only a second before he disintegrated in a cloud of dust that littered her floor.

She'd seen vampires killed before. They shriveled and eventually ended up as dust and nasty flakiness, but it took some time. She'd never seen a vampire disintegrate this quickly. It must have something to do with his unusually advanced age.

She turned her attention to Thogg, but he was already slipping out through the front door.

She stood in the middle of her living room panting, willing her heart to slow down. When her two gray tabbies casually waddled into the room from the bedroom, she realized she must truly be safe.

For now.

4
110,000 YEARS YOUNG

"**I** love your outfit," the male voice said from the shadows. Henrietta knew he was a vampire.

She didn't buy the compliment for one moment. She was a relatively young vampire in total age, but she had a lot of power at Squid Tower. She was the HOA board's secretary, not elected to the body but involved in all the day-to-day work. She also held a paid position as the nighttime property manager for the community. A human worked in the office during the day, oblivious to the sleeping vampires in the building, to deal with contractors and deliveries from the outside world. At night, when all the vampires were awake, Henrietta was on duty to deal with their requests and complaints. The latter always outnumbered the former ten to one.

Perhaps Henrietta's most important role was as Agnes' eyes and ears. In other words, Henrietta was the community busy-body, knowing all the dirt, gossip, and intrigue.

She understood when the male vampire complimented her

on her outfit that she should ignore what he said. The vampire, who had attacked the two missing residents, had used the same technique of flattery.

"Do you live here?" Henrietta asked the vampire who stood blocking her scooter's progress on the concrete pathway near the pool.

"I am a visitor," the male vampire answered. He vaguely matched the appearance of the vampire she'd seen on the security footage. Something about him looked like a caveman.

"Did you sign in at the front gate?"

"Yes," he said. She knew he was lying.

"You can't just fly in here. You have to sign in first."

"I admire your discipline," he said. "You must be why this property feels so safe. And it's meticulously maintained."

In truth, Henrietta rode the day manager hard to make sure the landscaping company did a good job. But she reminded herself not to feel flattered.

She was, however, growing frightened. She refused to act like it, though. She rolled her scooter closer to the vampire.

"Pardon me, but I have to pass through," she said.

"Wouldn't you rather stay and chat with me on this lovely night?"

He was trying to mesmerize her. Henrietta believed she was too hard-headed to be mesmerized.

"Thank you, but no," she said. "I have an appointment."

The vampire smiled. Then moved closer to her, still blocking her path.

She cranked the scooter to full speed and barreled right at him. He moved aside at the last moment, but the scooter rocked as it ran over his foot. She didn't dare stop now.

But now he was in front of her again. So she kept going,

missing his foot this time. Sure enough, he popped up in front of her again.

Vampires can move lightning-fast, even senior vampires to some degree. However, Henrietta suffered from rheumatoid arthritis in her knees and hips, a condition she'd had before she was turned. The supernatural self-healing powers of vampires didn't do squat for her health conditions she had before she became one. So Henrietta could only move as fast as her scooter.

"I wish you'd stop a moment so we could talk," the younger vampire said as Henrietta tried to go around him again.

It was ironic, she thought. She was much younger than him in body, but she sensed that his true age was ancient. Maybe it was the world-weary look in his eyes.

She jerked the handlebars and turned the scooter right at him. The world-weary look turned into fear. She chased him, briefly enjoying the spectacle of a disabled old lady chasing a powerful young vampire. But suddenly he leaped high into the air.

And landed on her scooter, sitting facing her on her handlebars. He was uncomfortably close to her. She stopped suddenly, hoping it would throw him off. It didn't.

"You're a strong woman," he said. "You deserve a strong leader."

"Agnes is a strong leader. And smart, too."

"Are you saying I'm stupid?" the vampire asked, his eyes narrowing in anger. "That's a stereotype. I'm just as smart as anyone."

Henrietta began rolling again. She turned off the path onto the lawn. The ride was bumpy, but the vampire held on. His expression softened and he gazed at her longingly, trying to mesmerize her.

"You are, perhaps, the smartest one of all," he said, right before getting knocked off the scooter by the low-hanging limb of a gumbo limbo tree.

Henrietta twisted the throttle and headed for the nearest pathway to make her escape. But the scooter wasn't fast enough. The full weight of the male vampire landed on her back and the scooter tipped sideways, dumping both of them on the grass. The vampire lay on top of her and whispered in her ear.

"I'm not stupid."

Then he sank his fangs into the side of her neck.

AFTER HER ADRENALINE FADED AWAY, Missy felt nauseous. And then the guilt poured through her like a wave.

She took an oath in nursing school to do no harm. And now she just killed a vampire. Or maybe the correct terminology was, "terminated its undead existence."

Either way, she did harm. Big harm. She couldn't excuse it away by saying she killed a monster. All her patients were monsters.

She could say, truthfully, that she destroyed the vampire in self-defense. Although, there might have been some way that magick could have ended the threat. But it didn't. And she didn't know any magick that could.

She tried to push her guilt aside and concentrate on helping the community at Squid Tower, her second family. She called Agnes.

"Agnes, I just terminated Thogg's henchman. They came to my house to kill me. And you should know Thogg wants to take over Squid Tower."

A pause. "I figured as much. He's taken Henrietta, too. The board is about to have an emergency meeting. You're welcome to attend."

Henrietta was taken. Agnes' closest friend. This was bad.

Missy said she'd be right there.

THE MEETING HAD ALREADY BEGUN when Missy arrived at the community room off the lobby in Squid Tower. At one end of the large space was a table where the five board members sat facing an empty room. For public meetings, there would be rows of folding chairs for the residents, but this was a board-only affair. The exceptions were Missy and the other non-board member, the HOA's attorney, a werewolf named Paul Leclerc. (Vampire lawyers are rare, except for those who only work in night court.)

"My special ops team could launch an assault as soon as we find out where they are," said Bill.

"As long as you remember your 'special ops team' is just a bunch of pretend soldiers with lots of guns," Agnes said.

"We can hold our own."

"How are guns going to help you against vampires, especially powerful ones like these?" Kim asked.

"We have to kill their human guards first before we get in range to use our stakes."

"Who says they have human guards?" Schwartz asked. "Are you talking about some movie you saw?"

"These vampires are really powerful," Missy said. Everyone looked over, noticing her for the first time. "But a stake in the heart will work. I can attest to that. And I think it might be better to send humans in during the day."

"In *where?*" Schwartz asked.

"My magick showed me they're in an enormous yacht moored somewhere along the Intracoastal Waterway. If someone could take me in a boat, I could search for it."

"I have a boat," the werewolf lawyer said.

"Paul, if you find the yacht, do you know where to get some humans who could break into it and rescue our friends?" Agnes asked.

"I think so. They would be rather unsavory characters, but who cares?"

"But they're not as deadly as my vampire crew," Bill said.

"Bill, will you knock it off with the macho posturing," Agnes said. "You can only attack at night, which means you'd have to fight who knows how many vampires, *plus* the humans. Paul can go in when the vampires are sleeping."

"You'll need a lot of firepower to take out the human guards," Bill said. "That's what we have."

"There might not be any human guards," Paul replied.

"I wish there was a way to resolve this without violence," Gloria said.

"There *is* a way to resolve this peacefully. You can all swear your allegiance to me."

Missy recognized the voice instantly. She turned around and there at the door was Thogg. He was brazen to show up like this. He strode into the room and up to the table where the board sat.

Bill lifted the bottom of his Hawaiian shirt to reveal a

handgun tucked in his shorts against his skinny body. Thogg smirked.

"Good evening, my young vampire friends."

"Who are you calling young?" Schwartz said.

"I may be thirty-three in body age, but I'm actually one hundred and ten thousand years old," Thogg said.

"You must have a lot of loyalty points on your credit cards by now," Gloria said.

"I lived during a hard, brutal time for hominids. And after I was turned, I've been through wars, famines, plagues, extinctions, and suffering you could never imagine. I've battled supernatural creatures that died out so long ago they don't even exist in human legends. I've seen and done it all. There is no one stronger than I and no one more suited than I to be your leader."

"This sounds like a campaign speech," Schwartz said. "The HOA elections aren't until next March."

Thogg laughed. "I don't care about your stupid HOA. I will be the leader of not just your community, but of all the vampires in Florida. And eventually of all of this continent."

"Well, I wouldn't vote for you," Bill said.

"You do not vote for me!" Thogg shouted. "You submit to me peacefully, or you submit under the sword."

"What kind of sword?" Bill asked. "I'm a bit of a collector myself.

Thogg let his frustration show. He didn't understand the only thing that frightened these vampires was the threat of paying a special assessment for building repairs.

"We want our friends back," Agnes said.

"Your friends are my slaves now," Thogg said. "But they are

also hostages. If your people don't offer fealty to me, I will stake them."

Gasps came from the board members.

"How dare you come here uninvited and threaten us!" Agnes said.

"The legend that vampires must be invited before entering doesn't apply to me."

"I meant seeking an invitation as a common courtesy before you stormed in here."

"I'm not stupid, you know," Thogg said, crossing his arms.

"I didn't say you were."

"But what about the bats?" Bill asked.

Everyone looked at him with befuddlement.

"The legend of vampires turning into bats. I thought that was bunk, but then you show up flying around like a fruit bat."

"Not a fruit bat, a *vampire* bat!" Thogg said. "My people lived in caves for tens of thousands of years. Inhaling all that bat guano. It's not surprising that when I was turned, I found I had this handy ability."

"Do you get rabies shots?" Kim asked.

"Enough of this nonsense! You people don't understand the gravity of this situation. I could kill you all right now."

Schwartz glanced at his watch. "I have a pickleball match in thirty minutes."

"You," Thogg pointed to Agnes, "as their leader, you will fight me in hand-to-hand combat."

"No, I will not." Agnes gave him a poisonous smile.

Thogg picked up the table, revealing five pairs of skinny senior legs in shorts, and threw it across the room where it smashed into the large-screen TV. The television's screen shattered. The male board members jumped to their feet in outrage. Breaking a TV was beyond the pale.

"You people are so wrapped up in your petty, small existence you don't understand that vampires can die as easily as mortal creatures. You can't appreciate the greatness I will bring to vampires as we conquer humans and rule the world."

No one answered. They were too upset about the TV.

"I give you two sunsets to make your decision. Submit to me or die."

Thogg turned into a bat, narrowly missed getting chopped by the ceiling fan, and flew out of the room.

"What a rude gentleman," Kim said.

Agnes shook her head. "We need to take him seriously. He has three of our people. Paul, please take Missy for a boat ride when the sun rises and try to find that yacht."

As Missy, Paul, and the board members left the community room, they came upon agitated residents milling about in the lobby and in the parking lot.

"The blood bus isn't here," Agnes said.

Sure enough, there was so sign of the red bus that took blood donations at public places around town and then brought them here to serve the vampires unwilling or unable to hunt for their meals. Normally at this time of the evening there would be a line of residents at the bus like humans in front of a food truck.

Some residents, when they saw Agnes, came over to complain. And complain they did:

"For crying out loud, where's the bus?"

"It's an hour late."

"We received no notice at all."

"I paid good money for my meal plan."

"This is inexcusable."

"My Marty always gets cranky when his dinner is late."

"We should fire these losers and find another supplier."

Agnes gave vague assurances that the problem would be corrected. But then she corralled the board members and moved them out of earshot of the others.

"This is serious. We need to find out what Thogg did to the bus. And we have to be ready to fight. The war has begun."

HENRIETTA WAS the only one who had the Blood Bus company phone number memorized, so Missy helped Agnes dig through the paperwork chaos on Henrietta's desk in the management office. Needless to say, the number was not listed publicly.

"We're supposed to have a master list of all our vendors and contractors," Agnes said.

Missy wished she knew a spell to organize the piles of papers and folders. Instead, she got lucky. There was a stack of fresh invoices near the top of the pile and one was from the blood company with its phone number below their logo.

Agnes called it with her phone's speaker on.

"This is Agnes Geberich at Squid Tower. Where's our blood?"

"You've got the nerve to use a tone with me?" an angry male voice said. "Your blood is on our bus, which happens to be in police custody. You know why?"

This didn't sound good.

"Because the bus was found parked on the shoulder of A1A

with two of my employees inside without their heads, that's why. So I've got the cops calling me, two employees dead, and two heads missing. Do you think your dinner time is at the top of my concerns right now?"

"I'm so sorry about your employees," Agnes said.

"I should have stayed legit and sold the blood to blood banks. The money isn't as good, but I wouldn't have decapitated employees to deal with now, would I?"

"You provide a critical service for our elderly residents. We need you."

"I convinced the police to keep the bus running to power the refrigerators. I told them I need to get the blood to a blood bank before it spoils. The bus is a crime scene so they could hold on to it for who knows how long. If I can get custody of the blood, I'll deliver it to you another way. You may not get it tonight, though."

Agnes thanked him and hung up.

"Thogg needs to be stopped," she told Missy. "We need to rescue Henrietta, Gladys, and Bernie. But he'll just retaliate. I'll have to reach out to other vampire groups for help."

"Like who?" Missy asked.

"I have friends in a vampire community of single-family homes west of town. Florida doesn't have a centralized alliance of vampires. We're all on our own. But that has to change if we want to be safe from Thogg. And as the wife and daughter of Visigoth generals, I can tell you the only way to end this is with another decapitation: Thogg's."

Missy had rarely seen Agnes with her inner barbarian showing like this. It was frankly scary.

Missy had spent her entire tenure with Acceptance Home

Care convincing herself that vampires weren't so dangerous. That they were simply individuals with special needs who needed empathy and understanding.

She was quickly changing her mind about that.

5

MISSY AND THE MISSING

"I have a cousin?" Missy asked.

"You were news to me, too," the woman's voice said over the phone. "Your mother never told us about you. I didn't know she had a daughter."

"I didn't know I had a mother until recently," Missy said. "Biological mother, that is. I mean, one who was alive."

"Families are all about strangeness in the bloodline," said the woman who had introduced herself as Darla Chesswick from San Marcos in North Florida, where Missy's parents had once lived. "Especially in our family. Your mother, my mother, me. We all have some magic in us. And a lot of neuroses, too."

"My adoptive parents were normal," Missy said. "Geeky, but normal. Then I find out my natural parents were witches who died when I was a baby. Next, I find out my mother isn't dead and is a black-magic sorceress who sells her services to the highest bidder."

"Yeah, Mom always complains about her and the clients she

does black magic for, like senators and reverends. At least, from what I hear, you had a normal life until recently. Unlike me."

"It wasn't totally normal. I managed to fall in love with and marry a man who left me for a gay vampire."

"Okay, I see what you mean. We really should meet soon and get acquainted, but the reason I called is your mother said you might be able to help me."

"How so?"

"My daughter Sophie is missing."

"Oh, my," Missy said. "I'm so sorry."

"Sophie has had some problems with drugs and I sent her to a rehabilitation center. But she ran away. Then she called me from another center that didn't sound legit. I tried calling her two days ago, and they said she ran away and no one knows where she is. But I don't believe them. I'm afraid she's in a sleazy sober home. Or worse. She could end up overdosing or being sold to a pimp. Or try to take her own life. I'm frightened to death."

"How can I help?" Missy asked.

"I was hoping you could look for her. The sober home is in Jellyfish Beach. That's where you live, right?"

"Yes." Jellyfish Beach wasn't just known for its snowbirds and retirees. It also was home to a small cottage industry of addiction recovery businesses. Many of them used their sunny Florida location to attract wealthy clients from northern cities.

"I run a bed and breakfast in San Marcos," Darla said. "I can't afford to hire a private investigator. And I can't get away from the inn until the end of the week to go down there. Can you at least ask around for her?"

"Of course I can. I have a friend who's a reporter. He can help me."

"And not to put you on the spot, but I understand you know a bit of the craft? I know a little myself, but I can't locate Sophie."

"I practice a little magick, yes. Email me Sophie's photo and I'll see what I can do on both fronts."

"Both fronts?"

"Making inquiries and casting spells."

Darla thanked her profusely and soon an email arrived with a photo attached. Sophie was pretty, in her early twenties, with dark hair and Irish dimples. Missy's mother, whom she had met only once, was also dark-haired with pale skin and Irish features. Missy didn't resemble either of them.

So maybe her satanic, black-magic mother wasn't really her mother?

Only if dreams come true.

"You expect me to knock on doors all over town to find Sophie?" her friend Matt Rosen asked incredulously as he played with his scrambled eggs.

The scent of the ocean in the air mixed with that hard-to-describe breakfast smell you only found at diners and certain cafes: coffee, butter on fresh-toasted bread, pancakes, sizzling bacon—a rich mixture accumulated in permanent layers over decades. Missy had tossed her vow to order an egg-white omelet out the window and dived right into a plate of waffles, fried eggs, and bacon. She'd been carrying her extra weight around so long it wasn't going anywhere. Besides, magick-making burned a lot of calories. Or so she told herself.

"I don't have time to investigate this," Missy said, dipping her bacon into the waffle syrup. "I have missing vampires to find."

"But Sophie is your first cousin once removed. And she's human."

"The vampires at Squid Tower are like family to me," Missy said. "My job is to care for them. I will not put that aside because I get a call from a cousin I didn't know I had about a niece I didn't know I had."

"But still."

"But still, she's an addict. It's more likely that she followed a source of drugs rather than being in danger."

"So cold, so cold," Matt said. He wasn't making a joke. "Yeah, she's especially vulnerable."

Matt's tactics were working. The guilt was seeping in.

"I didn't mean I wouldn't look for her. I need your help, that's all." Missy said. She took a bite of a waffle, hoping it would mollify her conscience.

"It's a hard world out there when you're in recovery," Matt said. "I've reported many stories on the people who fall through the cracks. There are some very reputable recovery centers in this area, but there are tons of scammers and low lives trying to make a profit off anyone who has health insurance or rich parents. If you leave, or get kicked out of, the high-end facilities, you could be chewed up and spit out by the criminals. They only want you so they can bill your insurance and don't care if you recover. Sometimes they keep you addicted so you never leave."

This was turning grimmer than Missy had hoped.

"What do you suggest we do?" she asked.

"We'll have to call every center we can find. And show her picture around to as many people as we can."

Missy cringed at the thought of how much work this would take. She realized she was taking advantage of Matt. He had great investigative skills. He also had the hots for her. She knew it was wrong to leverage that to her advantage.

She also knew, but didn't want to admit, that she had a bit of an attraction to him. She felt comfortable being with him and loved his wit. At times he was annoying, but she probably was, too.

They'd been good partners in investigating the freaky matters that arose from the supernatural creatures whom they both vowed to keep secret from the world. And she valued her friendship with Matt. She didn't want to lose it.

That's why she was reluctant to get into a relationship with him. With her former husband, she had fallen in love with and married a friend only to find out she hadn't known him as well as she thought. She spent years feeling unattractive and unloved, only to have him leave her for another man. A vampire who turned him and couldn't stop him from being staked by a cop. Her husband left her, left the human world, and then left the world altogether.

She had become accustomed to being alone and rather liked it. She had a couple of good friends, like Luisa the Santeria priestess who owned the botanica where Missy sometimes worked for extra cash. She had her elderly patients who truly depended upon her, even if they weren't human. And she had her magick, along with the growing sense that she was destined to be a great witch.

She didn't need a relationship with Matt right now. But she did need his help. Was she using him? No, not at all.

The check arrived. She snatched it before he could grab it.

"This is on me," she said. It was the least she could do after asking for his help. Although she was certain she'd be asking for more soon enough.

MISSY TOLD Matt that she would handle the phone calls to the recovery centers. They didn't get her anywhere. Every single one said that because of patient privacy laws, they couldn't tell her if Sophie was or had been a patient. Even when she explained that Sophie was her niece, they said no. Missy would have to be an immediate family member, with her name signed off by the patient, to receive any information.

"Okay," Matt said at the coffee bar when she explained why she came up dry. "We need to pound the pavement."

"How exactly? You mean walk around in the sun and get sweaty?"

"I mean talk to current and ex-patients. They don't have any legal obligation not to tell us stuff."

"And where do we find these people?"

"There are a few coffee bars in town where they hang out. Like this place. That's why I suggested meeting here."

Missy looked around the dimly lit cafe. It was almost empty.

"Then we try stealthier methods," Matt said. "We hang around outside the offices where they go for group counseling. When they go outside for smoke breaks, we just happen to walk by and say hello."

"Can we get in trouble for that?" Missy asked, feeling uneasy about this.

"At the worst, we would just be kicked off the property. And the final tactic we'll use is to stake out the sober homes."

Missy knew what those were. Recovery centers acquired

apartments or single-family homes in residential areas where they housed patients in the later stages of recovery who were transitioning to finding jobs again. These homes ranged from super-luxurious to dangerous dives. The owners made a lot of money this way, but residents protested against having the homes in their neighborhoods. Sometimes the protests were unfounded, because the recovering patients were quiet and responsible. Often the protests were deserved, when the homes were sites of drug dealing and prostitution.

"How do we know which homes are sober homes?" Missy asked.

"We look for druggie buggies."

"Say what?"

"That's the local nickname for the passenger vans used to transport patients between therapy sessions and the homes. If you're in a normal residential neighborhood and you see a van that holds twelve passengers in the driveway, you know the Brady Bunch doesn't live there."

This is more than I thought I was getting into, Missy thought.

"Okay," Matt said. "Time to get started. Watch what I do, it's very simple."

He took a handful of the flyers Missy had printed with Sophie's photo on them and approached the barista. The skinny, rodent-like man was shaved bald and every inch of his skin was inked.

"Excuse me," Matt said, sliding the flyer across the bar. "Have you ever seen this woman? She's my friend's relative and disappeared while she was in recovery."

"No, dude, sorry. Haven't seen her. A lot of people disappear like that."

"Can you hang onto this in case you do see her? My friend's phone number is on it."

"Sure, dude," said the barista as he took the flyer. "No problem. I hope you find her."

Matt returned to their nearby high-top. "See how easy that was? Now you try it with some customers."

There weren't many to choose from. Missy took a flyer and walked to a nearby high-top where an older woman sat drinking coffee from a tall cup. She had dyed her hair a ridiculous shade of pink and the bangles that hung from her ears looked so heavy they were stretching her ear lobes.

"Excuse me," Missy said.

"No, I haven't seen her," the woman said without looking up.

"Sorry?"

"I haven't seen the girl you're looking for."

"Oh, did you hear my friend talking to the barista?"

"No," the woman said, finally making eye contact. "I'm a telepath."

"Oh, my."

"And I know that you think my hair color is ridiculous and you don't like my earrings."

"No, that's not true," Missy needed to escape.

"And I know that you're a witch."

"Shhh. Please keep it down." Missy glanced around to make sure no one except Matt could hear.

"And I know that you think your friend there is cute."

"Indeed?" Matt asked.

"And don't get me started on you, young man. Your mind is deep, deep in the gutter."

"Can we go now?" Missy said to Matt.

"Yes, we're late for an appointment. Here, please keep this

just in case," Matt handed the flyer to the telepathic pain in the butt.

As they hurried to the door, the woman called after them, "Liar! You don't have an appointment."

Missy sighed in relief when they got outside.

"I thought you said this was easy?"

"Not when I'm with the woman who manages to bring me in contact with every freak in this town," Matt said.

6
NIGHT-VISION VAMPIRE

Paul Leclerc arrived in a center-console boat with an outboard engine. It looked to be about twenty-four feet long. He put the engine in idle and let the craft drift up against the dock. He helped Missy step aboard. Paul was one of those guys who wore his graying hair long and tied it in a ponytail while the front of his head was bald. Looking like he was in his early sixties, he had a short goatee and a sun-weathered face. He was thin with a potbelly and wore a blue fishing shirt with lots of pockets, tan shorts, and flip-flops.

Missy, who had skin almost as pale as her vampire patients', wore a wide-brimmed hat and lightweight top and bottom that hid as much skin as possible from the sun.

"Which way?" he asked.

"I have no clue. Wherever we'll find a private marina with an obscenely large yacht."

"It's probably at a community of condos or townhomes."

"No," Missy said. "I saw single-family homes."

"Okay. The wealthier ones are to the south."

He pushed the throttle forward, and they chugged along at a no-wake speed through Jellyfish Beach. They passed two waterfront restaurants, older condo towers, and then individual homes. All places where Missy could never in a million years afford to live. They crossed under a bridge leading from the mainland, to their right, to the beach on the barrier island to their left.

"Keep an eye on this community coming up on the left," Paul said, pointing.

A dozen three-story homes lined the seawall. They were modern with boxy features and lots of windows. There was a dock with several slips, half of which held boats. A couple of the boats were ridiculously large, but neither was the one from her vision.

"It's not here," she said. "What if it spends most of its time at sea so it can't be found?"

Paul frowned. "That would be prohibitively expensive. A boat of the size you described burns through nearly a half million dollars of fuel a year. Let's keep looking."

They continued south, not passing many boats since it was a weekday during the summer when the snowbirds and tourists weren't around. Paul wasn't able to go very fast because there were several no-wake zones to protect manatees. Missy had seen sea cows swimming in this area with propeller scars on their backs.

They left Jellyfish Beach behind, and as they passed through cities to the south, there were plenty of obnoxiously large boats, but none matched the one in her vision.

"How far south do you want to go?" Paul asked.

They could keep searching all the way down to Fort Lauderdale, Miami, and even the keys. But even vampires that can fly as bats can travel only so far in an evening.

"I think we should search to the north of Jellyfish Beach," Missy said.

Paul turned the boat around, and they traveled back the way they had come, eventually passing the dock where she had come aboard. The Intracoastal Waterway north of Jellyfish Beach was less developed. There were fewer condo buildings, more single-family homes, and more stretches of untouched mangroves growing from the water, birds perched in their branches.

"What's in there?" Missy asked, pointed to a large opening in the mangroves on the mainland side.

"Just some homes," Paul said. "I haven't looked in there for years."

He turned the boat left and slowly eased into the opening between the trees. The channel curved and then opened up into a small bay. Six ostentatious waterfront homes shared an arrangement of docks.

And at the outermost pier, a gigantic yacht was moored. The one from Missy's vision.

"This is the one," she said, practically whispering.

She pulled out her phone and opened a mapping app, noting that the homes were at the ends of three streets. The yacht was missing from the satellite view of the area, so it must have arrived fairly recently.

They drifted closer to the yacht. The name *Man Cave* was painted on the stern. The vessel had to be more than 100 feet long, with portholes along the hull. Interior shades blocked all the portholes. Two decks of living space rose above the main deck, not counting an open flying bridge at the very top. Above deck, every window was obscured by blinds. A large tender covered with a tarp hung from davits on the rear deck. There were no signs of anyone moving around.

No one was in the yards of the homes, either. One home caught Missy's eye because blinds covered all its windows, even though it was daytime. Whoever lived there really didn't like daylight.

"What do you want to do?" Paul asked.

"I don't want to alert anyone that we're snooping around. We'll only have one chance to search the boat and we'll need your guys with us." She took a photo of the yacht's name and registration number as they drifted by.

"My sentiments exactly," Paul said, putting the engine in gear and steering his boat gently out through the channel.

"I'm going to do some research on those homes," Missy said. "Maybe I'll find some names that lead me to helpful information."

"We need to search the yacht soon, though. Agnes called me last night about it. They're getting frantic at Squid Tower."

"I don't blame them. I feel the same way. But we need to be careful that we're not blundering into a trap."

Missy had an idea. "I think I'll come back here after sunset, on a kayak so I have a low profile."

"Do you have night-vision goggles?"

"I'll bring the next best thing: a Schwartz."

VAMPIRES HAVE MUCH BETTER vision than humans. And Leonard Schwartz, seventy-five years old in body age and nearly two hundred years old in total, had the best eyesight out of all the vampires who were involved in the war with the Neanderthals. In Missy's mind, that was unfortunate. Not only was Schwartz disagreeable, he was the vampire least likely to want to be in a kayak.

"I'm from Brooklyn," he protested. "I'm allergic to nature."

But Agnes pressured him into going on the mission, both because of his superior night vision and his inherent ability to detect other vampires. Missy also felt it would be safer having a vampire along when scouting on vampires.

Matt also came along. Mostly because the kayaks were his. Missy, an experienced paddler, wanted to be able to maneuver easily and didn't want to be stuck with transporting Schwartz in the second, two-person, kayak. That was Matt's job.

They launched from a park close to where the yacht was moored. There was no moon visible, so Missy and Matt used headlamps to see by while they untied the two kayaks and lifted them from the roof of Matt's car. They carried them one at a time through the parking lot and set them on the sandy bank of the Intracoastal. Matt handed Missy and Schwartz life vests.

"I'm not wearing this thing," Schwartz said. "Vampires don't drown."

"Just wear it," Missy said. "It used to be a 'fact' that vampires can't cross rivers. Well, you guys drive on the bridge across the Intracoastal every time you go shopping in town. And even if it's true you can't drown, it doesn't mean you're a good swimmer."

"I go in the pool from time to time on a nice evening."

"Put on the vest."

Chagrined, Schwartz obeyed. "I look stupid," he said.

They each got a paddle, then Missy and Matt pushed the

kayaks, Schwartz already sitting in the front seat of the tandem kayak, into deeper water before climbing in themselves.

"That thing in your hand, Mr. Schwartz?" Matt said from behind Schwartz. "That's a paddle. Feel free to use it. I seem to be the only one moving the boat forward."

"I've never paddled anything in my human life," Schwartz said. "The only boat I was ever on was the Staten Island ferry. Is this thing going to tip over?"

"I can't believe I'm kayaking with a vampire," Matt said. "A vampire who isn't helping with the paddling."

Missy knew that Matt was nervous, though he tried not to show it. He didn't have nightly contact with the undead like Missy did. In fact, he didn't have any contact at all with supernaturals unless one was trying to kill him. She had given him an amulet to wear around his neck that would ward off vampire attacks, in case Schwartz couldn't suppress the urge. It didn't help Matt feel any better.

They paddled south toward the cove where the yacht was moored. They had the tide at their backs, so it was easy paddling. A slight breeze made the temperature comfortable and there was no boat traffic at this hour. Lights on residential docks helped them navigate, though Schwartz didn't need them to see.

"Okay, Mr. Schwartz, this is the plan," Missy said. "I'll let you know when we're approaching the marina. You tell me when we're near enough for you to sense vampires. Then we'll sit and observe, trying to get a feel for how many there are."

"So if Mr. Schwartz can sense them, can't they sense him?" Matt asked.

"Don't be a putz," Schwartz said. "If there's a group of them, they're much more easily detectible than a single vampire."

"I should have known that," Matt said. "I think I had a class in high school about it."

"Vampires can also detect sarcasm," Schwartz said, turning around and giving Matt an evil glare. "It makes us thirsty."

Even in the darkness, Missy could tell Matt's face went pale. She couldn't help being amused at the sight of her nervous friend struggling to paddle the kayak while the stooped figure of Schwartz, his pot belly pushing the life vest up into his chin, sat in front of him unmoving, his giant nose protruding like the figurehead of a ship.

The homes dwindled, and they came upon the preserve where a mangrove forest cloaked the shore, perched on roots rising from the water like stilts.

"We're very near," Missy whispered. "Everyone stay quiet."

They drifted with the current, and soon an opening appeared in the wall of trees. Schwartz raised his hand.

"Vampires up ahead," he said.

"How many?" Matt asked.

"How am I supposed to know, you numbskull? I'm not clair-voyant. I can only sense there's more than one."

"Then why am I padding your dead weight all the way over here?" Matt muttered.

"I heard that," Schwartz said.

Missy carefully steered along the channel that led into the cove. As soon as she saw the first dock light, she stopped and held onto a mangrove branch to stop her drift. She gestured for Matt and Schwartz to go ahead of her. Matt's kayak passed her, Schwartz leaning forward, sniffing the air like a dog.

"I can see the giant boat," Matt whispered, "but it's too far away and too dark to see anyone on it."

"Two humans are rolling a cart from a house onto the dock,"

Schwartz said. "Now they're carrying supplies of some sort onto the yacht." A few minutes later, he added, "Now they're leaving, walking really quickly. They're frightened."

They sat on their kayaks in silence for a while. The only sounds for a human like Missy were the rattling of mangrove leaves in the light breeze and tiny splashes of fish feeding nearby. Schwartz, however, could hear much more.

"There's a lot of activity in the house those humans came out of. Wait . . . four vampires are leaving the yacht, walking along the dock. They look like freaking Neanderthals. Okay, now they're going into the house. I smell blood."

"I hope you're not smelling mine," Matt whispered.

"Shut up, you imbecile. There was a lot of blood flowing in that boat. Several vampires were feeding."

Missy shivered at the thought.

"You got enough info?" Matt asked. "Can we go now?"

"Do you sense Gladys, Henrietta, or Bernie here?"

"I can't tell. I said I wasn't clairvoyant," Schwartz grumbled. "But there are more vampires still on the yacht. And humans, too."

"If we got closer, could you tell if they're our vampires?"

"Not without seeing or hearing them. If one of them was my maker, or my child, sure. And, fortunately, none of them are."

Schwartz suddenly swung his paddle in the air above him. The paddle, that had sat in his lap unmoving for the entire journey, was now flailing desperately in the air.

A bonk rang from the fiberglass and a stunned bat dropped into the water.

"I got the little bugger!" Schwartz exclaimed with joy.

"Let's get out of here," Matt said.

And then a spray of water hit them all as a large male

vampire shot out of the water, roaring like an enraged bull gator.

The vampire landed on the mangrove branches above them. He crouched there, looking down upon them with anger in his eyes. He bared his fangs and hissed.

"For crying out loud," Schwartz said. "Of all the bats in Florida, I had to hit the one that was a vampire." He pointed at the vampire in the tree. "You're not supposed to be able to do that, buddy."

The vampire dropped from the tree onto Schwartz. Matt screamed and fell into the water.

Missy instinctively paddled backwards away from Schwartz as the vampire battle began.

The two creatures thrashed at each other so quickly that their movements were a blur. There was hissing and growling, punching and slashing. She didn't believe Schwartz was capable of such athleticism and speed, but she assumed he was doomed at the hands of the younger vampire.

She didn't have a spell in her arsenal that would help Schwartz in this fight. Everyone was moving too quickly to be a target, anyway.

"I can't believe they haven't capsized the kayak."

Missy jumped at the voice. Matt was floating with his hand on her kayak, his vest keeping his head and neck above the surface.

He was right to wonder that, because the kayak was getting dunked beneath the water and buffeted from side to side. She guessed that the Neanderthal vampire didn't want to go into the water.

Schwartz screamed in pain and blood sprinkled on the water's surface.

Missy had to do something. She grasped the power charm she always carried in her pocket since the Red Dragon was safely locked away at home. And she cast the first spell that came to mind, a temporal adjustment spell. How this would help, she had no idea. She just did it.

And the blur of motion that was the vampire fight slowed down. Now she could see what was going on in what seemed like real time to her. The slow-motion Neanderthal was pinning Schwartz backwards, trying to get his jaws upon Schwartz's throat. Both creatures were covered in cuts and puncture wounds. But Schwartz's pot belly had pushed his vest up to his chin, and the other vampire struggled to get past it. Schwartz had his thumbs in the Neanderthal's eyes and struggled to push his head backwards.

Something was swimming quietly up behind the vampire death match. She couldn't tell what it was in the darkness. It wouldn't be an alligator because this was saltwater. Was it a manatee?

No, it was Matt. He was sharpening a broken tree branch with an emergency knife attached by a cord to his vest. Missy watched with dread as Matt kicked forward through the dark water, to the slow-motion battle atop the kayak, and raised the branch in both hands.

And plunged it into the upper back of the Neanderthal vampire.

The vampire reared backward and screamed silently, blood shooting from his mouth like a geyser. The sharpened tip of the branch barely poked out of a hole in the vampire's shirt.

Matt disappeared beneath the kayak.

Schwartz pushed his assailant from his chest just as the

vampire shed its undead existence. Its clothing collapsed as the body turned to dust and poured into the water.

Matt's head popped out of the water. He looked like he was in shock.

"Is it . . . gone?" he asked as his teeth chattered, even though the water wasn't cold.

"What took you so long?" Schwartz said, sounding like his speech had been digitally slowed to half its normal speed.

Missy waved her hand and said the words that broke the temporal adjustment spell.

"You almost let me get killed," Schwartz said in a normal voice.

"You're welcome," Matt said. "No one asked you to pick a fight with the bat."

"I was afraid it was going to get caught in my clothes," Schwartz said. "But you should thank me. He was probably spying on us and was flying home with his report."

"You could be right," Missy said.

"Then let's get the heck out of here, Matt said. "Hold onto that branch and try to keep the kayak steady while I pull myself on."

After Matt was back aboard, they paddled back toward the launch. Unfortunately, the tide hadn't changed, so they were going against the current the entire way. Schwartz finally helped with the paddling this time.

"I'm going to need your help with looking into that home that had all the activity. And if there are humans staying on the yacht," Missy said to Matt. "I bet they're being held prisoner."

"Do you think they're being used for. . ." Matt left the question incomplete.

"Food," Schwartz said. "Yeah, probably."

"We need more info before we try to rescue our friends, so we don't get ambushed. And I want to find out where these vampires came from," Missy said. "Why has no one heard about them before?"

Schwartz chuckled. "They came from somewhere else. Just like everyone else in South Florida."

"Hey, I'm a native," Matt said.

"Why would you natives ever allow so many freaks to move to your state?" Schwartz asked. "Including me."

7

BETTER DAZE

"Why do you want to settle in Jellyfish Beach?" Sal Amato asked. "Or settle anywhere. I thought you guys were hunter-gatherers who wandered the land."

Thogg slammed his fist on Sal's desk. It had obviously been the wrong thing to say. Sal tried to act calm after his butt leaped two inches off his chair.

"Stop stereotyping us," Thogg said, looking like he wanted to snap Sal's head off. "We adapt with the times. Despite what anyone says, we can adapt. During the agrarian eras, we tended mushroom farms at night. During the industrial revolution, we owned coal mines. They reminded us of our former caves. Nowadays, we're into private equity. Which, when you think about it, is sort of like hunting and gathering. Like I said, we adapt."

"Adapt but not evolve," Sal mused, studying the shape of Thogg's head.

"Undead creatures can't evolve," Thogg said. "And speaking of evolution, someone ought to remove you from the human gene pool if they don't want human intelligence to decline."

Sal resented that, but he would not pick a fight with a 110,000-year-old vampire. Especially since the vampire's hand, the one not used for slamming Sal's desk, was clamped around the throat of Sal's intern, holding the poor kid a foot above the floor. The kid's job was to fetch Sal's coffee and dump out the clients' urine samples. He was fairly expendable.

"You never answered my original question," Thogg said.

"About the blood?"

"Why else would I be here?"

"How many of your clan are moving here?"

"Twenty or so now. More will come later."

Florida already had too many Neanderthals as it was, in Sal's opinion, and they weren't even actual Neanderthals.

"I'll see what I can do," he said, "but some of the patients I think have no ties turn out to have a relative who pops up out of nowhere wondering what happened to them. If the authorities get involved, it'll be bad for you and me both."

"Handling such things is why we pay you so well," Thogg said, menacingly.

How had he gotten himself into such a mess? Sal wondered. He knew the answer. Short-sighted greed. That was always what got him into trouble.

Sal had been in construction, like everyone else in Florida who didn't work in landscaping, hospitality, or making money off the retirees' finances. But his buddy Bert came to him with a get-rich-quick scheme. All they needed was an office, some houses, and an employee with a medical license of some sort who knew how to bill health insurance companies. And, presto! "Better Daze Recovery Center" was born.

It was easy money. Charge the patients inflated fees for room and board. Drive them to group-therapy sessions that over-billed insurance and shared a cut with Better Daze.

But the big money-maker was the pee. Better Daze took urine samples from its clientele for drug testing every chance it could get. Once a week would be plenty, but he demanded they pee every day. Sometimes more than once a day. Ostensibly, it was to ensure that the folks were clean and weren't using again. But he didn't even test the pee. He sent it to Whizz Laboratories, which he and Bert owned. "Sent" meant dumping it in the toilet or in his neighbors' yards. Then he over-billed his clients' insurance.

Sal had a good thing going, but then he had to get even greedier. When Thogg showed up with his proposal, Sal didn't hesitate a second before taking him up on it. If urine was so profitable, then blood samples would be even more so. He just needed a part-time phlebotomist to draw the samples. And the difference here was that he wouldn't send them to a fake lab. He would send them to Thogg. At the time, Sal didn't know what Thogg wanted the blood for and he didn't ask. Thogg came across as much smarter than he looked, so Sal had turned a blind eye.

Then Thogg started demanding more blood than Sal could supply. You could ask a patient for urine three times a day, but you couldn't do the same for their blood.

And the problem was, Thogg's clan needed more than a few test tubes of additional blood. We're talking pints and pints more.

"Okay," Sal said. "I'll send a few more clients over to Seventeenth Street."

"You need to find a way to scale this operation," Thogg said. "When I'm ruling my vampire empire, I'll have thousands of soldiers to feed."

Sal knew Thogg was nuts, but he had to play along.

"At that time, you'll have thousands of prisoners to serve your needs."

Thogg nodded. "True."

"Do you mind if I ask, why don't you guys go hunting at night and feed on your prey?"

"Adaptation," Thogg tapped his head. "That's not a sustainable way to feed in these modern times with police and streetlights everywhere. So we adapt our ways."

"Ah, very smart."

Thogg yanked the intern higher in the air.

"Are you being sarcastic?" he asked with a scowl.

"Not at all, my Lord of Darkness."

Sal rued the day his greed got him involved with these bloodsucking cavemen. Why hadn't he just stayed with his urine scam?

After Thogg finally left, and the intern was excused to go to the ER to see if his larynx had been crushed, Sal left his office and drove to his largest residential facility. It was a two-story apartment building that may have been a motel once, the kind in which all the studio apartments opened onto breezeways facing the parking lot. Seven residents sat smoking cigarettes in plastic chairs arranged next to the druggy buggy van.

"Hello, kiddies. I've got some good news for . . . Peter, Maria, and . . . Sophie," Sal said, pointing to each of the skinny, strung-out young adults: an arrogant, white, rich dude; a gay

68

Hispanic tough girl; and a pretty, pale chick with lots of piercings. He chose them because he was pretty sure they hadn't been using. Thogg's vampires didn't appreciate drug-laced blood.

"You guys are moving up in life today," he told them. "You get to stay in a waterfront luxury home."

The three looked up at him, assessing if he was serious.

"It's true. Grab your stuff. You're going now."

The plastic chairs scuffled against the asphalt as they jumped to their feet and dashed to their rooms.

A tall, muscular man leaned against the wall of the building. It was Walter, the onsite supervisor. As the operation grew, Sal had to hire more people like Walter, who guarded the clientele and shuttled them around in the van. The Walters of the world also bought drugs for the patients who had gone clean and were about to graduate. That kept them here for another profitable term of treatment.

"Walter, take them to Thogg's house on Seventeenth Street."

"What about the group I took there two weeks ago?" Walter asked.

"They're going to move onto greater things."

SOPHIE THREW her pitifully small amount of possessions into a backpack in the moldy studio apartment. She was excited to be moving on to a sober home. She finally had been taking her recovery seriously. It was too bad that it was her boyfriend dying of an overdose and her spending a week on the streets that made her adjust her attitude. She hoped it would stay adjusted for good this time.

She shouldn't have run away from the fancy recovery center her mother had sent her to. It was an expensive place.

At twenty-four, she was still on her mother's health insurance, which covered a lot of the center's cost, but her mother had spent a lot of her savings to send Sophie there. The place had been nice, but too regimented. She didn't enjoy having a roommate and the strict schedule of therapy sessions, workshops, and fitness classes. An innocent romance with Victor, a moody architect, was her only escape from the tedium.

Victor, skinny as a bone with long, 1980s rock-star hair, and such serious, soulful eyes, convinced her to run away with him. He claimed his brother in New York was going to pay him a large sum to design an office building. But Victor had to begin immediately. He couldn't wait until he completed his treatment. Victor was going to catch an Amtrak train to New York the next day. Would Sophie please come with him? He said he couldn't live without her.

The next day she met him at a cheap motel, and he was off his rocker on heroin. An hour before the train departed, he stopped breathing. The paramedics used Narcan, but it was too late.

She was distraught. She was lost. The first night sleeping in the park in Jellyfish Beach was horrifying. Subsequent nights didn't make it any easier. A kind, older homeless woman showed her where to find a church that gave out free lunches each day. And a seemingly kind, sleazy man gave her some opioid pills and brought her to a place to sleep. It was supposedly a recovery center. They examined her insurance card and asked her to pee in a cup before they even asked how she was doing. After spending a few weeks constantly high in a dirty studio apartment, she decided to go clean again. She rode the van to the group therapy sessions every day. And she peed in a cup constantly. She'd been clean for a month.

"Sophie, get down here!" Walter shouted. He had been hitting on her since she first arrived at Better Daze Recovery. She hoped she wouldn't see him again.

She climbed into the van with Peter and Maria. Peter had his usual self-satisfied expression. Maria looked wary, as usual.

"Finally, we get decent accommodations," Peter said.

"Why are you even at Better Daze?" Sophie asked. "I had you pegged for someone who could afford a better place."

His preppy face darkened. "I tried other places. It didn't work out. There were disagreements."

"Walter, why are you taking us to a sober house? I feel like I have a lot more work to do on my therapy," Maria said.

Walter looked back at them in the rearview mirror. "You will still have your therapy. The boss figured you guys would do better in a more comfortable environment."

Maria looked like she didn't believe him. Actually, Sophie was beginning to feel suspicious, too. And wasn't staying in a nice house going to cost a lot more? She hoped the house had a phone so she could call her mom. Living without a cell phone was impossible.

The van took U.S. 1 north through downtown Jellyfish Beach and a few miles further before taking a right and heading east on a residential street. At the very end was a giant banyan tree with a shady canopy and aerial roots dangling from its long limbs. On the wide cul-de-sac were modern-style luxury homes. Between the homes, she could see water.

"Welcome to paradise," Walter said, parking the van in the house's driveway behind the banyan. It was two-story with square lines, large windows and chrome accents. The garage looked like it could hold four cars. Walter waited until the three patients climbed out of the van, then led them to the front door of the house. He pressed the doorbell.

Sophie spotted security cameras everywhere—above the door looking down at them, on the banyan tree facing the house, and another on a lamppost next to the front walk.

The double front door opened. A middle-aged woman with jet-black hair stood there.

"These clients are moving in," Walter said. "See ya later." He went back to the van without even introducing them.

"I'm Jan," the woman said with a German accent. "I'll show you to your rooms."

Sophie gazed in wonder at the two-story-tall foyer with a large but minimalist chandelier. The floors were dark slate with white throw rugs. Modern art hung on the walls. This place was big-money.

"How many bedrooms does this place have?" Peter asked.

"Seven," the woman answered. "With eight bathrooms."

Sophie was the last to be shown to her accommodations. It was a room for kids with bunk beds. A seven-bedroom house and they needed bunk beds? She knew she shouldn't complain. The bunks were actually wooden and built into the wall with privacy curtains. There was only a desk and two chairs, but they were high quality. She opened the closet to toss her backpack in there and discovered it was a walk-in with twin dressers. She was reluctant to unpack. Who knew how long she was going to stay here?

She wandered to the kitchen. Jan was there, chopping chicken breasts.

"It's pretty quiet in this house," Sophie said.

"It's always quiet during the day," Jan said. "Things are more active at night."

"Who else lives here?"

"I live here and there are two other clients staying here at this time. They will be finishing the program soon."

"Good," Sophie said, no longer paying attention as she studied the sumptuous kitchen: two sinks, two ovens, two stainless-steel refrigerators. The countertops looked like they were white quartz. Marble tiles on the walls below the white cabinets. She couldn't tell if the floor was real hardwood or laminate. In San Marcos, her mother's home was from the seventeen hundreds. It did not have a kitchen like this.

"So when do we get picked up to go to therapy?" she asked.

"Not today," Jan said. "Today you all will rest and eat. You are all too skinny. You can't recover if you don't eat." She smiled and shoved a bowl of mixed nuts across the counter. "Eat these."

Sophie felt obligated to take a handful. "Are we allowed to help ourselves to waters and sodas and stuff?"

"Take anything you want. I am making lunch for you now. Sit down." Jan gestured to the stools alongside the center island.

Peter wandered into the kitchen. He looked like he had showered and changed.

"That's a freaking awesome yacht out there!" he said, running his hand through his straight blond hair. "Does the owner of this house own it?"

"Yes, but you can't go near it," Jan said. "The owner stays on the boat with some friends. It's off-limits to us."

"Can I go fishing from the docks?"

"Yes. There is fishing tackle in the storage closet facing the pool. If you catch fish, I will cook it for you. Fish is full of iron, which you need," Jan said as she prepared an elaborate meal with chicken and dark greens. "But don't go near the yacht. And don't go into the garage."

"Why? Does he have a rare car in there?"

"No. He has dogs. Killer dogs. Don't even think of opening the door. It's too dangerous."

"I hope the dogs aren't kept for fighting," Sophie said. "Are they well cared for?"

"Believe me, they are spoiled. But they don't like strangers."

The smell of chicken sautéing in olive oil with onion must have attracted Maria. She sat next to Sophie and hungrily eyed Jan's cooking.

"Some garlic would go great with that," she said.

"No garlic!" Jan slammed a wooden spoon on the skillet. "No garlic in the house. Some of us are allergic."

Peter laughed. "Are you vampires or something?"

Jan gave him a dark look that made Sophie nervous.

"So what's our schedule here?" Maria asked Jan.

"I will make one for you. The rules are different for those who are fortunate to live here. You will rest and relax, eat and regain your strength. Your group therapy will be here in the house. And since we are not near anything worth walking to, you will stay here for the first week."

Sophie and her two comrades sat on stools at the island and devoured Jan's lunch of chicken and rice with beans. Sophie downed a tall glass of sweet iced tea. Then the group broke up and dispersed in the giant house. The sound of a television came from a distant room.

Sophie wandered through the living room's mid-century modern furniture and glass tables. Giant, floor-to-ceiling sliders revealed a large swimming pool, docks, and a water view. It was a cove off the Intracoastal Waterway, sheltered by mangroves. It was nice looking at nature only, without houses across the water.

The exception was the yacht. Its stern facing the house, it was tied to the end of a long dock jutting perpendicularly from the seawall. The vessel had to be at least a hundred feet long. It had sleek, angular lines, but was tall and fat like a mini cruise ship. The name on the stern was *Man Cave*. She wondered why the owner lived aboard instead of in the house.

"Beautiful, isn't she?" Peter said from behind her right shoulder, startling her.

"I didn't hear you come out."

"My parents had a cabin cruiser when I was young," Peter said. "They would cruise all over Cape Cod Bay each summer and we would live aboard. I thought it was delightful. But when we were cruising, it cost hundreds a day in fuel. My dad always complained about that. Then my father got arrested, and the Feds confiscated the boat."

"Sorry," Sophie said.

"I still miss that boat. Even though the Mexican drug lord that gave it to dad had horrible taste in interior design."

"Hopefully, the owner of this boat isn't a criminal," Sophie said. "The house is tastefully decorated."

"You'll get your chance to meet him tonight. Jan said he and his buddies hang out with the patients at night."

"That's odd."

"Jan said he's a part owner of Better Daze. He has recovery training, so it's okay for us to mingle with him."

It didn't seem right to Sophie that some rich dude would be hanging out with vulnerable addicts.

Peter added, "He gives inspirational talks, Jan told me."

8
EVENING WITH THOGG

Dinner was a sumptuous feast of Chateaubriand as well as flounder and Florida lobster tails. There was spinach and plenty of beans. Sophie ate ravenously.

"Are you trying to fatten us up for slaughter?" Maria joked. Jan smiled.

The two other housemates had joined them after sleeping all day. They were women in their twenties who once had been pretty before living too roughly. Both were white. In fact, they were ghostly pale with dark circles under their eyes. They looked like heroin addicts who hadn't ever been clean.

"Hi, I'm Sophie," she had said when the girls appeared at the table without a sound.

They studied her with sad expressions.

"Lise and Francine don't speak English well," Jan said.

They must be European, Sophie thought. That's why they wore fashion scarves around their necks.

By the time dessert arrived, it was fully dark outside. Abruptly, the two women left the table and went outside.

"Nice talking to you, girls," Maria said.

"Where are they going?" Peter asked.

"They have a therapy session with Mr. Thogg. He's the owner of the house and yacht."

"Thogg?" Peter asked.

"Theodore Thogg."

"What kind of name is Thogg?" Peter seemed obsessed with ethnicity.

"American," Jan said.

Jan said there would be a group therapy session later that evening, but gave no time. The girls still hadn't returned from their private therapy session on the yacht. So after the small talk ran out, Sophie and her two fellow patients broke off and went to their bedrooms. Sophie lay on the bottom bunk and read a paperback, a romance novel about werewolves. Wouldn't life be cool if supernatural creatures existed? Especially hot guys with six-pack abs who would fight with other monsters to protect her.

Just as she was getting sleepy, loud laughter from unfamiliar voices erupted from the common areas. She got up to investigate.

The sliding glass doors were wide open and on the pool deck four people sat in chairs arranged around a fire in a portable fire pit. They laughed and swigged from bottles of wine. They looked up as Sophie approached.

Three men and one woman smiled at her in a knowing, creepy way. They were a strange-looking lot. Muscular and stocky, large heads with pronounced features. Wide noses and rugged jaws, sloping foreheads, and unkempt hair. But they all dressed nicely in designer resort wear.

One man, brandishing a bottle of Scotch, stood. He was the oldest of the group, but only in his thirties. He was clean-shaven with short, dark hair and a face that was slightly handsome in a rugged way.

"I'm Thogg," he said. "Welcome to my home."

"Hi. I'm Sophie," she said shyly.

"This is Mona, Gar, and Carldophilus. Just call him Carl."

Thogg followed Sophie's eyes to the bottle in his hand.

"Ah, we set a terrible example." He hurled his bottle over the pool and into the cove. "Come, my friends, let's show some respect for our guests are in therapy."

Mona and Carl tossed their bottles into the water. Gar clutched his own bottle to his chest and growled when Thogg pointed to him.

Sophie's faith in Better Daze Recovery sank to even lower depths than when she was staying in the former motel peeing in a cup three times a day. How could these party animals who looked like Neanderthals possibly know anything about therapy?

Peter and Maria came out onto the pool deck.

"Ah, more tasty young guests!" Thogg exclaimed.

Maria shot an alarmed glance at Sophie. Sophie was concerned, too. Thogg sounded like a perv.

Thogg introduced his friends. "Come, pull up chairs and join us," he said.

Hesitantly, Maria and Peter dragged patio chairs to the circle around the fire pit.

"That's a sweet yacht you have," Peter said.

"We love it," Thogg said. "We sail it to Florida from Canada every season. But we think our years as snowbirds have come to an end. We will be staying in Florida full time. You have no state income tax!"

"How long is she?" Peter asked.

"One hundred and ten feet. We'll invite you to tour her one night soon."

"That would be excellent."

Mona giggled. Carl was making hand shadows with the light of the fire. Carl was younger than Thogg and wore a short goatee. He had a scar under his right eye.

"Ah, an elephant!" Sophie said.

"No," Carl said. "Wooly mammoth."

"Of course. Dumb mistake."

"You know what this is?" Carl created a four-legged creature that was sleek and of shorter stature than the mammoth.

"A dog?" Sophie asked. "Wolf?"

Carl slapped his hands on his thighs in exasperation. "A cave hyena. I thought it was obvious."

"Look at this," Peter said, making his own hand shadow.

"Ah, jackrabbit," Carl said sadly. "How I miss a good rabbit stew."

"Let's not talk about meat," Thogg said.

Were those fangs showing beneath his lip? Sophie wondered. My God, yes.

Thogg noticed her stare, pressed his lips together and smiled.

"So you guys are Canadian?" Peter asked. "Jan said you're American."

"We are American," Thogg said. "We roam around a lot. We like to go to Canada for hunting."

"I love hunting," Peter said. "My dad used to take me to

Africa." He stared at Thogg intently. "You look kind of East European to me."

"Peter, don't be rude," Maria said.

"I've lived in America for thousands—I mean, my family has been in America for generations. Since the beginning."

"Oh, they sailed over on the Mayflower?" Peter said defiantly. "I actually had a relative who did."

"No, they walked over. Across the Bering Strait. Long before your relative ever got on a boat."

Peter and Maria laughed. Sophie wasn't so sure Thogg was being sarcastic.

"We were supposed to go to Central America, but we took a wrong turn," Carl said. "We eventually hit a dead end. Florida."

Their four hosts laughed at an inside joke.

"That was the first time we came to Florida and we find that we just keep coming back," Thogg said. "The hunting is so much better now. That's why we're staying full time."

"What do you hunt here?" Peter asked. "Wild boar? Deer? Turkey?"

"Everyone," Thogg said.

His friends laughed.

"Are we going to do any group therapy tonight?" Maria asked. "I've been making good progress, but today was a hard day."

"We will have individual therapy sessions," Thogg said. "Would you like us to begin with you?"

"Like I said, today was a bad day. Too much time alone with my thoughts and memories. I keep trying to look at the good inside me, but I feel so full of self-hatred."

Maria was turning this into a group therapy session, Sophie thought.

"You are boring me, darling," Thogg said.

Maria looked like she had been slapped in the face. "What?"

"Don't you worry about Thogg," Carl said, scrolling on his phone. "You have my full attention."

"What they're trying to say is your individual therapy will be so much more effective," Mona said. "You'll have the four of us and just you. It's better than talking and talking."

"And talking until you kill the entire evening," Thogg said.

Mona stroked Maria's arm. "You have beautiful features."

"Why is your hand so cold?" Maria said, drawing away.

"You know, I think you share some of our genes," Mona said.

"What are you talking about? What genes?"

"American," Thogg said.

"She might fit in quite well with us," Carl said.

Gar grunted in affirmation.

"What are you guys talking about?" Maria asked, annoyed.

"Maybe you'll work with us someday," Mona said.

"At a recovery place? I want to go to law school."

Thogg laughed.

"You're supposed to be supportive of my ambitions."

"Don't worry about Thogg," Mona said. "He has a strange sense of humor, but his charisma will win you over."

"Charisma? What charisma?" Maria folded her arms and pouted.

"This conversation has become tedious," Thogg said. "Let's go aboard and have some *therapy*. Are you ready, Maria?"

"I don't want any therapy with you guys."

Mona stroked her arm. "You have such an independent spirit," she said in a soothing voice. "You are a strong woman. Strong enough to overcome your inner demons."

Maria's expression dramatically softened. She smiled.

"Thank you," she said softly.

"You should be proud of your strength," Thogg said, suddenly affectionate.

Maria's blissful expression seemed almost drug induced. Sophie exchanged a questioning look with Peter.

"Are you ready to talk more about this?" Mona asked, stroking Maria's arm.

"Yes. That would be nice."

"Then let us reconvene on the *Man Cave*," Thogg said, standing. He nodded to Sophie and Peter. "It was a pleasure meeting you. I hope you will find our home comfortable. We'll speak again tomorrow night."

He led the way to the dock where the yacht was moored. Gar followed, tossing his empty bottle of wine in the water. Mona and Maria walked side by side and Carl took up the rear. He glanced back at Sophie and Peter, studying them. Then he smiled and waved.

"Man, they are seriously whacked," Peter said.

"Is it safe for Maria to be alone with them?"

"Those other two girls, I forget their names, they're still on the boat?"

"Lise and Francine. I think they are. But they didn't look like they would be much help."

"Maria's a pretty tough girl," Peter said.

"But there's four of them. We should check on her."

"We're not supposed to go near the yacht."

"We won't go on it. We'll just tiptoe up to it and try to see inside."

"Okay, but let's wait a few minutes."

They sat and watched the fire die down in the metal fire pit. The night was silent except for a boat passing in the distance on the Intracoastal Waterway. No sounds came from the yacht.

"Okay, let's go," Peter whispered.

They walked carefully down the dock until they were close enough to get a glimpse in the large windows of the vessel's lounge on the aft deck. Sophie crept a little closer and craned her neck to see.

Inside the well-lit lounge, Maria sat on a couch next to Mona, smiling dreamily. The back of a male head was against the window. Nothing appeared to be going on other than talking.

Sophie gestured for Peter to follow her to the house.

"Seems harmless," he said when they reached the fire pit.

"I don't know. Something feels off."

"Well, what can we do? Barge in there? They'll kick us out of the house and Better Daze will drop us and we'll end up homeless."

"Yeah, you're right."

The two said goodnight and went to their rooms. Sophie read two chapters of her werewolf romance novel and went to bed.

The noises came from outside just as she was falling asleep. Deep snuffling breaths and heavy footsteps in the yard just outside her window. A low, moaning growl.

She was too afraid to move.

More snuffling and sniffing near her window. A giant shadow darkened the blinds and shut off the moonlight that seeped through.

It knows I'm in here. It smells me.

This wasn't a dog or multiple dogs. This was a gigantic creature. She had to be dreaming.

A large object pressed against the window with wet inhalations.

No, it wasn't a nightmare. This was real.

She lay in bed unmoving, trying to breathe as quietly as possible, her heart pounding and her head throbbing. She didn't dare call out for Jan or the others. She didn't want to provoke this creature. A mere window would not hold it back if it wanted in.

And then the dark shadow passed. The footsteps and snuffling receded into the distance. She waited, still frozen, for what seemed like hours, until she dared to turn her head toward the clock by the bed.

3:17 a.m.

An hour later, she realized sleep wasn't going to happen. She found the courage to get out of bed and separated the window blinds ever so slightly with her fingers. Nothing was outside except the lawn, shrubbery, and a stone wall blocking the view of the neighbor's house.

She went to the kitchen and grabbed a bottle of water from the cavernous fridge. As she was sipping it, the sliding glass door opened in the living room. She crept through the family room and took a look, hiding beside a wall.

Gar walked inside with two bodies slung over his shoulders. They were Lise and Francine, passed out or drugged. He disappeared into the hallway where the guest bedrooms were located and soon returned. He went outside, closed the slider, and walked toward the dock.

Sophie found the girls' room and quietly opened the door. They each lay on their separate beds. Sophie was relieved to see the rising and falling of their breathing.

"Hey," she whispered.

No response.

"Are you guys okay?" she asked in normal volume.

Still no response.

She approached Francine's bed and shook her shoulder gently. The young woman made a faint moan.

"I'm checking to make sure you're okay," Sophie said. "Are you on something?"

Francine still didn't respond. Her breathing was steady but shallow. Sophie bent over to study her face.

And saw the puncture marks on her neck.

She gasped and stepped backward in fright. Yes, those were puncture wounds.

She crossed the room to Lise's bed. She had wounds on her neck, too. And there were several on her inner forearms as well.

Vampire bites? Were Thogg and his crew bloodsuckers?

Sophie didn't believe in vampires, though legends of them abounded in San Marcos. Sophie's mother had mentioned them occasionally in the past, but they hadn't seemed like serious references and she never gave straight answers when Sophie questioned her.

And now it appeared that the creatures did exist.

It began to sink in what this meant for Sophie and the others.

She left the bedroom and quietly closed the door. Farther down the hallway, just past her own room, was Maria's. The door was closed. She opened it, not wanting to risk the noise of knocking.

The bed was vacant. Maria was still on the yacht.

This was bad, very bad.

Sophie next went to Peter's room at the end of the hallway.

She tried the door handle, but it was locked. She knocked lightly. No answer. She knocked again.

The door opened a crack. Peter looked out.

"My, it's Sophie. What unexpected good fortune. Come on in."

He opened the door with a mischievous smile, revealing that he wore only boxer shorts. She felt suddenly uncomfortable in an extra-large T-shirt over her panties.

"Listen," Sophie said, "Thogg and his gang are vampires."

"Get out of here!"

"Shhh." She pushed past him into the room and closed the door. "Put some clothes on."

He reluctantly grabbed a pair of jeans from a chair and stepped into them. He moved to turn on a small lamp on the dresser, but she signaled for him not to. There was enough light to see from the face of the clock radio and she didn't want Jan to see that anyone was up.

"I woke up just now and got some water in the kitchen and saw Gar come inside carrying Lise and Francine. They were unconscious. Remember, they went to the yacht after dinner and we never saw them again last night."

"Yeah, so what? They passed out and Gar brought them back. It's too bad Thogg and his people let them get high or drunk or whatever they were on."

"Peter, they have puncture wounds on their necks. Multiple wounds. And Lise has them on her arms, too."

"Weird. Is that some sort of self-mutilation? Like a mental illness thing?"

"Peter, don't be a moron. We're living here with Jan trying to fatten us up. The owners are sequestered on a yacht and only appear at night. I got a glimpse of Thogg's teeth, which looked abnormally long and pointy. And now they dump these two women who are unconscious and covered with puncture wounds. Do I have to spell it out more clearly for you?"

"Are you saying . . . vampires? No way."

"Yes."

"I can't believe this," Peter said, rubbing his hands on his face. "They have to be some of those goth types who pretend they're vampires."

"I don't think so. God, I wish they didn't confiscate our phones. I should have known something was up."

"It was so we couldn't call up a dealer and order drugs."

"We'd already progressed enough to earn our phones back before we came here. The only reason they took them away again was so we couldn't call for help."

Peter's face went pale. The gravity of the situation was sinking in with him.

"We have to rescue Maria and then get out of here," Sophie said.

"We don't owe Maria anything."

"Don't be a jerk. She's one of us and she's in danger with them." She cocked her head in the yacht's direction. "If the tables were turned, you wouldn't want us to abandon you to the vampires."

He rubbed his face. "I don't know. We'd have to wait until daylight. That is, if they're really vampires. But during the day, Jan will be keeping an eye on us. And there might be a guard on the yacht."

"If we act right at dawn, maybe Jan won't be up yet. Same with the guard."

"I don't know. It's really risky."

"All we need to do is grab our stuff, take Maria off the boat, and keep walking until we get to a bus stop."

"My parents spent big bucks on my recovery," Peter said. "This would be the third place I failed."

"They didn't pay all that money for you to be passed around like a toy by four vampires who will drain your blood until you're unconscious and anemic. And end up dead."

"Well, if you put it that way."

"Look in the outdoor storage closet for things we can use as weapons."

"You mean like stakes to kill the vampires? I don't think I can handle that."

"No," Sophie said. "We're going to let the vampires sleep. We need weapons in case there's a non-vampire guard aboard. Now go, and be quiet."

About ten minutes later, Peter returned with a shovel and a hammer.

"This was all I could find. It doesn't look like Thogg does any gardening."

Sophie took the hammer. She went to her room to gather her belongings. Then she realized she should do the same for Maria's. She brought the two backpacks to Peter's room and sat on an extra chair while he sat on the bed. They waited for the agonizingly long hours to pass until dawn without speaking, only staring at the window for signs of light in the sky.

At 6:00 a.m. the sky turned purple and then orange. Sophie and Peter left the house through a side door near the garage so Jan wouldn't hear them. But as they exited, that deep snuffing

sound she'd heard before came from the garage. The garage door buckled outward slightly as a massive weight pushed against it.

"What is that?" Peter asked worriedly. "That doesn't sound like a dog to me."

"Don't think about it," she said. "Let's hurry."

Sophie had her backpack strapped on and carried the hammer in her right hand. Peter was burdened with both his and Maria's packs on his back and had the shovel grasped at the middle of the handle. Rounding the giant house, they crossed the pool deck past the metal fire pit filled with ashes.

Before they walked onto the dock, Sophie turned to Peter and held her finger to her lips. Then she led the way down the dock, past three empty slips, toward the massive vessel that held four vampires and their friend.

The dock made agonizingly loud creaks with each of their footsteps. The mooring lines groaned, and the foam bumpers squished as the yacht shifted with the current. Fog clung to the surface of the dark water around the roots of the mangroves that sheltered the cove.

A fish splashed, and Sophie nearly jumped out of her sneakers. She turned to check on Peter, who looked a little silly wearing the two backpacks and carrying the shovel.

They were close to the yacht now, and she stopped and listened. No voices or sounds came from the boat. Aside from the flying bridge on top, all windows and portholes were covered by curtains or blinds.

She couldn't delay any longer. She removed her backpack and placed it next to a piling, then climbed aboard using a short gangway that led to the main deck. A few steps away was a door. She tried the handle. Of course it was locked.

She walked forward toward the bow on the narrow deck that ran along the side of the vessel. Hopefully, there would be another way in. She tried to get a glimpse inside the windows she passed, but all were thoroughly covered, no doubt to prevent sunlight from entering.

At the bow, a large sundeck included a hot tub. There was a door here, too, but it was locked. She made a complete circuit of the deck, but the other two doors she found were locked as well.

Now she was back at the gangway. Peter shifted nervously on the dock below her. She was about to give up when she saw the tiny gap at the edge of a sliding window. She carefully eased it open and pushed the curtain aside.

The cabin was pitch black. She couldn't see anything. But the window was large enough to allow her to crawl inside, if she had the courage.

She leaned in and hoped her eyes would adjust to the darkness. She could barely make out the shapes of chairs and end tables.

"Maria," she whispered. "Maria."

Sophie would have to crawl in. She turned to get Peter's attention, waved for him to come aboard. He nodded, but suddenly his face registered alarm.

Strong hands seized Sophie and yanked her through the window into the darkness.

The shovel made a loud clang as it hit the dock amid the pounding of Peter's feet running away.

9

MISSED THE BOAT

Missy drove north with Matt in her passenger seat. Her new car ran like a charm, compared to her old one that had disappeared in a sinkhole thanks to a magick attack. Her "new" car was actually about to hit six figures in mileage, but it seemed in mint condition compared to the old one which had more than double that. If it weren't for the longevity of Japanese cars, Missy wouldn't be able to afford to drive at all. Home health nurses for stingy supernaturals don't exactly rake in the bucks.

"This is the street," she said, turning right on a residential street just past a dubious-looking strip center. The first houses they passed weren't much to look at, but as they headed east, closer to the Intracoastal Waterway, their street appeal increased dramatically. Where the street ended in a cul-de-sac, the homes on the water were mini-mansions.

And there, just beyond a massive banyan tree, sat a white passenger van. A druggie buggy.

Missy checked her mapping app. "This is the place," she said.

She drove further into the cul-de-sac at an angle that allowed a glimpse around the side of the house to the water beyond it. Part of the yacht was visible.

"Yep, this is it."

Earlier, she had researched the home on the county property tax appraisal site. The house was owned not by an individual, but by Mammoth Enterprises, LLC. The home next door was also owned by this entity. A public records search revealed that they had purchased the properties with cash. She spent an hour on the internet trying to come up with information on the company to no avail. The only useful tidbit was a filing in public records that also mentioned Better Daze Recovery Center. According to her notes, that was one of the companies she had called in her fruitless search for Sophie.

"So, it looks like the house might be a sober home," Matt said.

"It certainly does."

They sat in the car, engine running, staring at the house. What were the odds that the vampires were held captive in a yacht behind the house where Sophie was staying? Stranger things have happened.

"We should probably do something," Matt said.

"We probably should."

The problem was, she didn't know what to do other than walk right up to the house and ask if Sophie was there. So that's what she did.

She rang the doorbell. It was an elegant-sounding harmonious ring that befitted a multimillion-dollar home. After a long wait, the door opened and a stressed-out woman with her hair in a tight bun looked out.

"Hi, I'm looking for Sophie Chesswick," Missy said.

"She does not live here," the woman said in a German accent.

"Do you know where she might be?"

"I have never heard of this woman. Have a nice day."

The door closed in Missy's face. She wasn't surprised.

"The woman who answered the door claims she never heard of Sophie," Missy said as she got back in the car. "But that means nothing. She could be lying to protect Sophie's privacy."

"It would be too much of a coincidence for Sophie to be here," Matt said. "There are a lot of sober homes around here. Maybe it's not so odd that the yacht filled with vampires just happens to be moored at a sober home."

"No, it's a common place for yachts filled with vampires to be."

"You don't have to be sarcastic," Matt said.

"You don't have to be so touchy."

"Hey, I staked a vampire last night. My feelings are a little raw."

"And I staked one, too, a couple of nights ago. We should form a support group for vampire killers."

"Seriously, what are we going to do now?"

"We continue our search for Sophie. And we get Paul Leclerc to engineer a raid against the yacht to rescue our vampires."

"How are we going to steal a one-hundred-and-ten-foot yacht from a heavily populated area in broad daylight? I'm glad you asked," Paul Leclerc said to the Squid Tower HOA board and

Missy. "Because 'we' are not going to do it. I don't want to get disbarred from practicing law, and you folks obviously can't do it in broad daylight.

"Instead," he continued, "a crew of the most dangerous, ruthless thieves you have ever imagined will do it. In case you haven't guessed, I'm referring to a boat-towing service. The guys you call when your engine dies and you're adrift far out to sea and they demand a king's ransom before they'll even tie a line to your boat."

The vampires exchanged glances.

"Vampires generally aren't into boating," Bill said. "So we're not entirely clear what you're saying."

"I'll put it simply," Leclerc said. "A crew of amoral mariners will pilot their boat to the yacht and tow it away, giving the appearance of bringing a broken-down vessel to the marina for repairs. If there are human crew aboard, they will be dealt with by my cousin Simeon."

"That's what I was hoping to do," Bill said, "with superior firepower."

"Wait a minute," Agnes said. "So now you have a yacht filled with bad vampires and the good vampires we want to rescue. Now what?"

"Simeon will expose the interior of the boat to sunlight and go from cabin to cabin staking any sleeping vampires who weren't destroyed by the sunlight."

"You don't see the flaw in that plan?" Agnes asked. "How will Simeon know which are the good vampires and which are the bad?"

"You'll provide photos and descriptions."

"And you have a misperception of vampires that will get Simeon killed," Kim said. "We're not in a coma when we sleep.

We wake up in the middle of the day sometimes. Marty wakes up more than once to pee."

"To pee?" Schwartz was astounded. "I pee only once every three days."

"He doesn't actually pee when he wakes up," Kim explained. "He just thinks he has to. An old habit and prostate trouble from his human days. But the point is, staking a vampire could be noisy, and then the others will wake up and kill Simeon if he comes in their cabins."

"I'm just a humble werewolf country lawyer," Leclerc said. "I'm no expert on vampires."

"You will have the boat towed to an out-of-the-way dock where several vampires and I will board and fight Thogg's crew," Agnes said.

"I don't want to fight another vampire," Schwartz said. "I had to be rescued by a human last time."

"We'll have overwhelming numbers," Agnes said. "And a few tricks up our sleeves."

"And guns?" Bill asked hopefully.

MISSY STOOD in the towing boat's stern as it chugged up the Intracoastal toward the cove where the yacht was moored. Why was she on this vessel with the bloodthirsty pirates that Leclerc had defamed? Because he had begged her to go.

"They might need a little of your magick to make sure nothing goes wrong," he had pleaded.

"You think it's too risky for you to go yourself. Why should I go?" she asked.

"Your friends are being held captive," Leclerc said. "And I can't afford to jeopardize my career if we get arrested."

"Oh, and *I'm* expendable?"

"You're a home health nurse for supernaturals. You're not even licensed."

"I'm still licensed for treating humans. But, yeah, what governing body would license nurses for monsters? Anyway, I don't want to be arrested either."

"Your magick could save some lives today. Those low-life hustlers need you."

Missy did, in fact, want to see how this would go down. So she agreed. And the black-hearted cutthroats that Leclerc went on about were well-behaved. Maybe it was because she was a woman.

The towing boat was like a smaller version of a tugboat. It resembled a commercial fishing vessel small enough to maneuver in a marina. When Missy alerted the captain, he dropped the speed and turned into the gap in the mangroves that was the entrance to the cove. They followed the narrow channel, rounded the bend, and emerged in the cove with the dock behind the high-end homes. The water glimmered in the early morning light.

The dock was empty. The yacht had left.

"We got here too late," the captain said.

Missy felt like the wind had been knocked out of her. It had taken a lot of strength and energy to pull off the spell that located Gladys on the *Man Cave,* and it had required conventional searching to find the vessel. Now she had to start all over again. The mission was scrubbed.

She texted Agnes to let her know. Agnes didn't sleep much

and even if she was asleep at the moment, she'd see the text before dusk and call off transporting the vampires to the location where they were planning to attack the yacht.

The towing boat drifted toward the dock, then reversed as the bow swung around. Objects on the dock caught her eye: a green garbage bag and a pink backpack.

"Can you pull up to the dock, please?" she asked the captain. "I want to check out those bags."

The captain complied, and once the craft touched the dock, a crew member slung a rope around a piling to keep the boat steady. Missy climbed onto the dock.

The plastic garbage bag looked like it had been dropped there in haste when the yacht departed. She opened it to find only empty wine, liquor, and water bottles. No food remains or packaging.

And a bloody rag. Her stomach clenched.

The backpack lay in the middle of the pier a little closer to shore. It looked like it belonged to a young girl with its pink color and an illustration of a Disney princess on the front. Inside, however, were a woman's underwear, adult T-shirts, and shorts. A few toilet articles and a paperback romance novel were at the bottom of the bag.

Then she noticed the luggage tag tied to a carrying strap. Large, loopy lettering read:

"Sophie Chesswick."

Underneath was a phone number. Missy pulled her phone from her pocket and called it.

"You have reached Better Daze Recovery Center. Our office hours are nine a.m. to six p.m. If this is an emergency, please call nine-one-one."

Missy disconnected, grabbed the backpack and hopped back on the boat.

Sophie was on the yacht with the vampires, Missy was certain. And Better Daze had lied about Sophie when she had called them. The housekeeper lied, too, when Missy inquired at the house.

In fact, asking for Sophie most likely tipped off the vampires and caused them to flee. Now she had to live with that.

As the towing boat headed back to its marina, Missy wished she could do a locator spell to find Sophie, but she couldn't because she'd never met her. The photo she had was not sufficient to create a full visual in her mind. Perhaps the contents of her backpack would provide enough of Sophie's spirit energy to use the spell that had found Gladys' location, but Missy doubted clothing would retain enough energy for the spell to work.

The best strategy would be to get Gladys' phone and use that again for the spell, and hope it would locate her and the yacht again.

Her phone buzzed. It was a text from Agnes:

"Please try locating the yacht with your magick."

No kidding, Missy thought.

"I need access to Gladys' phone again to do the spell. Please unlock her condo," Missy texted in response.

Once they docked, Missy drove directly to Squid Tower. It wasn't even noon yet, so all the vampires were asleep, but Agnes had nevertheless unlocked Gladys' condo.

Missy picked up the vampire's phone from the table and repeated the spell-casting ritual she had used before. Gladys' spirit energy was slightly faded, she noticed. Your energy might cling to an object that's important to you, but it won't last forever. It will fade with time, like the body heat you leave in a chair. Fortunately, Gladys' energy was still strong enough to complete the spell. Missy sent the glowing orb in pursuit of its owner.

She had to wait much longer this time. And when she finally received the image of the yacht, it was faint and filled with static, like a bad video connection.

Her heart dropped when the image came into focus. The yacht was off the coast of Jellyfish Beach, far out to sea.

She called Paul Leclerc and filled him in on the recent developments, including their new captive, Sophie. She asked if the vessel could be taken.

"This is a whole new ballgame," Paul told her. "The mechanics of pulling this off are much more difficult on the rougher water of the ocean and when the yacht is under power. Plus, they'll have a crew member on watch at all times, so we can't just sneak up and steal the boat. This would have to be like a classic pirate attack. There would be violence and we could have casualties."

"What else could we do?"

"They'll eventually have to go to a port somewhere for fuel. And more blood."

The image of Sophie being harvested to feed the vampires sickened Missy.

"We should wait and see where they go," Paul said. "I sincerely doubt they're crossing the ocean. Maybe they're headed for the Bahamas or the Keys. Or back here when things cool down."

Missy believed they would return to Jellyfish Beach. Because this was the territory Thogg wanted to rule. She explained that to Paul.

"I think you're right," he said. "So we just have to be patient. The good news is it's unlikely they'll kidnap anyone else. Or come to attack you. Bats aren't designed to fly in ocean winds."

"What if they left some vampires behind to do it?" Missy asked.

Paul paused. "Then we're in deep doo-doo."

At 3:00 a.m., no humans were on the beach or lounging on the balconies of oceanfront condos. Still, the yacht had its running lights extinguished and all interior lights off. The only illumination was from the instruments in the bridge where its human captain brought the vessel as close to shore as he dared, only 150 yards from the beach and perilously close to a reef. But the winds were dead, and the ocean was flat—easy conditions to anchor and keep the yacht steady.

A stateroom window opened, and a bat flew out. Flapping furiously, it made it to shore without a problem, thanks to the lack of a breeze. It flew to the nearest building, which happened to be Squid Tower Condominiums.

It fluttered above the swimming pool where a session of vampire water aerobics was in progress. No one noticed the bat. It flew past the shuffleboard courts where a heated argument over scoring took place. And then it hovered above the multiple pickleball courts where vampires played mixed doubles matches.

Darting up and down like an insect, the bat headed for the lobby. A hunched-over male vampire on a scooter rolled through an automatic handicap door and the bat passed overhead. The vampire pushed the elevator button, and the bat perched on a wall sconce until the doors opened. The bat followed him into the car.

The bat telepathically whispered into the vampire's brain: "Four, please."

The scooter vampire dutifully pressed the button and then the fifth floor for himself. Only then did he look up at the hovering bat with a confused expression on his face.

When the door opened at Four, the bat flew out. It headed down the hall to Number Seven. And then it transformed into a humanoid vampire.

It was Thogg. He rang the doorbell.

The door opened. When Bill recognized Thogg, alarm passed over his face.

"You're that Neanderthal vampire!" Bill said.

Thogg struggled to control his temper. At least Bill wasn't using Neanderthal in an insulting manner.

"Good evening, Bill. I'm glad I found you at home."

"I believe we're enemies," Bill said. "Would you wait a moment while I get a stake from my weaponry room?"

"That's exactly why I'm here to speak with you. You have a reputation for being the wisest and most dangerous warrior of Agnes' vampires. Am I wrong?"

Bill puffed up with pride. But he still gave Thogg a side-wise glance of suspicion.

"I have been around for millennia," Thogg said. "I have seen brave men and those who only pretend to be brave. And when the saber-tooth tiger charges your hunting party, the pretenders suddenly disappear. You, Bill, are one who remains stalwart. You stand your ground and dig the butt of your spear into the dirt as the creature, larger than four men, leaps at you. This, I know from meeting you."

"You're just flattering me. Tricking me," Bill said.

"Tricking you how? I'm here to make a proposition. I need a brave vampire like you, who doesn't just have a gallant heart, but also lots of weapons. Who also collects obscure firearms and Japanese swords, not to mention uniforms from the American Civil War, and velvet paintings of dogs playing poker. You are just the sort of vampire I need."

"How do you know all this about me?"

"Because I admire you, Bill. I do my research."

"I agree that I'm a rare find, but I'm quite happy enjoying my retirement."

"How long have you enjoyed it? A hundred years? Two hundred? Don't you think you'll be bored after a thousand years or so?" Thogg asked. "I offer you the chance to be immortal not just in years, but in legends."

"You flatter me, but I'm just a simple guy—"

"Enough! You are the opposite of simple. You are the vampire I need to help me create an empire of greatness. A golden era of vampire glory. We vampires were created to rule the world, and why haven't we?"

"Because of taxes and regulations?"

"No! Because of cowardice and settling for the status quo. I am at the cusp of creating this empire. And all I need is brave warriors like yourself to fight the glorious battle at my side!"

"I was never actually in the military," Bill said. "But I have a lot of the firearms. And, like you said, some of the uniforms."

"You have fangs. And brilliance. And courage. That is all you need."

Thogg dialed his mesmerizing up to eleven. And it seemed to work.

"What exactly do you want me to do?" Bill asked in a soft voice.

"Fight with me. Follow me. Obey me."

Bill nodded, his eyes losing their focus.

Thogg leaned in close to his face. "Go for the glory."

Bill smiled and nodded. He closed his eyes.

And Thogg buried his fangs into his jugular vein. The blood was actually rather tepid.

After Thogg fed, Bill staggered backwards and sat on a living room chair. Thogg pulled a dagger from his belt and Bill flinched.

Thogg opened a vein in his own right arm just below the elbow. He thrust it into Bill's face.

"Drink and recover your energy. Then join me on my luxury yacht. Do you know how to swim?"

Bill nodded, smiling from his taste of Thogg's blood.

"Go to the beach. My boat is very close. You can swim to it very easily. I will be waiting for you, my gallant friend."

Thogg stepped back into the hallway. Just for insurance, he locked eyes with Bill and gave him a penetrating stare that could mesmerize a giant. Bill ate it up.

"Do you mind opening the doors to your balcony?" Thogg asked.

Bill rose and shuffled like a zombie into his living room,

where he unlocked and slid the glass doors open on their tracks.

Thogg stepped onto the balcony and shifted into a bat. He flew to his yacht, eating some bugs along the way.

Sure enough, an hour later, a crew member helped a wet and exhausted old vampire named Bill climb onto Thogg's yacht.

And Thogg's retinue of slaves grew larger.

10

MAGICK IN DEMAND

Missy's last home health visit of the evening was cancelled. The patient was Agnes, who needed a check of her vital signs because of all the stress she'd been under lately. The reason for the cancellation? Even more stress. The HOA board called an emergency session to discuss the disappearance of Bill.

"I was at the pool and he walked right past us like a zombie," Gloria said. "And I've seen zombies before, down in Miami. I know of what I speak."

"Stanley Gatz was using his metal detector on the beach," Kim said. "He told me he saw Bill walk straight across the beach and into the water with all his clothes on. Then he swam out to the boat—it was an enormous yacht just offshore with all its lights off. Stanley said Bill made it to the boat, and some guys helped him climb aboard. Then the boat left."

Agnes glared at Missy. It's not a pleasant experience when a vampire glares at you, even when she's in the body of a ninety-year-old.

"You said the yacht was heading to the Bahamas," Agnes said.

"I said the Bahamas was a possibility. The boat was far out to sea heading east when I had a vision of it. There was no way I could have known it would turn around and come here."

"What do you suggest we do now?" Agnes asked.

"The yacht will need to refuel somewhere. That's when we'll attack."

"In the unlikely event we can get there before they're finished fueling," Schwartz said. "Chasing after the boat is a waste of time in my opinion. I say we enter into negotiations with them."

The room filled with astounded intakes of breath from half the members and angry hissing from the other half.

"How could you even suggest that, Leo?" Agnes asked, directing her deadly glare at him this time.

"They've taken four of our residents and disrupted Blood Bus deliveries," Schwartz said. "What have we done to them? Zilch."

"Excuse me," Missy said standing up. Not being a member of the board, she was required to wait until the part of the meeting for public comments, but she had to say this. "We staked the vampire you were fighting on the kayak, Mr. Schwartz."

"Kayak?" Gloria muttered.

"And I staked one of Thogg's vampires in my home," Missy continued. "In front of Thogg, I should add. We've definitely damaged them."

"But we're still on the defensive," Schwartz said. "They're

outsmarting us and taking more of our vampires hostage. They're obviously much richer than us."

Everyone nodded and murmured how impressed they were by Thogg's immense yacht and obvious wealth.

Agnes slammed the table with the piece of wood that served as a gavel during board meetings. It was part of a stake that had executed the first vampire at Squid Tower to be penalized for breaking the bylaws: a scofflaw who insisted on putting tacky holiday decorations on her door. Over the decades since then, the sharpened chunk of wood symbolized the brutal rule of law.

"My fellow vampires, Thogg is a thug," Agnes said. "He's a caveman, for Pete's sake. Vampirism kept him alive when his people went extinct and he became a wily survivor. But he's an animal compared to us. A cave bat dropping his guano on our idyllic community. I'll never submit to that brute. We need to stay strong and fight back."

"Maybe Leo has a point," Kim said. Kim was from Amish country in Pennsylvania, though she hadn't kept up the tradition. Amish vampires are known to be particularly fearsome.

"I do?" Schwartz wasn't used to Kim agreeing with him.

"Yes. The world is changing. The population of vampires is growing in Florida. It's only a matter of time before we come under pressure from someone else to be ruled. Like the vampire mafia. Or the Miami Cuban vampires."

"I'll remind you all, our bylaws state that we're an independently chartered entity," Agnes said. "The vampires of Squid Tower won't be ruled by anyone. We will enjoy our retirement in freedom."

"Here, here!" Gloria said. "Bill would be pounding the table right now in support for you. If he were only here." She wiped a bloody tear from her eye.

"This is going to lead to all-out war," Schwartz said. "I fought one of Thogg's vampires and I was not winning, even though I'm from Brooklyn and I fight dirty."

"We have no choice," Agnes said. "They're taking our friends. They're trying to cut off our blood supply. They have to be stopped." She stood, all four-foot-something of right-eousness. "And we have something they don't have."

"Pickleball?" Schwartz asked.

"Magick," Agnes said. "We have Missy."

Uh-oh, Missy thought, swallowing.

The vampires agreed to a strategy session the following evening, then retired before dawn. And Missy did, too.

At 10:00 A.M., the doorbell awakened Missy. She threw on a robe and answered the door to find out her life had just gotten much more complicated.

Her cousin Darla stood on her front porch, smiling. Her cousin, whose daughter Missy had been unable to locate and was now in peril. The timing of this visit was rather unfortunate.

"Missy!" She leaned in to give Missy a brief hug and air kiss. "At last we meet. I brought you bread. Sourdough."

"Um, thanks. It's great to meet you in person, Darla. You didn't tell me you were coming today."

"No, not precisely. I said I couldn't leave my shop right away, implying that I would do so *after* right away, which I would call 'presently.' So here I am! Let me get my bag from the car."

"Your bag?"

"You won't mind my staying for a night or two, would you? As soon as we find Sophie, I'll be out of your hair."

"Sophie. Ah, yes. You might be here for more than a night or two." Missy didn't know how to break the news that Darla's daughter was a captive of vampires who were most likely feeding on her. And these weren't just any vampires. They were Neanderthal vampires. And they had Sophie on a yacht sailing to Lord knows where.

"Lord knows where?" Darla asked.

"Huh?"

"Oh, I'm sorry," Darla said, patting Missy on the arm. "I neglected to tell you I'm a telepath. I didn't read your thoughts on purpose; they just popped into my head uninvited. That happens from time to time at unpredictable moments. Those of us in the Chesswick clan have the paranormal in our genes. I know you must, too. I also have psychometric abilities."

"What's that?" Missy asked.

"When we hold objects, we leave a psychic residue on them. I can read it. When I touch said object, I read the thoughts the owner was having when she touched the object. I essentially relive her experience. More about that later. First, tell me about these vampires."

Missy was flummoxed. Psychometry had similarities to the spell she used to find Gladys.

"Please come inside," she said. "I hadn't planned on telling you about Sophie while we were still standing on the porch."

"I know. It was my fault. My abilities have created many an awkward social moment."

Missy led Darla inside to the living room and seated her on the couch.

"Lovely place you have," Darla said. "It's historic?"

"Nineteen-twenties Craftsman style. Built during Florida's first real estate boom."

"My home is from an earlier boom. Seventeen hundreds."

"Right, sometimes I forget it all began in San Marcos. Can I get you some tea?"

"Please."

While Missy was boiling the water, Darla entered the kitchen. She wouldn't sit still. She was petite with black hair, a pert nose, Irish dimples, and light freckles. Missy saw the resemblance to Sophie's photo, and, ever so slightly, to her own mother, the sorceress.

At the moment, worry lines creased Darla's forehead.

"How did you find Sophie?" she asked Missy.

Missy explained her and Matt's attempts to track Sophie down through recovery centers and how it was pure coincidence that they located the young woman while in pursuit of Thogg and his vampires.

"And you used magick to find the vampires?"

"Yes," Missy said.

"I'm not at all surprised you're a witch. As I said, the paranormal runs through our genes. I have many questions for you later. But first, I'm interested in Sophie's backpack you said you found. Do you have it here?"

"Yes, I was going to send it to you. I'll be right back."

Missy retrieved the childish pink bag from the guest room and brought it to the kitchen. Darla took it gingerly and examined it.

"I don't recognize it. She must have bought it down here after she went into therapy."

Darla's examination of her daughter's bag was more like the way a blind person might do it. She ran her hands over the bag's exterior, then along its inside surfaces. She opened the small, exterior zippered pockets and touched the lipstick, mascara, and compact. She touched the writing pen and the small notebook that was probably a journal, but she didn't open and read it. She removed each item of clothing, rubbed her hands upon it as if smoothing out wrinkles, then held it to her face, drinking in the scents.

It was poignant to watch. It was as if Darla was inventorying these possessions after her daughter had died. Missy wanted to tell her to keep the faith, that they would find Sophie, but she wisely kept her mouth shut.

Finally, Darla pulled the paperback romance novel from the backpack. It had a bare-chested man on the cover and the story was something to do with werewolves. Darla examined the book, opened it to the page saved by a business card used as a bookmark, and then ran her fingertips over the pages of the spread. She made a sharp intake of breath.

"Sophie was afraid on the night she last read this book. She had met the vampires. Three male and one female. They didn't identify themselves as vampires, but she suspected it. One claimed to be an owner of the recovery place. He owns the house where she was staying. And a yacht. A very large yacht. She was forbidden to go on the yacht, but the vampires brought one of Sophie's recovery patients aboard with them. They pretended that they were going to give this young woman therapy, but it was clear they didn't know anything about therapy. It was all an act.

"Sophie believed she was the only one of the three recovery patients who knew the true identity of the vampires. There were two other recovery patients staying in the home, but they had gone to the yacht earlier in the evening and hadn't returned. Sophie was very concerned."

Darla looked at Missy with eyes brimming with tears. "We have to find her right away."

"I know," Missy said, touching Darla's hand.

It was interesting that the book held so much of Sophie's energy.

"Can I see the book?"

Darla handed it to her, and as Missy held it, she probed it with her mind. It did, indeed, contain a great deal of energy. Sophie must have been truly engrossed in, and delighted by, the book.

"I have a spell I can use with the book that might help us locate Sophie. I used the spell before to locate a kidnapped vampire. A good vampire."

"You never explained why you were looking for the yacht in the first place."

"Well, it's complicated."

Missy explained about Thogg, his quest for domination in South Florida, and how he had been capturing vampires from Squid Tower to force the residents there to capitulate.

"Wow," Darla said. "It sounds like the Wild West down here. In San Marcos, the vampires have a very orderly, sophisticated society."

"I know. I've met one of them. But if Thogg has his way, San Marcos would be ruled by him. The vampires, at least. He says he wants to rule the humans of Florida, too, but he didn't say how. Even our governor can't quite manage to govern the humans."

"If you find Sophie, how will we rescue her? I assume down here, it's the same as in San Marcos: The human authorities cannot be involved."

"Absolutely. We'll have to rescue her ourselves. And by 'we,' I mean you, me, and the elderly vampires of Squid Tower. Our lawyer also has some thuggish humans at his disposal. We had plans to raid the yacht, but it escaped the night before."

Missy didn't mention that her inquiries about Sophie probably tipped off the vampires.

"No, don't blame yourself for inquiring about Sophie."

Oops.

Darla dropped into a chair at the kitchen table and took a big sip of tea. She looked exhausted.

"My fear was that Sophie was using drugs again. Or being sexually exploited. I was afraid she'd ended up with sleazy crooks pretending to help her. And she did. But I never imagined she'd be used as food by vampires."

"Now, we don't know if that's the case," Missy said.

"Why else would the vampires take her? Either for blood or sex. Or both."

"Let's not allow our imaginations to get out of control. Give me some time and I'll perform that spell to try to find her."

Missy retrieved the Red Dragon talisman from its hiding place in the false bottom of a cat litter box. The index card with the spell was hidden in her underwear drawer. Back in the kitchen, she began drawing a magick circle on the floor with chalk. Until being watched bothered her.

"I'm sorry," she said to Darla. "Do you mind waiting in the living room? I can't fully concentrate unless I'm alone."

"No problem." Darla took her cup of tea and left the room.

Missy brought Sophie's novel into the circle and began the spell-casting ritual. The energy level of the book was high. Holding the talisman with her left hand, the power surged through her and she read the words translated from the Spanish that Don Mateo had written centuries ago.

Before she knew it, a glowing orb floated in the air at eye level.

"Find Sophie," Missy whispered.

The orb disappeared. Missy put herself in a trance and waited.

Finally, a vision filled her head of the yacht, viewed from above. At that very moment it was sailing offshore. She made the orb get closer to the vessel so she could view the surroundings from the boat's perspective. To the right, land could be seen, which meant the yacht was headed south. It couldn't have traveled too far after picking up Bill off the beach at Squid Tower. And, sure enough, she recognized a water tower on land. The boat was south of Jellyfish Beach, hopefully headed for the next inlet, though that was just a wishful guess.

The woman whose spiritual energy was sought by the orb was somewhere on a lower deck of the vessel.

And she was in great distress.

Missy broke the spell and cleaned the chalk from the floor before going to the living room.

"I received a vision of the yacht," she told Darla. "It's not too far from here."

"What do we do?" Darla asked.

"I'll call the attorney with the thugs and we'll try to intercept the yacht with a faster boat. The yacht will need to refuel at a marina at some point, so I'm hoping it will enter the Intracoastal Waterway where we'll have a better chance of catching it."

"And you're sure Sophie is on this boat?"

"Yes," Missy said. Leaving out the fact that Sophie was distressed, and blocking the thought from her mind to prevent Darla from reading it.

11
YACHTING LIFE

Maria had four different pairs of puncture wounds in her neck, two on each side along the jugular veins. Based on the little Sophie could get Maria to say in her semi-conscious anemic state, the four vampires had fed upon her not long after bringing her to the yacht. Even worse, there were additional vampires on the vessel, held prisoner on the lower deck. The two younger women, Lise and Francine, and been given to them.

Sophie had a feeling that Thogg and his buddies got the fresh meat. When they had tired of it, the prisoners got the second helpings.

Was Sophie going to be the main course tonight?

She and Maria were in a locked lounge on an upper deck. There was a small sitting room, a bar, and a TV mounted to the wall. Maria slept on a sofa, Sophie sat on a chair nearby, though she mostly paced around the room. Through the blinds, the open ocean stretched to the horizon; a distant shore was visible from the other side of the boat. The engine rumbled from far below as they cut through the chop.

Sophie felt vaguely seasick. She fought the feeling. This was not the time to become incapacitated with her head over the toilet.

The door opened, and she jumped. It was the burly guy with the shaved head, the one who had yanked her through the window and tossed her in this room. He carried a tray of plates covered with metal lids that he placed on the coffee table.

"Where are we going?" Sophie asked.

He ignored her and left the room, locking the door.

The plates contained grilled cheese sandwiches and spinach salad. Sophie took a bite of the sandwich. It was all she could stomach.

"Maria, have some lunch. You need the calories."

Maria mumbled and rolled over on the couch.

So this was it? Sophie wondered. We just wait until the day ends and we're served for dinner? She didn't know how she could do it without losing her mind.

How bad would the vampire bites hurt? Did the vampires have bad breath? That Gar dude looked like he would have some serious halitosis. Would the bites cause infections? Would she become a vampire herself?

Too bad she didn't have her crucifix anymore. She had pawned the last of her jewelry for drug money ages ago.

These thoughts were going to drive her nuts, but what else was she going to think about until dusk?

She turned on the TV. Hopefully, there was a satellite connection to get regular programming. Instead, a lame video came on with an aerial shot of the yacht cruising on the ocean.

"Welcome to the S.S. *Man Cave*," said a female voice with an

English accent. "Thank you for being our guest. If you are a human, we kindly ask you to refrain from smoking while aboard. Please discard any garlic or crosses you may have brought with you. Please refrain from consuming alcohol or drugs four hours before sunset. Each cabin contains life vests. Please make note of their location. In case of an emergency, put it on and say a prayer because you're on your own. Thank you for sailing with us. For our vampire guests, kindly switch to Channel Five."

Sophie did so.

"Thank you for being our guests, honorable lords of the night. Your safety and enjoyment are important to us. Please refrain from transforming to bat form when on deck, as high winds could sweep you away. Please do not nest in the engine room to avoid self-combustion. Humans will be provided for your nightly nourishment. Please refrain from feeding on any crew members. Should you have special dietary needs, the *Man Cave* is stocked with fresh, whole blood in all blood types, as well as platelets and plasma.

"If you are awake during the day, Deck 3 midship, is completely sealed off from natural light so you can safely wander about and amuse yourself with table tennis and vampire video games. Please avoid the bridge during daytime. We are not responsible for burns from sunlight exposure. We hope you enjoy your stay with us."

Sophie flicked through the other channels. One featured championship poker, and the others had movies. They were all zombie movies, except for *Gone with the Wind*.

This was going to be a long day.

As she had done after being captured, she checked all the windows in a fruitless effort to escape. But to where? To float in the ocean in her life vest until the sharks ate her? Maybe sharks were preferable to vampires.

There was nothing left to do but take a nap on the other sofa.

SHE AWOKE with a start when the door opened. Mona was standing in the doorway smiling at them, and Sophie's heart sank as she realized it was fully dark out. Maria still slept fitfully.

"And how are my delectable little humans tonight?" Mona asked.

"Are you going to kill us?" Sophie blurted out. "Are we going to turn into vampires?"

"Aren't we inquisitive? You, the naughty one who was spying on us."

"I was trying to rescue Maria," Sophie said.

"Maria doesn't need rescuing. She has a very promising future ahead of her."

"A future of what? Being your blood-cow to be milked every night?"

"We are very special vampires, my dear," Mona said, closing the door and sitting on a chair across from Sophie. "We are possibly the oldest vampires on the planet."

"Why should I care?"

A flash of anger appeared in Mona's face, but she smoothed it away.

"With great age comes incomparable wisdom," she said. "And power. Vampires don't become weaker with age, like living creatures. We become stronger."

Sophie didn't care, but nodded anyway to avoid Mona's wrath.

"Thogg is a great leader," Mona continued. "He will be the king of all the vampires in Florida, and, soon, of the world. By then, all the humans will be our slaves and he will reign in glory."

"It doesn't sound very appealing to me."

"We shall see. Maria will share in that glory."

"Oh, no. You're turning her into a vampire?"

"We are what you modern hominids call Neanderthals. Not only will Thogg rule the world, but he will return our kind to prominence after we were cruelly wiped off the planet. As vampires, we can't reproduce like living humans. But we can make more vampires. In particular, with people who have an above average percentage of Neanderthal DNA."

"Say what?"

"Modern humans have traces of Neanderthal genes from when our species interbred tens of thousands of years ago."

"Yuck."

"My feelings exactly. I don't know what my ancestors saw in you guys."

Mona looked fairly normal in Sophie's eyes. A little ethnic, kind of heavy facial features, stocky, wide hips. She looked pretty much like Brenda Sarwiski from high school.

"Maria has Neanderthal genes?"

"Yes," Mona said. "I'm guessing maybe three percent. I wish it was a hundred percent, but we've got to work with what we've got. The test results should come in soon."

"What test?"

"My-Neanderthal-Ancestry-dot-com."

"Then what happens?"

"If she's above two percent Neanderthal, we turn her into a vampire."

"How?" Sophie asked, but instantly regretted it.

"We drain her to the point of death, then revive her with our own blood."

Sophie's stomach turned to stone.

"What will happen to me?" Her voice was barely above a whisper.

"You will remain our honored guest." Mona smiled. Her fangs were showing.

Laughter came from the corridor, then Thogg, Carl, and Gar entered the lounge.

"Ah, breakfast!" Thogg said when he saw Sophie. "Whoa, what is that smell? Patchouli? I hate patchouli. Are you some kind of hippy, girl?"

"Thogg, watch your manners with our new guest," Mona said.

"But our new guest was trying to break into our yacht."

"I wanted to rescue my friend," Sophie said. "Anyone would do the same thing."

"And there are many humans who would have shot you if they owned the boat. We, on the other hand, are making you our guest."

"Your breakfast. You already admitted it."

Thogg and the two males sat on a third couch. Four vampires and two humans, one of whom was still half asleep, waiting for something to happen. It was as awkward as teens at a party wondering when the making out would begin. Sophie wanted to steer the subject away from feeding.

"At your home, I heard an enormous creature outside of my window. Do you know what it was?"

"Ah, that was Lucy," Carl said. "We keep her in the garage and let her out at night."

"Lucy didn't sound like a dog," Sophie said.

"She's not a dog," Carl said. "She's a cave bear. A vampire cave bear, to be exact. She's been our beloved pet for thousands and thousands of years."

"And guess who has to clean up after her," Mona said.

"How can a bear become a vampire?" Sophie asked.

"From a very irresponsible Neanderthal vampire," Mona said.

"Do not forget I am your leader," Thogg said. "I have impaled thousands of victims upon stakes, both human and vampire, for disrespecting me."

"And you've been using that line to threaten me for like a hundred thousand years."

"I miss poor Lucy," Carl said. "We need to get home soon before she starts wandering the neighborhood."

"Jan will feed her," Mona said.

"But when Lucy gets lonely, she acts out."

"Technically, a vampire cave bear only drinks blood," Thogg explained to Sophie. "But boy, does she mess up who or what she feeds upon."

"Mess up?"

"We have to clean up pieces of them from all over the street."

"Why did we leave your house, anyway?"

"Don't you worry about it," Mona said. "Just some nosy people."

Nosy people? Sophie hoped it had been someone looking for her, that she was not completely gone and forgotten.

"So," Thogg slapped his hands on his knees. "Enough of this vapid chit chat. This is worse than when we're pretending to do therapy." He squinted and scrunched up his nose. "That patchouli is simply wretched."

"Thogg, please behave," Mona said.

"Vampires have hyper-sensitive olfactory nerves. My nose is burning up."

But then his eyes locked upon Sophie's. It seemed as if he had known her for her entire life. A light-headedness overtook her. When Thogg smiled, she smiled and heard his heart beating along with hers. Her eyelids drooped from sleepiness and she settled back on the sofa cushions.

Then all she knew was the beating of two hearts, of blood pulsing through arteries and veins.

Sophie awoke lying face-up on the sofa. It was still night outside and she and Maria were the only ones in the lounge. Her right ankle stung.

She snapped fully awake and jerked upright. There was a pair of puncture wounds high on her ankle. She ran her hands on her neck. No wounds there. Of course, that's where she had put dabs of patchouli the day before. She'd had no idea it would serve as vampire repellant.

But when she looked at Maria still sleeping on the other sofa, her heart raced. Maria had more wounds, this time on her forearms and ankles, as well. Their vampire captors had fed heavily on her.

A loud banging, clattering sound from below and just forward of the lounge startled her. Was it the anchor being lowered?

Sophie peered between the blinds. The yacht was crazy

close to shore. The lights of a condo tower burned about a football field's length away. What were they doing here?

She searched the shoreline for familiar landmarks. She didn't recognize any, but a painful longing arose in her at the sight of land. If she could only get out of this room, she could probably swim to shore. To safety. To life and a future. She'd hitchhike home to San Marcos. Heck, she'd walk if she had to. Anything to get out of this nightmare.

A dark speck of movement on the beach, a person, was wading into the surf. In the moonlight, it appeared to be a man, though he was far away. Now he was swimming toward the yacht. That was odd. As he got closer, she saw the white hair of an old man.

Crew members appeared at the railing of the deck below. One of them had one of those long-handled hooks you see at public swimming pools. The crew members leaned over the railing and soon pulled the fully clothed, soaking-wet man up onto the deck.

They immediately carried him into the boat and out of view.

Then footsteps thudded in the corridor outside the lounge and the door rattled as the key was slipped in.

12

ULTIMATUM

"The gang is back together again," Missy said sarcastically as the towing boat chugged up the Intracoastal Waterway. "And you've graced us with your presence."

"I have no reason to expect it will go any better this time," Paul Leclerc said as they stood at the rear of the pilothouse behind the captain and the mate. "It's not as if you gave us exact GPS coordinates and we could use sailing speed to predict where we'll intercept the yacht. This is completely guesswork."

"It's hard for that yacht to hide."

"How do we know they didn't refuel somewhere and now don't have any need to come in from the ocean?"

"You don't have to be grumpy about it. The HOA is paying for the fuel and labor."

"It would have been so much easier if we had called the cops," Paul said.

"If it was only Sophie who was kidnapped, we would have.

Not when there are four kidnapped vampires also aboard. So, how exactly are we going to take the yacht?"

"It will be a challenge to board it while it's underway and hijack it. I told the captain that if we find it, we'll follow it. If it docks in a secluded place, we'll steal it. If the only opportunity to take it is at night, vampires from Squid Tower will have to attack it."

"Oh."

"Yeah, the plan is too open-ended. I don't like having to improvise on matters where someone might get killed."

"Oh, my!"

"What?"

"Look." Missy pointed off the starboard bow where a gigantic yacht was passing in the other direction. It was the *Man Cave.*

The captain noticed, too, and after the yacht was safely behind them, he yanked the wheel and turned the towing boat around in pursuit. Keeping the yacht far ahead of them to avoid suspicion, they followed it as it moved south slowly enough to avoid casting a large wake as it passed the docks of condominiums and expensive homes.

The captain motioned for Paul to come to him. Missy followed.

"In about a mile there's an undeveloped stretch of waterway with a park on the east and a preserve on the west and no homes," the captain said. "Boat traffic is light today. If we overtake them there, we can probably jump on board without being seen."

Paul nodded. "Let's do it."

Oh my, Missy thought. This really is going to be a pirate affair.

The captain conferred with his mate and three other crew members who were sitting in the stern. They all pulled out handguns and checked the clips.

The waterway bent gradually to the left. As it straightened out, the captain slammed the throttle forward. Engines roaring, the boat practically leaped out of the water and raced forward. Soon, they were almost upon the yacht.

Both shorelines were now nothing but mangrove trees as the towing service boat caught up with the yacht, slowed to the yacht's speed, and pulled up against it. The yacht's deck was higher than the towing boat's, but the three crew members scrambled onto the roof of the pilothouse. Two of them easily jumped onto the yacht while the third aimed his pistol at the bridge. The two disappeared into the yacht and the third man jumped aboard. Meanwhile, the mate had secured a line from the towing boat to the larger vessel.

A few minutes went by. Missy held her breath, hoping no guns would fire. Then the yacht abruptly slowed.

One of the towing boat's crew appeared, leaning over the deck rail above them.

"It's empty," he said.

"What?" The captain was incredulous.

"There's no one aboard except the captain and two crew members. We're still searching, but their captain said the passengers moved to another boat last night while at sea."

"Where did they go?" Paul asked.

"She wouldn't say. She said she called the Marine Patrol on us, so we need to get out of here."

"Make sure you search in the hold," Paul said. "And the engine compartment."

The man nodded and went back inside. Not long afterwards, he and his two companions were back aboard the towing boat, the line was untied, and the towing boat turned around and headed north.

"That's strike two," Paul said to Missy.

She would have to try another spell to find Sophie and the vampires. But Thogg could always stay one step ahead of her and move again.

She arrived home to an empty house. Darla, fortunately, was out. So Missy immediately set to work on the spell. First, she connected with Sophie's spirit energy residing in the romance novel. It was still strong. At the culmination of the spell casting ritual, she went into a trance and followed the glowing orb that sought the source of the spirit energy: Sophie.

Soon, her consciousness hovered above a house. The spark of connection burned within in her, telling her that Sophie was in the house. This one was on the water, on a canal that ran perpendicular to the Intracoastal Waterway. It had to be expensive, based on its waterfront location, but it was smaller than the previous home the vampires used. It was a ranch-style model with a screened-in pool behind it and a dock. No boat was moored there. The roof was barrel tile. There was nothing unique about the house.

She willed herself in this astral travel to come down to ground level, so she could see an address on the mailbox. It wouldn't work. She wasn't fully in control of this. She tried floating higher to look for nearby landmarks. That didn't work. The only feature of the property that seemed unusual was an abnormally large outbuilding or shed attached to the house's rear. It was the kind of addition that probably wasn't to code.

She committed her vision to memory to assist her in her search for the house, though it wouldn't be easy to find.

Once she ended the spell, she was exhausted. But she realized she would also need to do one for Gladys. With Thogg and his vampires on the run, there was no guarantee that all the captives would be held in the same place.

She drove to Squid Tower to access Gladys' condo. That's where the vampire's cellphone remained because Missy hadn't felt right about removing it. She'd wanted to believe that somehow Gladys would make her way back on her own. Not much chance of that happening, though.

She had cleaned up the chalk that had marked her magick circle the last time she'd done this, hoping that there wouldn't be another time. So she took Gladys' phone and drew a new circle. She knew the words of the spell by heart now.

The vampire's spirit energy was still strong on the phone, but something unexpected happened. The magnetic-like pull of the force inside Gladys herself was too weak. The glowing orb she'd conjured wouldn't go in search of it. It simply remained hovering above the phone with nothing to pull it.

Was something wrong with Gladys?

She tried putting more power into the spell, yet still nothing happened. So she gave up and ended it.

Just then, she received an urgent text from Agnes. The vampire requested her presence at another emergency meeting of the HOA right after sunset.

IF YOU COULD IMAGINE vampire faces even more pale than death-white, that's what Missy saw when she entered the community room at Squid Tower. Four HOA board members, minus Bill, sat side by side at the long table facing the audience which in this case was a single vampire: Thogg. He sprawled in a folding chair that looked about to buckle under his stocky frame. He looked up when Missy entered the room.

"Your human?" Thogg asked. "Why do you need your human for a vampire matter?"

"She's our nurse."

"There's nothing a nurse can do for you now. You summoned her because you think her witchy powers will help you. They won't."

Thogg turned his red-rimmed, glowing eyes to Missy. "You killed one of my clan. You will pay for that."

"Why, exactly, did you want me here?" Missy asked Agnes.

"I have delivered an ultimatum to your geezer friends," Thogg said to Missy. "Submit to me tonight, or one of my captives will die at dawn."

"He tied up Bernie the gate guard on the roof," Kim explained. "If we don't pledge our servitude to this brute here, he'll keep Bernie up there until dawn when the sun will kill him."

"I say let the moron fry up there," Schwartz muttered.

"Leo! How dare you," Agnes said.

"You know I never liked him. I wanted him fired since the moment he showed up here. Then he gets turned and suddenly he's your favorite vampire."

"You know it's impossible to get a decent guard for the overnight shift," Gloria said. "Humans never last long, and vampires don't want to be stuck in a little booth all night when they could be hunting."

"Thogg, will you allow us some privacy to discuss this?" Agnes asked.

"I don't know why you would need to discuss whether to sacrifice someone's life."

"We want to agree on terms to negotiate with you."

"Negotiate? Ha! Good luck with that. I'll remind you that if you allow your gate guard to die, I have three more of your vampires to destroy."

Thogg stood, clenched his fists, and shook his body like a wet dog. Then a bat was in his place, hovering briefly before flapping away into the hallway.

The vampires were silent for a while.

"He made a mistake choosing Bernie to extort us with," Schwartz said.

"Shut up, Leo." Gloria said. "We're not sacrificing our vampires one by one to this brute."

"Then we're surrendering? That's what you're saying?"

Agnes pounded the table with the piece of wooden stake. "Why haven't Thogg and his thugs attacked and conquered us already?" Agnes asked. "Why is he reduced to extorting us? Because he doesn't have enough manpower."

"Vampire power," Kim corrected.

"We've killed two of his vampires," Agnes said, "and—"

"Technically, the humans killed them," Schwartz said. "Even though I seriously wounded the vampire I was fighting."

"Whatever, Leo. You see the point I'm trying to make. Thogg has vampires guarding the roof right now. How many more do you think he has? Enough to guard his captives. I'm hoping not many more than that. That's why Missy is here."

"Um, what?" Missy asked in a low voice.

"You will use your magick to find the new location of our vampires. Our best fighters will go with you. Hopefully, you'll face minimal resistance and be able to free our vampires. And you have to do it before dawn, so we can then free Bernie. I know it's a lot to ask. I hope you didn't have any other plans tonight."

"I was going to binge-watch *Buffy the Vampire Slayer*," Missy said. "But Agnes, there's a slight problem with what you're asking. I already used the spell to try to locate Gladys, but her life force was too weak for the spell to work."

"What does that mean?" Agnes asked.

"It means she's dying. Maybe she's refusing to feed."

"Then try the spell with Henrietta or Bill," Agnes said. "You need a cherished object of theirs to do it?"

Missy nodded.

"Then let's go to Bill's condo. He has a fetish for his weapon collection. I'm sure his guns and knives will hold more than enough spirit energy for you to use."

That vampires are especially stylish is a false cliché from the movies. Bill's condo had all the interior design aesthetics of an army barracks. Missy didn't know when he had been turned, but based on a framed photo of a young, human Bill, he was around when men wore bowler hats and muttonchop whiskers. There was a glass hutch with a variety of pistols and knives displayed from different eras.

"I wouldn't know where to begin," Missy said.

"His most cherished guns are probably in his gun safe," Agnes said, "so those won't do us any good, but he often bragged about a Prussian cavalry sword he had. I think it's that one there. Under the painting of the dogs playing poker."

Wall brackets held the sword in its metal scabbard, right below the image of a bulldog with a cigar in its mouth and a pair of aces. Missy removed the sword from the wall.

Her training in magick and education of the spiritual world

had made her especially sensitive to auras and human energy. Merely touching the sword told her it contained a great deal of Bill's spirit energy.

"This will do nicely," she said.

She excused herself and brought the sword to the kitchen where she took the chalk from the tote bag of medical and magickal supplies. Once inside the circle drawn on Bill's tile floor, she invoked the spell.

The glowing orb was full of energy, and it quickly found the creator of its energy. Missy's mind filled with an image of a large recreational vehicle. The camper was on the move along suburban streets. The glowing orb that Missy's consciousness was riding followed closely behind it.

Could she maintain the connection long enough until the camper arrived at a destination? She clenched the Red Dragon talisman more tightly. It grew warmer in her hand, almost to the point of painfully hot. But the resulting surge of power coursing through her body allowed her to maintain her astral connection with Bill.

The camper might be hundreds of miles away, but the neighborhoods it passed through looked more and more familiar. She gasped in surprise when it turned onto a street she recognized and parked in front of a large home.

It was the home on the water where the yacht had been docked.

She maintained the vision long enough to see a male who looked Neanderthal-like exit the RV with a sharpened wooden pole. He pointed it at Bill as he stepped out, hands bound in front of him. He jabbed Bill with the spear and prodded him into the house. A second vampire guard emerged with a folded wheelchair that he set up and then assisted Henrietta down the steps and into the chair. Her hands were bound as well. He repeated this with a second wheelchair and carried Gladys from the RV and into the chair. She appeared to be barely conscious. The first guard returned from the house, and the two of them wheeled their prisoners inside.

Missy wondered why the Neanderthals brought their prisoners back here. Then she realized that there were probably new recovery patients living here now. The prisoners were being brought here to feed.

Missy recited the lines that ended the spell, then cleaned the chalk from Bill's floor. Agnes was still in the living room. Missy told her what the spell had revealed.

"Okay. Let's hope there aren't more guards. Oleg is downstairs loading his SUV. He's going to lead the raiding party. I would go with you, but I need to stay here in case Thogg wants to talk to me. We can't let him know what we're doing."

You might believe an SUV full of vengeful vampires was scary, but Missy doubted the Neanderthals would be shaking in their Guccis at the sight of marauding geriatrics. Hey, but we go to war with the army we have, not the army we want, she thought.

The "army" was Oleg, a cavalry officer under Catherine the Great; Sol, a vampire from Brooklyn who looked like Nosferatu; Randolph, a 227-year-old who was more comfortable collecting stamps than killing Neanderthals; and Wilbur, who was said to be an expert in hand-to-hand combat back in the day— "the day" being somewhere during the 1890s.

The rear of the SUV was filled with sharpened garden stakes and rebar from the local home-improvement store. Bullets aren't of much use against vampires unless you happen to shoot one in the heart and the bullet lodges there. What you needed was to impale their hearts with the classic wooden stake, but a metal one would do, too. The other options are total immolation by fire or decapitation. Two axes lay in the back of the SUV, but Missy wondered who among them would be savage enough to use it. Destruction by sunlight was the only other way vampires were killed, as far as Missy knew. Saving Bernie from that fate seemed rather iffy at the moment.

It was left unsaid that Missy came on the mission because of her magick, even though she had made it clear that she didn't use attack spells, only defensive ones. That was her ethic as a practitioner of white magick and as a nurse. Of course, she had violated that when forced to stake one of Thogg's vampires to save her own life.

Missy sat in the middle seat between Randolph and Wilbur. It was odd sitting close to two men and not feel body heat coming from them.

"You three will have to squeeze into the third row on the way home," Oleg said in his Russian accent. "We must put the hostages in the middle seat for easy access."

At least he was being optimistic, Missy thought.

The drive to the upscale sober home was sobering in itself. Oleg was the only one who had actually been in combat, though it was over 250 years ago. Missy had been with Sol and Randolph once before when fighting a few punk vampires. Going up against powerfully strong Neanderthals who had, when alive, wrestled wooly mammoths was a much more daunting proposition.

No one spoke until Oleg broke the silence.

"Randolph and Wilbur, you go in through the front door," he said. "While the Neanderthals are distracted by you, Sol and I will take the house from the rear."

"What if they don't let us in?" Randolph asked.

Oleg looked at him in the rearview mirror. "Of course they won't let you in. What vampire would open their door to men carrying stakes? One of you holds the stakes and stands out of sight while the other rings the bell and pretends you're a Jehovah's Witness. If they open the door, jam your foot in there, and the one with the stakes pushes inside. If they don't open the door, that's what your ax is for."

"Do Jehovah's Witnesses believe in vampires?" Wilbur asked.

Oleg gave a big sigh and kept driving.

When they entered their destination street, Oleg killed the headlights and they rolled slowly to the end of the street. Fortunately, the RV still sat in the home's driveway.

Missy took a deep breath and tried to slow the hammering of her heart.

13
VAMPIRE RAIDING PARTY

G eraldo's two pit bulls were the terror of the neighborhood. He thought they were sweet and adorable. Except that they didn't like little yappy dogs. It wasn't their fault the time they killed the obnoxious Pomeranian owned by the old lady down the street. If he were a dog, he would have killed the furry rat, too.

The old lady lived in one of the super-sweet homes at the end of the long street, the homes on the Intracoastal. They were selling for millions nowadays. Geraldo's home was at the opposite end, near the main road, behind the bar where the bikers got into brawls. He liked to walk his dogs to the rich end of the street and watch the residents pick up their rat-dogs and retreat inside when they saw him coming.

Tonight he was walking them way later than usual because he had been out partying. Brutus, the bigger dog, picked up a scent ahead. Guapa did, too. They strained at their leashes, pulling him along with them.

Was it a raccoon? No, something bigger. It was on the other side of a ficus hedge in the house just ahead. Brutus and Guapa were growling now. He'd never seen them so agitated before. What was that animal?

As Geraldo and his dogs approached, the hedge rustled violently. The dense, tiny-leaved trees were trimmed to eight-feet high and were impossible to see through in the darkness, but whatever was messing with them was tall. Too big to be a dog, coyote or deer. Bigger than a panther, too. Was it a bear? This area was too urban to have bears, though.

If it was a Florida black bear, though, wouldn't it be cool if Geraldo's dogs caught it? Man, just think of the video he could shoot on his phone. It would totally go viral.

They were close to the hedge now, but still opposite where the creature was. The dogs were going crazy. Geraldo unclipped them from their leashes and let them pursue their prey. They raced away from him and around the end of the hedge. Geraldo jogged after them, hoping to capture video of what was happening on the other side.

There wasn't the sound of a battle going on, just constant barking. Maybe they had the beast at bay.

But then two pit-bull rockets launched from the end of the hedge and almost knocked him over as they fled down the street toward home. Geraldo stood there befuddled.

Until the bear rounded the end of the hedge and saw him. It stood upright, towering over him more than twice his height. It was as big as a city bus. It opened its mouth, big enough to fit Geraldo in his entirety, and roared like a freight train inches from hitting him.

Then it charged.

Geraldo didn't even have time to wet his pants. If he had, it wouldn't have mattered because his pants and legs ended up in the Morris' yard while the rest of him rained down on the Goodmans' viburnum and into the Sanchez's swimming pool. All the scattered parts were completely devoid of blood.

WILBUR RANG the doorbell of the expensive home. The fancy-sounding chimes echoed from within the spacious interior.

No answer. He tried again.

Randolph, hiding ten feet behind him around the corner of an exterior wall, whispered for him to try knocking. So knock he did.

The front door opened outward a crack.

"Who is it?" a woman's voice asked in a German accent. "What do you want?"

"I'm here to talk to you about Heaven and the joys that await the faithful. And I have pamphlets, too."

"It's three in the morning. You guys only come by on Saturday afternoons."

"There's never a bad time to talk about Jesus," Wilbur said as he tried to wrench the door open.

The woman on the other side, a stout middle-ager in a robe, tried to pull it shut. But Wilbur got his foot inside to block it open and Randolph rushed toward the house with the wooden stakes and rebar. Wilbur grabbed a stake and slipped through the door.

Then the door closed. Randolph stood there, stakes in hand, momentarily confused. He tried to open the door. It was locked.

Missy had been hiding with Randolph where the house jutted out in front, crouching to stay below the window level. She joined him after watching Oleg and Sol pass along the side of the house to the backyard. After giving them enough time to get in position, Wilbur had strolled up the front walk, pretending to be an earnest missionary. Once the door was opened and Randolph left his hiding place, Missy stepped onto the walkway to watch.

Just in time to see the door slammed in Randolph's face.

Missy headed for the door to give whatever aid her magick could provide.

But then the door opened, and Randolph rushed away from it, knocking her backwards. He disappeared around the corner of the house, dropping stakes as he went.

Missy was getting to her feet just as three Neanderthals ran out of the front door. As they were about to barrel over her, her hand touched one of the sharpened rebars that Randolph dropped.

She raised it at the charging vampire, who was an arm's length away, and he impaled himself upon it. Black blood bubbled from his chest before he crumpled to the ground and disintegrated.

The other two vampires sprinted past, unaware of what just happened, trying to catch up with Randolph.

Missy quickly summoned a protection spell for herself. This operation was going south in a hurry, she realized. And making her violate her oath to "do no harm" yet again.

Picking up the other stakes, she rounded the part of the house that jutted out and saw the battle raging in the driveway. Randolph had locked himself in the SUV while the two Neanderthals ran up to it. Sol and Oleg ran from the side of the house with four Neanderthals right behind them.

Oh, and she just noticed the 1,500-pound bear loping up the street. Yeah. Perfect.

The newspaper delivery person picked the wrong time to do this part of his route. Rolling slowly down the street, tossing papers in plastic bags onto driveways, the driver didn't see the charging bear until he clipped it in the head with *The Jellyfish Beach Journal*. The vampire cave bear was not amused. While it was poor timing for the driver, it distracted the beast from coming after Missy.

While the cave bear was tearing the doors off the delivery man's Hyundai, Missy took the opportunity to cast a sleep spell onto the bear. Fortunately, she had the Red Dragon talisman with her. The small, metal figure provided a lot more juice than her old power charm, and she felt it surging through her body as she built the layers of the sleep spell. She'd used it on humans and an ogre before, but not on a mammal that weighed nearly a ton.

The cave bear was winning its battle with the Hyundai, trying to extract the driver like a nut from its shell.

In the final step of the spell, Missy waved her hands across her eyes, pointed them at the cave bear, and uttered the last words of the invocation.

The cave bear dropped the car. It sat down on the street human-style and its head dropped until its muzzle met its chest. Then it keeled over asleep.

One down. Six Neanderthal vampires to go. But when she returned her attention to that battle, she was dismayed to see that her side was losing. Already outnumbered, her team had their backs against the SUV while the Neanderthals repeatedly lunged at them. It didn't help that Randolph had locked himself inside the vehicle and was in the fetal position on the back seat.

Sol and Oleg were using stakes as spears, thrusting them at their attackers. The fundamental problem was that Neanderthals really knew how to use spears. Millennia ago, they had made spears by hand and used them for hunting and fighting. Right now, they were demonstrating that they knew how to avoid being stabbed by spears. Sol and Oleg knew how to hunt with fangs and fight using lawyers. This battle was not even, and as soon as one of the Neanderthals grabbed one of the stakes from Sol and Oleg it would be a disaster.

Scratch that. It was already a disaster. A spear hit the hood of the SUV, burying its point in the metal. It was a real spear with a flint point. A seventh Neanderthal ran up to the battle carrying a bundle of spears.

Missy prepared another sleeping spell, though it would be hard to target only the Neanderthals and not her own vampires.

But, just then, Oleg made a successful feint and stabbed a vampire—

No, he didn't stab him. The vampire turned into a bat at the last instant and flew out of reach. It hovered above the melee, then dropped a steaming splat of guano on Sol's bald head.

Sol cursed and pulled a pistol from a holster under his shirt.

"Bullets can't kill vampires but watch what it does to a freaking bat!" he yelled.

He fired two shots, missing the bat. But a third hit it. Missy expected an explosion of bat guts.

Instead, a naked Neanderthal fell from the air and landed heavily atop the SUV.

The car alarm went off at an ear-piercing volume.

"Guys, we have to get out of here," Missy said. "Gunshots and a car alarm? You know that a neighbor called the cops."

The Neanderthal scrambled off their roof, apparently uninjured by the bullet, and ran toward the house. His companions, now armed with spears, hesitated.

Flashing strobe lights appeared at the end of the street on the main road. The rest of the Neanderthals ran to the house.

"Let's go!" Oleg shouted.

Missy and the two vampires piled into the vehicle, forcing Randolph out of his fetal position.

"Where's Wilbur? We can't leave him behind."

"We have to. He's their prisoner now," Oleg said, gunning the engine and turning the SUV around.

But as they moved up the street, three police cars poured in from the main road, blocking them.

"It doesn't help that we're driving a gangster rig," Sol said.

"Nonsense. This SUV has a minimum of bling," Oleg said. "I'll play the sweet, old grandpa." He rolled down his window and stuck his old bald head out, smiling and waving at the police.

"Please get out of your vehicle," said a voice on the loudspeaker.

Oleg complied, acting as slow and frail as he could. He put his hands on the hood and blinked in the spotlight shined on him.

"Busted like a group of teenagers caught drinking beer in Dad's car," Missy said.

Two officers approached on foot.

"Good evening, officers," Oleg said. "A hotrod just drove down this street shooting a gun. We're the ones who called 911. I'm so frightened."

"Where do you live?"

"In Squid Tower on the beach. We were driving home and I just can't figure out these GSP machines. I took a wrong turn, and when I heard the gunshots, I realized I picked the worst neighborhood to get lost in."

"You're out rather late."

"No, we're up early. We old people can't sleep past three a.m."

The other cop was walking around the SUV, looking in the windows. Missy had an idea of how to distract them.

She focused her mind, gathered energy, invoked the words.

And released the cave bear from the sleeping spell.

The ground shook from its footsteps as it charged the obnoxious flashing lights. The officer interrogating Oleg turned his head to see what the noise was, and his jaw dropped open. The other cop yelled an expletive. They quickly retreated to their patrol cars.

Gunshots rang out. Then the creature, seemingly the mass of a cruise ship, galloped past the SUV and the sound of a major highway collision rang out. Metal was torn as if it were the wrapping on a present.

"Maybe it's time to go," Missy said.

Sol put the SUV in gear and slipped past the battle of prehistoric mammal vs. Ford Explorer. More shots rang out and

Missy braced for their vehicle to be hit. But nothing happened, and they made it to the main road.

"Certainly glad that is over," Oleg said. "It's getting near dawn. Anyone feel like hunting for a human?"

"Oleg, we have to get back to Squid Tower," Missy said. "We need to save Bernie before he gets sun-killed."

"I don't think I want to hang out with you guys anymore," Randolph said.

14

HERE COMES THE SUN

Missy, Oleg, Sol, and Randolph returned to Squid Tower minus Wilbur, their mission a failure. Missy texted Agnes during the drive back to let her know. Agnes was waiting in the lobby, a pained expression on her face. The four foot eleven, ninety-something-year-old vampire was scary when she looked pained.

"We were greatly outnumbered," Oleg said. "And they have a vampire cave bear. That's like a regiment of heavy cavalry."

"The board is meeting right now," Agnes said. "There's not much time left before dawn. We will vote on whether to submit to Thogg. Missy and Oleg, please give us your recommendations based on your particular expertise."

They followed her into the community room where the rest of the HOA board members waited at the conference table. Bill's seat was empty. Missy grabbed a folding chair and sat facing the group. Oleg remained standing at attention. Agnes took her seat in the center of the table.

"Oleg, as a former military officer, what is your assessment of our chances of beating Thogg in combat?" she asked.

"They have more vampires than we realized, and might have more still that we're unaware of. Our total number of vampires at Squid Tower surely exceeds theirs. The problem is, we were all elderly when we became vampires. Many of us have disabilities. Neanderthals had short life expectancies, so none of them are older than their thirties or forties. They're strong and hearty. They were all hunters when alive. How many of us here know how to fight, or would be willing to?"

"You're saying they could all kick our butts," Schwartz said.

"Yes," Oleg replied. "They outclass us five to one. But they can be staked just like any vampire. Sol and I staked one in their house."

"I staked one on their front walk," Missy said.

The board members looked at her with surprise.

"In addition to the one in my home the other night," she added. "Not that I'm proud of it, being a nurse and all."

"Don't feel badly. In war, medical teams must defend themselves when attacked," Oleg said.

"Remember, Missy's friend, the reporter, staked one, too," Schwartz said.

Agnes made a steeple of her fingers and rested her chin upon it. "Okay, they are not invincible. But they have outsmarted and out-maneuvered us at every turn. They know where to find us, but we rarely know where to find them."

"And they can turn into bats and fly," Oleg said. "That's an immense tactical advantage. And as Sol discovered, bullets don't stop them in bat form either."

Agnes turned her attention to Missy. "Can your magick stop them?"

"I don't know. I have an extremely powerful talisman that amplifies my magick. I'm hoping to find the right spell to stop them, but so far, I haven't had the chance. The talisman sometimes gives me the ability to command creatures to obey me, but it doesn't seem to work with vampires."

"Vampires don't obey anyone, believe me," Agnes sighed. "Trying to get them to follow the association bylaws is hard enough."

"I motion we vote now," Schwartz said. "Submit to Thogg or let the moron Bernie Burdine fry."

"Wait," Missy said. "Give my magick a chance first. Maybe I can save him."

"Well, you can't get on the roof," Agnes said. "Thogg's goons have blocked the door. I don't know how they got into the building to bring him up there."

"They probably turned into bats and flew him up there," Gloria said. When everyone looked at her like she was nuts, she added, "I'm sure if you had enough bats working together, you could lift him."

Missy glanced at her watch. "Excuse me. I'm running out of time. Let me get to work."

Missy left the community room and went to an empty card-playing room. It would have had a spectacular view of the ocean if the hurricane shutters hadn't been closed, covering every inch of glass. Apparently, vampires needed to play pinochle when the sun was shining. She closed the door for privacy.

The first thing she needed to do was find out exactly where on the roof Bernie was. Not having a personal connection allowing her to bind her magic to him, she put herself into a meditative state, gathered her energies and those of the elements, and recited an astral travel spell.

Few witches could pull this off, but she was born with natural paranormal abilities for mental feats such as astral travel and telekinesis. Her magick spells strengthened them and switched them on.

Her mind searched for Bernie's mind; her spirit searched for his. Normally, she'd have no desire to get near Bernie's brain, but she had a job to do. Soon, she sensed him up there on the roof.

Her spirit detached itself from her body and she was in the sky, looking down on the roof. He was on his back spread-eagled, each limb tied to air conditioner condensers and duct work. The sky in the east was lightening, going from shades of purple to orange. The Neanderthal vampires stood inside the stairwell, ready to close to the door when the sun became strong.

Though Missy was detached from her body, she registered the boom of Thogg's voice in the community room next door to the card room. He demanded a decision from the board before Bernie was destroyed.

"Hey guys? You still there?" Bernie called out. "Guys? The sun's about to come out. I'm feeling a little toasty here. You've made your point. You can untie me now."

She had to do what she had never attempted: perform telekinesis, not directly from her mind, but from the astral projection of her mind. Don't try this at home.

"Does anyone smell smoke? I'm smelling smoke," Bernie whined. "I'm smelling smoke coming from me. This is not a joke, fellas. It's not funny anymore. I'm about to combust here, I'm telling you. Don't leave me to be vampire barbecue."

His increasingly frantic voice was disturbing her concentration. Must he always be obnoxious, even at the verge of death?

The Neanderthals retreated into the stairwell and closed the door. Missy executed a simple binding spell to lock the door. The power for the spell came from her mind, body, and spirit on the ground floor, but it was directed by her consciousness floating above the roof.

Next, she used her telekinesis to untie the knots on the ropes that bound Bernie. It was easier to do than she had expected. Also, the Neanderthal's knot-tying ability was very primitive. Bernie sat up, rubbing his freed wrists in confusion.

Her final heavy lift was exactly that: getting Bernie off the roof and onto the ground. She transferred these words into his ears:

Bernie, this is Missy. Relax, and my magick will carry you off the roof and lower you to the ground.

He swiveled his head in search of her.

I'm invisible, she explained. *I'm going to lift you now.*

She increased her concentration. With her corporeal body, down on the ground floor, she grasped the Red Dragon talisman, its power electrifying her, amplifying her strength, and sending it to her astral projection.

The clarity of her astral vision increased, every color was more vivid, every object was crisper. Her self-confidence surged. She focused all of her power on Bernie and visualized him rising from the roof.

And he did. Still in a sitting position, he hovered two feet above the asphalt roof covering.

"I don't know about this," he said. "I'm afraid of heights."

She moved him across the roof and over the lip at its edge.

Now he hovered ten stories above the ground. The swimming pool looked like a postage stamp below.

"Holy moly, I'm gonna fall! Don't let me fall!"

The sun's corona was just now peeking over the horizon.

"Ow!" Bernie cried. Faint tendrils of smoke rose from his exposed skin.

Missy had to get him downstairs and inside quickly.

Her astral consciousness stayed close by as she slowly lowered him. Any faltering of her concentration, any weakening of her energy, would break the connection and he would plunge to his death.

"Oh my God, oh my God," he cried. "I'm going to burn or be smashed to a pulp on the ground. Make that, my burning carcass is going to be smashed to a pulp."

Shut up, Bernie, you're making me lose my concentration.

She lowered him a few more stories.

"I think I'm going to pee myself," he said, whimpering.

They were more than halfway to safety. And that was when the door to the card room crashed open. Her body jumped in surprise. Her concentration faltered.

Bernie dropped a good fifteen feet before her mind stopped him.

"Witch! I knew I should have killed you before."

It was Thogg entering the card room as Missy bent over her knees on the floor within her magick circle. Completely defenseless.

She couldn't cast a protection spell. She couldn't run away. Every fiber of her being was occupied in lowering Bernie from the sky and not dropping him.

Thogg swung a heavy boot and kicked her in the thigh, sending her sprawling across the floor.

And she dropped Bernie.

THE SPELL WAS BROKEN, her astral projection shattered, and her telekinetic bond to Bernie severed. She hoped his death wasn't painful.

Painful like the second kick Thogg landed on her ribcage. It knocked the wind out of her and left her wheezing with the sharp pain of a possible broken rib.

"Why are you always interfering with me?" Thogg shouted, standing over her prone body. "Vampire affairs do not concern you. Whatever powers of magic you may have, you are not a vampire. You're not supernatural. You're just a mortal. You're a pest, like a rat. And I'm going to kill you like the vermin you are. I will beat you to within an inch of your life, then drain you until you're a lifeless husk."

"Wait." It was Agnes' voice. "Spare her and we will agree to be ruled by you."

Thogg turned to face her. "Why do you care about the life of a human?"

"Here at Squid Tower, we consider Missy to be one of us. Even though she isn't a vampire. She's given us compassionate medical care and has gotten us out of a bind many times."

"You're crazy," Thogg said. "But I will spare her life and accept your submission."

"Deal," Agnes said. "Now if you could send over the paperwork, I'll have our attorney review it and he'll call yours with any points of contention."

Thogg laughed. "There is no paperwork. You will kneel before me. Now!"

Gloria and Kim tiptoed into the room past Thogg's vampires, and each took one of Agnes' arms, helping her bend to her knees.

"Kiss my ring."

His large golden ring had an unrecognizable symbol embossed on it. Thogg pushed the back of his hand into Agnes' face. She hesitated, then kissed it quickly.

"And now," Thogg said, pulling a small dagger from a sheath attached to his belt. "You will drink my blood."

He drew the knife across his inner forearm. A trickle of dark, almost black, blood appeared. He thrust his arm in Agnes' face and she put her mouth over his wound. She swallowed and then hung her head in shame.

"See, no paperwork," Thogg said. "You will be my vassal for eternity now. And pick up my dry cleaning each week."

Kim and Gloria helped Agnes to her feet and led her out into the lobby. Missy limped after them before Thogg could change his mind and kill her.

"I will keep the hostages until you've demonstrated your obedience to me," Thogg called out after them. "Though now that you've tasted my blood, you'll find it impossible to disobey me."

He laughed, and his Neanderthals joined in.

Agnes and the others waited by the elevator. Red tears streamed down Agnes' face.

"You made this decision without the board?" Missy asked.

"When Thogg attacked you, we knew he'd kill you," Kim said. "We voted then and there to accept the terms if it would spare your life. Even Schwartz. It was unanimous."

I<small>T FELT</small> as if Missy were holding him as he slowly descended from the roof of Squid Tower. Bernie couldn't see her or feel her arms supporting him. Yet her presence was undeniable.

Until it suddenly wasn't. And his stomach bottomed out as he dropped in free fall.

Why did she let him go?

Oh, yeah, and his skin was burning, too. Frying and falling to his death.

His back hit the water with a crack like being slapped with a wooden plank and he sank into chlorinated water. The swimming pool! Hallelujah!

His butt hit the bottom of the pool and for a moment he was afraid he'd inhale water and drown. Surviving the fall only to drown? But he managed to kick his way to the surface and take a huge gulp of air.

And then get blasted by the burning rays of the sun. He howled in pain.

The rising sun was at such an acute angle that there was still a shadow in the eastern side of the pool beneath the concrete lip. He took shelter there. The cool water soothed his burns, but whenever any part of him extended out of the shadow, the burning sensation was intense, even under water. The shadow wouldn't be enough to save him for long.

The whirr of a weed trimmer came from nearby. The landscaping guys were human, of course, and didn't know that vampires lived here. The ones who grew to suspect it always quit. So the vampires' secret was safe.

Except for now, when Bernie was about to be incinerated unless the guy with the weed trimmer rescued him.

"Hey!" Bernie shouted. "*Buenas dias*. Help!"

Huddled in the diminishing shadow, Bernie heard the trimmer stop.

"Help me! I'm in the pool."

Footsteps approached. A man in work clothes looked down at him, a dark silhouette in the rising sun.

"Man, your skin is burning," the worker said.

"Yeah, I noticed. I need your help, or I'll die. I have a rare skin condition and the sun can kill me."

"Really? What's it called?"

"Vampire-dermatitis—who the heck cares what it's called! I need you to cover me in some chair cushions and drag me inside."

The man continued staring at him.

"There's smoke coming off you,"

"Please?"

The man shrugged and disappeared, returning with long blue cushions from the sun loungers. Bernie covered himself with two of them as best he could. The landscaper grabbed him by the biceps, pulled him from the pool, and dragged him across the concrete pool deck. Bernie's feet, partially exposed, erupted in flames, but the landscaper swatted them out with a large rag.

He yanked Bernie through the glass doors that were covered with blackout coating and deposited him on a rug next to the table with the placard announcing the evening's planned activities. At least he had survived to see another Bingo Night.

"Thanks, man," Bernie said. "Try not to let the sun in when you go out the door."

Agitated voices came from down the hall.

"Hey!" Bernie shouted. "Can I have some help here? Vampire down, vampire down!"

"You're alive!" exclaimed Randolph standing over him. "How did you get off the roof?"

"Missy used her magick to untie me. It was weird. I couldn't see her, but I heard her and sensed her presence. It was like she was a ghost. We were floating in the air and she was slowly lowering me down the building. But then she dropped me."

"She was attacked by Thogg."

"Well, luckily I landed in the swimming pool. But I got burned pretty bad."

"Yes, no offense," Randolph said, "but you look horrible."

"Thanks. I appreciate it. How come I'm not healing yet? I'm new to this vampire game, but I know we have healing powers. They worked with my acne."

"Sunlight is different. Mortal injuries don't heal just like that. I knew a guy from Philly who still had burn scars three hundred years after he was exposed to the sun."

"I get gigs at bars playing keyboards for tourists on weekends," Bernie said, a whine creeping into his voice. "I can't do that looking like a monster. I mean, there's hot chicks at these bars."

"Make an appointment with Missy. Maybe she knows of a treatment." Randolph looked down the hallway. "Agnes, look what the cat the dragged in."

Agnes clopped over with her quad cane.

"I'm glad you survived, Bernie," she said. "Was it bad while you were a prisoner?"

"They kept me on a boat in a cabin the size of a closet. Every night they'd bring a human for me to feed on. Sad folks who'd already been fed on a bunch of times before. They were awfully anemic. And then Thogg would stop by and tell me to proclaim my subservience to him. He would try mind tricks with me, but tricks don't work on my mind. Nothing works on my mind."

"I'm afraid you'll continue to be subservient to Thogg," Agnes said, wiping a tear from her eye. "We're now his vassals."

"What?"

"Thogg is now our leader. I report to him and we all serve him at his pleasure."

15

NEANDERTHAL DADDY ISSUES

Missy returned home to shower, eat, and sleep. She also planned to see if Don Mateo's addendum to *The Book of Saint Cyprian* had any spells that would heal a sun-wounded vampire. She had been immensely relieved to learn that Bernie hadn't died in the fall—she had lowered him above the pool just in case—but was horrified by his burns. Only magick could help him.

When she opened the door, her home smelled of olive oil, garlic, onions, peppers, and potatoes.

"You're finally home," Darla said from the kitchen. "I hope you don't mind I'm cooking omelets."

"Of course I don't mind." Missy was starved. Fighting vampires works up an appetite, and it's not as if her vampire hosts had food lying around to feed her.

Missy entered the kitchen, and Darla gave her a big smile as she chopped tomatoes. A kettle was waiting with boiling water, so Missy made herself a cup of tea.

"Were you seeing patients last night?" Darla asked.

"No, we were fighting Neanderthal vampires, trying to rescue hostages. But we failed."

"Oh," Darla said, sounding chipper, as if what Missy said was perfectly normal. "Are Neanderthal vampires particularly dangerous?"

Missy didn't want to answer that and tried not to think about how much they scared her so Darla wouldn't read her mind.

"They have a vampire cave bear," she said instead.

"I don't know what that is, but I wouldn't want to mess with it."

"No, you wouldn't."

Darla began whipping eggs in a bowl. "These are the same vampires that have Sophie?" she asked.

Missy sighed. "Yes. They also abducted some of my vampire patients who they're holding as hostages at a different location from where Sophie is."

Darla's face darkened. She beat the eggs with added fury.

"It sounds like a coincidence that she would be involved with these vampires," Missy said, "but they're a criminal enterprise. Like the Mafia. When they come to town, they affect everyone. Their leader is an owner of the recovery service that gave her to the vampires."

Darla still hadn't said anything, but a storm was brewing beneath her darkened expression.

"Sophie will be okay," Missy said. "We'll get her out of there."

"I don't believe you."

Missy put her arm around her cousin. "Yes, we will bring her home. My spell located the house she's in. I just have to find exactly where it is."

Darla allowed herself only a few tears before she poured the bowl of eggs into the skillet with the sautéed vegetables. She stirred briskly.

"I filed a missing-persons report with the police," Darla said.

Missy wished she hadn't. She never wanted the police involved in supernatural affairs. But she couldn't blame Darla for doing it. If she were Sophie's mother, she'd call the police, too.

"We can't depend on the police," Missy said. "We'll have to find her ourselves."

What she didn't mention was the problem of extricating Sophie from the house. As she learned last night, these Neanderthals weren't a bunch of pansies. She would need to devise some heavy-duty magick to pull off a rescue.

They ate in silence. The eggs were good, though. Darla had thrown in some Datil peppers, grown in San Marcos. They added a sweet-spicy touch. When they were done eating, they didn't clear the table yet. Darla sipped her coffee and Missy her tea.

"Tell me about Sophie," Missy asked.

"She's a very sensitive girl. I'm not surprised she got into trouble with drugs."

Darla sat back in her chair and gave a brief tale of Sophie's girlhood in a home where magic and paranormal were always present, just beneath the surface. Her father, Darla's first husband, was a ne'er-do-well whom Darla eventually divorced. Her second husband disappeared in mysterious circumstances that Darla didn't explain. But she tried to give her daughter a normal life of school and soccer mixed with the eccentricities of living in a tourist town laden with history and filled with the Florida pleasures of boating, fishing, and going to the beach.

"But then, of course, she fell into the wrong crowd in high school," Darla said. "She went to college locally, and in retrospect that was a mistake because she kept in contact with her druggie friends."

Darla took a long sip of coffee and smiled bitterly.

"She was doing well in recovery," she said. "Or so I thought. I don't know how she ended up with those low lives who betrayed her."

Uncomfortable silence followed until Missy changed the subject. "How much do you know about my birth parents?"

"Not that much," Darla said. "Like I'd told you, I didn't know they had you. Though our mothers were sisters, they couldn't be more different. For Mom, witchcraft was just a hobby. Your mother was into it big time, especially after your father died. It was like an addiction. Your mother and mine grew apart. I think Mom was scared of your mother."

"Because of the black magic?"

"Yes. I know that she'd tinkered with it early on, but she got deep into it after she married. Which was odd, because I've heard your father never touched it."

"The little I know about him, I'm certain he was a benevolent witch," Missy said.

"Maybe that's why he died."

"What do you mean?"

"His magick was in opposition to your mother's. I was told that was why she killed him."

Missy stopped breathing. She felt like she was going to throw up.

"Are you all right?" Darla asked, searching Missy's face. "You didn't know?"

"I knew nothing about it until recently. But the Arch-Mage

WARD PARKER

Bob and an old wizard named Wendall told me that Dad was killed by a demon summoned by black magicians who were later driven from town."

"Your mother was one of them," Darla said.

Missy put her face in her hands.

"Look, I don't know for sure," Darla said, stroking Missy's arm. "It's what my mother believed. I'm sure plenty of people will tell you otherwise."

"My mother denied killing him, but of course she would."

"I'm sorry that I brought this up. I didn't know you've never heard about it. Again, I could be wrong."

"You're probably right. I met my mother for the first time recently. She's a real piece of work. She'll do anything for the money, including summon demons. Now, I really want to find out what happened."

"You should let the past stay in the past."

"I'm worried about what kind of bad stuff she could be up to. But I'm not eager to confront her again. She tried to kill me last time, and it wasn't fun. Believe me, you don't want to fight with a mosquito the size of a delivery truck."

"I think you should put her behind you," Darla said.

"If I put her behind me, she'd stab me in the back. But I will put it aside for now. We need to get Sophie to safety."

"Do you think . . . she's been bitten?"

Missy did, but she didn't want to say so. "It's in the Neanderthals' best interest to keep her alive and well."

"So they can feed on her."

"Let's not think that way," Missy said. "Let's concentrate on getting her back."

Sophie quickly discovered that the patchouli was her best friend. The Neanderthals hated it. It revolted them (along with many humans). She would apply it heavily to her neck, arms, ankles, and other places they loved to bite. It kept them at bay like bug spray does for mosquitoes. The vampires would order her to wash it off, but the scent was so intense that soap and water couldn't vanquish it completely. They confiscated it from her, but she had smaller vials she concealed in her room and on her person. She used the patchouli like her life depended upon it, because it did.

When the test results came back from MyNeanderthalD-NA.com, she learned that she had very little Neanderthal in her. That meant her captors wouldn't want to turn her into a vampire. Which was good. But it also meant that her only value to them was as a food source and that she was expendable.

She had just finished dabbing patchouli on her neck when the door to her small room rattled as it was unlocked. She braced herself as she sat on her bed. Mona entered the room.

"I am here to check on your vitality," Mona said.

It was like a parody of nuclear family life. Here Sophie was in her bedroom of a suburban home with a mom-like figure coming in to check on her to make sure she's doing her homework on a school night. Except that this home is owned by Neanderthal vampires and used to hold the human prisoners who are essentially their herd of livestock.

"My vitality is fine until I get bitten again," Sophie said. "How is Maria?"

Mona paused and looked away. "It is difficult."

"What do you mean?"

"She has not turned yet. I have been chosen to turn her and I find it difficult."

"You're not a cold-blooded killer?"

"Oh, yes, I am. I am cold-blooded. And I kill. No problem. But it is different when you take someone's human life and replace it with the eternal life of a blood feeder. It's a great responsibility. Even more so than when you have children as a human. I care for Maria and it is difficult to take her life, even if I'm enabling her to live forever. What if she doesn't want to live forever? What if she finds eternal life to be a curse?"

Mona's eyes turned haunted.

"I have been alive for over eighty thousand years. I have seen all the clans of our people wiped out. I have seen the beasts we hunted die off and the earth grow warmer and become covered in concrete. Sometimes I grow weary."

"Did you have children when you were human?" Sophie asked.

"I had five. Two died while still suckling and the three others were healthy. They were still young when I was turned. They were raised by others in the clan because I was banished for being a blood feeder."

"I'm sorry."

"I wandered alone for many years before I found Thogg's clan. I slept in a hollowed-out tree during the day and hunted what I could at night. My maker did not stay around to help me."

"Before meeting you guys, I had no idea vampires existed in pre-history."

"It wasn't pre-history for us. And, yes, tales of blood feeders were told around the fires at night since I was a child. There have always been blood feeders among the races and species of humanoids and the primates from which we evolved. Since the beginning of time, there were creatures who lived on the blood of others and didn't die. Who had this spark inside that gives us supernatural powers. Some call it evil. I think it is neither good nor evil, this spark. But it has been around since the first life."

"Are you saying there were single-cell vampire organisms in the primordial soup of early earth?"

Mona looked at her like she was crazy. "No. Vampire amoebas? Are you nuts, girl?"

Sophie tried to change the subject.

"You and your clan seem highly educated and savvy," she said. "How were you able to learn and keep up with the world when it has changed so much since you were turned?"

"I tell you what. They say Neanderthals died out because we couldn't adapt. That's wrong. We were wiped out by disease and genocide. Thogg, our clan, and I are proof that we can adapt just fine. And how did we learn? Easy. We took prisoners. We forced them to teach us new things as languages changed and new tools and weapons appeared. We have evolved just fine."

"Why does Thogg want to rule all the vampires?" Sophie asked.

"He has daddy issues."

"Say what?"

"Thogg's father was the leader of his clan. He put a lot of pressure on Thogg to be a great hunter and capture hunting grounds from other clans. But he never showed Thogg any love."

"That's so sad."

"And now he is hungry for power and domination. Neanderthals weren't into conquering and pillaging like more modern humans. But Thogg is. You can thank his daddy."

The door opened and Thogg towered over them.

"Speak of the devil," Sophie muttered.

"I am not the devil," Thogg said. "The devil is afraid of me."

"Of course he is," Mona said.

"Whew, that horrible smell again," Thogg said, waving his hand in front of his face. "I came by for a little snack, and now I've lost my appetite. Mona, make sure this human washes that stink from her."

"I will, Thogg."

When he left, Mona got up from the bed.

"You can keep that stink on you if you wish," she said. "I will not be feeding on you because I have to feed on Maria. And if the stink keeps the other guys away from you, that's their problem. Enjoy your night."

She left the room, closing the door behind her.

Sophie reflexively rubbed her neck and ankles where the fang marks were healing. As far as she knew, she had been bitten only twice since her captivity. Something about the process made her fall asleep with no memory afterwards of what happened. So she didn't remember who had attacked her and how traumatic it had been. She was determined to keep it from happening again.

But if the vampires figured out that she wasn't being put to use, what would they do?

16

YOU ARE THE MEAL PLAN

After spending the day poring over Don Mateo's addendum to *The Book of Saint Cyprian*, Missy was frustrated. The spells that appeared to be for healing supernatural entities were in archaic Spanish. She couldn't read even modern Spanish very well, so this was hopeless. Once again, she tried to call Don Mateo's ghost to come to her. Once again, he ignored her. He seemed to prefer appearing at night, but she tried to force the matter by using the power of the Red Dragon talisman. In the past, that had always worked to fetch him, even in daylight.

But not now. There was only one thing left to try.

She opened the underwear drawer of her new dresser and pulled out her lingerie.

"Don Mateo, I summon you to— "

An explosive crack made her whip around only to see her underwear drawer break apart and crash to the floor. A man was sitting in the drawer. The ghost of a man, to be exact. A man with a fetish for lingerie.

"Oops," Don Mateo said. "Sometimes I miscalculate my mass when I materialize."

"But most of the time you're a normal, wispy, semi-transparent ghost," Missy said. "What's the deal?"

"To fully appreciate the silky smoothness of your lady-garments' material, I needed to materialize myself."

"You're a real freak. I need you to help me with a spell from your addendum. A healing spell."

"Oh, that would please me greatly."

"Join me in the kitchen," Missy said.

The grimoire lay open atop the kitchen island. Don Mateo was hovering above it in traditional, wispy ghost form when Missy got there.

"I have a vampire patient who has first- and second-degree burns from sun exposure," she said. "Healing from sun exposure is a power vampires don't have. These spells here," she pointed to a page filled with tiny, dense handwriting in ink, "look like they might be the solution. But you didn't translate them into English. I have trouble with the Spanish from your era. And your penmanship."

"My penmanship was excellent. You're just too accustomed to reading typeset materials on your little mechanical devices."

"Whatever. Just help me with the translations."

Don Mateo slowly recited the spells in English while Missy jotted them down on a notepad. Each spell consisted of instructions on how to cast it as well as the words of invocation. Most of the invocations had to remain in the original languages for the spell to work, particularly when there were Latin phrases.

There were portions in the native Timucuan language that she had to write phonetically.

"Try both spells," Don Mateo said. "At least one of them should work in healing your patient."

"Why did the Timucuans know so much about healing supernatural creatures?"

"Because there were plenty of them back in those days: creatures that already lived here before humans and those of their own people who had supernatural characteristics and abilities."

Don Mateo reappeared on the stool across from the island.

"The Native Americans understood the supernatural much better than we Europeans did. We distorted our knowledge by associating the supernatural with the devil and evil. The Native Americans understood that the supernatural originates in the natural. We Europeans believe the supernatural doesn't follow the rules of nature, but it does. It simply doesn't follow the rules of our narrow minds and simplistic rules of logic."

"I like it when you put it that way," Missy said.

"The secrets to healing supernatural creatures, and harming them, are found in nature. Remember that. With the supernatural, nothing cannot be healed. Yet nothing is invincible."

Missy brought her notes and her tote bag filled with magick supplies to Squid Tower that evening. At first glance, it seemed like a normal evening. Pickleball games were in progress. A vampire swam laps in the pool while others lay upon lounge chairs soaking in the moonlight.

But somehow things felt off. Of course, over all the time she had spent there, never had a motorcade of giant, black SUVs with tinted windows pulled up and parked in front of the lobby entrance. The Neanderthal drivers, wearing suits, jumped out and opened the doors of each vehicle. Instead of vampires, bats emerged and flew together in a flock to the balcony of one of the penthouse condos.

There was a feeling of tension in the air. The sensation of being watched. As much as the residents tried to act otherwise, they were under an occupation. They were under the control of an authoritarian force.

They were now the vassals of Thogg.

Bernie was at his post in the gatehouse when Missy came by.

"This hour the traffic is usually slow," he said. "It's a good time to examine me."

He looked horrible. The red welts and brown patches of his burned skin made her cringe, not only because of their ugliness but out of empathy for his pain. This would be the case for all of eternity unless her spells could heal him.

Bernie looked over his shoulder at the looming tower.

"I hope I don't get in trouble for having a guest while on duty," he said.

"This is a medical visit. I'm sure they'll understand."

"I'm not sure those Neanderthals understand anything except blood and money." He cringed in regret for speaking his thoughts aloud.

"Is it really that bad? They've only been in charge for a day."

"And they've already condemned someone to be staked."

Missy was shocked. "Oh, my. Who?"

"Oleg Kazmirov. He led the raiding party that tried to rescue the other hostages."

Missy was sick to her stomach with concern for Oleg. And for herself. She had been part of that raid, too.

"Did they detain him?"

"I think so. I don't know where, though."

Missy needed to speak with Agnes about this right away.

"Is Agnes okay?"

"Yeah. They know better than to harm our community mother."

Missy wondered why Agnes hadn't contacted her about this terrible turn of events. But Missy had to focus on the task at hand and heal Bernie. She opened her tote bag and pulled out supplies.

"What is that?" Bernie asked.

"Aloe."

"I knew aloe is good for burns, but I never knew it was magic."

"Be quiet. I need to concentrate."

Missy squeezed the gelatinous pulp from the aloe leaves and rubbed it over Bernie's blisters. He winced in pain. Then she sprinkled a fine powder made of ground-up dried native herbs over his skin, which adhered to the shiny layer created by the aloe.

Then it was time for her magick.

Don Mateo had instructed her to use the Red Dragon talisman with these spells. He had never had the talisman, but its extra power might be needed to heal such intractable burns. As its energy went through her left hand like an electric shock and made its way up her arm, she began reciting the first spell. It was meant for the healing of the skin and blood vessels. Supposedly great for poison ivy, acne, and dandruff while somehow also healing peripheral artery disease. Go figure.

Before she was halfway through it, Bernie seized up, and his eyes rolled backward in his head.

She was concerned, but had to keep concentrating on the spell. She continued reading the invocation from her notes, trying to remember the proper pronunciation of the Timucuan words.

When she completed it, she looked at Bernie. His eyes were still rolled up. His breathing was slow but steady. Yet something was odd.

The odd thing was that he looked perfectly normal. His skin had healed with no signs of burns at all—no blisters, redness, or swelling.

Wow.

This was the first time she had healed a vampire of an ailment that their supernatural powers or human medicine couldn't heal. Her eyes teared up as pride and gratification swept through her. Bernie's burns hadn't been dangerous to his existence, but he would have had the pain and disfigurement for eternity. Now he had been spared that suffering.

At a time like this, she didn't mind how crappy her job paid.

She didn't need the second spell. Don Mateo said it had something to do with how one's body adapted to severe heat or cold. Among other things, it was supposed to help the body heal from insect stings, snake bites, and bad breath.

A sharp rapping on the guardhouse door made her jump.

"What are you doing in there?" demanded a Neanderthal. "Leave the guard alone while he's on duty."

"I was giving him medical care. I'm a nurse," Missy said. "I work for Acceptance Home Care, which has a contract with Squid Tower."

"What's wrong with him? Is he asleep?"

Missy snapped her fingers by Bernie's nose. He didn't wake up. So she slapped him in the face.

"What? What's going on?" Bernie asked, groggy. He looked at his hands. "My wounds are gone." He smiled at Missy. "Thank you."

She packed up her tote bag and slipped out of the booth before the Neanderthal asked any more questions. She headed straight for Agnes' condo.

When the elevator opened in the lobby, it was packed with old, cranky vampires. A bald guy with a walker blocked the opening, and the other vampires impatiently waited to push past him as he exited. Agnes was at the very rear of the car, hidden because of her short stature.

"What's going on?" Missy asked her. "Is it Bingo Night?"

"No," Agnes said with a martyred expression. "Our new supreme leader wants to address us tonight. Attendance is mandatory."

Missy knew this must be painful for all the vampires, especially Agnes who had been their leader. Until now.

"I'm going with you," Missy said.

Vampires were converging upon the ground floor of the building, lining up to enter the community room. Rows of folding chairs filled the room. A folding wall at the rear had been opened to the adjoining card rooms for extra space.

There were seniors in wheelchairs, scooters, walkers, canes, and orthopedic shoes. Some were in stylish sandals. All of them moved slowly. Senior citizens, even with enhanced supernatural vitality, were simply not fast on their feet. Unless it was Bingo Night or a Free Blood Bag Giveaway. Listening to a speech from their conqueror was not high on their excitement list.

Missy sat away from Agnes, in the overflow area in the back, to avoid standing out. She didn't want to get any more boots in her ribs.

At the front of the room was a rarely used lectern. Neanderthals in black suits stood at attention behind it and beside the doors.

Thogg flew into the main room in bat form. He was probably trying to impress the crowd by showing off an ability the modern vampires didn't have. But, in truth, he looked a little silly. A majestic eagle flying in would have been cool. A flying rodent skittering through the air just wasn't.

When the bat reached the podium, it transformed into Thogg seamlessly. He wore a black blazer over an open-collar white dress shirt. He looked like an intelligent business executive who just happened to have a pronounced brow ridge over his eyes.

"My fellow vampires," he said into the microphone. "Welcome."

There was a whine of feedback. One of his minions raced from the front row to adjust the microphone, but let's face it, Neanderthals just aren't cut out to be techies. They can adapt all they want to changing times, but technology was not in their DNA. Thogg touched the mic and more feedback screeched out. Vampires in the crowd turned down their hearing aids. But Thogg pushed on.

"In case not all of you have heard, I am Theodore Thogg and I am now your ruler. Together we will embark on a glorious adventure. The undead are destined to dominate this world, and I will be the emperor. You, as my loyal subjects, will be the privileged citizens of this new vampire empire. Remain loyal, and I will reward you with riches and special privileges."

He surveyed the crowd and his bushy eyebrows furrowed atop his protruding brow.

"But if you show even a trace of disloyalty, you will regret the day you ever became a vampire. I will fill the parking lot and shuffleboard courts with the staked bodies of vampires who betray me."

Whispering broke out in the crowd. A loud woman asked, "What did he say?"

"Something about baked toddies in the parking lot," her companion said.

"How do you bake a toddy?"

Finally, they were shushed by the vampires sitting around them.

Thogg walked back and forth in front of the crowd, with dramatic hand gestures, as if he were giving a vampire TED talk. Missy half expected a PowerPoint presentation to be projected on the wall.

"I am using my immense wealth to fund the cataclysmic war against the humans," Thogg said. "But even my untold riches are not enough. We need to raise additional revenues."

Dark murmuring ran through the crowd. Living for eternity, these vampires could spot fee increases a mile away.

"There will be a special assessment to the general fund to cover the extra security needs. And," he raised his voice above the growing clamor, "the HOA fees will increase for everyone by one hundred dollars a month."

Angry voices roiled the crowd.

"Quiet down," Thogg told them.

"HOA increases should be a matter that's voted on," shouted a vampire named Marvin from Cleveland. He stood not far from Missy, shaking his fist in anger. "I refuse to pay a penny more."

Senior citizens on a fixed income tend to be frugal. Missy found that senior vampires were downright stingy. Many had amassed considerable savings from centuries of compounded interest. But once you've lived into your hundreds, it's hard to convince the Social Security Administration that you're still alive and should receive payments. Knowing that your savings had to last until the end of time would make anyone cheap.

Thogg glowered at Martin, then exchanged a glance with one of his minions.

Two bats appeared and flew above the crowd, hovering above Marvin.

"Sit down, Marvin," a vampire senior whispered to him.

"I will not be intimidated," Marvin said, his voice quavering with passion. "I've been an owner here since Squid Tower was first built."

The two bats transformed into Neanderthals, dropping to the floor on either end of Marvin's row. Then they pushed through the crowd toward him stepping on toes without regard.

Marvin realized what was about to happen. He bared his fangs and hissed at the Neanderthals. But they were not deterred.

Each grabbed an arm and dragged Marvin out of his row and toward the front of the room where Thogg was waiting. The crowd erupted in cries of protest and dismay.

"You're going to hear from my lawyer!" Marvin shouted.

While his thugs held Marvin in place, Thogg walked up and grabbed his throat in both hands.

"My authority is absolute," Thogg said. "No one shall challenge it."

He lifted Marvin from the ground, squeezing his neck while the frail senior struggled. As far as Missy knew, vampires couldn't be killed through strangulation. But it wasn't pretty watching Marvin's face darken as he struggled, his hands trying to loosen Thogg's, his legs twitching two feet above the floor.

"Any more such insolence will be punished with staking," Thogg said.

Then he threw Marvin across the room. Marvin landed on a card table in the very back covered by a half-completed jigsaw puzzle some residents had been working on. It had been a creepy illustration of a castle in Transylvania. Marvin collapsed the table and sent the jigsaw pieces scattering.

The crowd was suddenly silent.

"I spent hours on that puzzle," a woman said.

"You have all of eternity to start over again," another one added.

"Have I made myself clear?" Thogg asked the crowd. "Disobedience will not be tolerated. Neither will late HOA fees. Or parking in handicapped spots without a permit. My justice will be harsh. The first public staking will be this Friday after sundown."

He ran his glowering eyes across the cowed faces of his new subjects.

"Pool aerobics begin in forty minutes," he said before striding from the room with theatrical energy.

MISSY SPENT hours staring at satellite views of the city. She knew the home was on a canal leading to the Intracoastal Waterway, but there were dozens of those. While she had memorized the magick vision she'd had of the house, it wasn't all that helpful. From above, it looked pretty much like most of the one-story ranch homes with barrel-tile roofs. The only homes that stood out on the satellite views were the modern McMansions that were built to replace older homes that had been knocked down. The large outbuilding behind the home in her vision was distinctive, but there were other homes that had a similar feature.

It's too bad she couldn't make a digital photo of her magick vision so she could compare it side-by-side with the homes on the mapping website.

Then it occurred to her with a sinking feeling that the home wasn't necessarily in Jellyfish Beach. It could be anywhere in the nearby towns as long as it was close enough to be conveniently reached by Thogg and his thugs.

She needed some more information—the smallest of details, even—to help her narrow down the search.

SOPHIE AWOKE at dawn feeling weak and groggy. For the briefest moment she thought she was back in her childhood bed in her mother's house, safe and content.

Then reality intruded. She was a prisoner of vampires who were using her as their meal plan. She touched two sets of fang punctures on her neck from last night. They were sore and made her feel disgusted. She remembered nothing of what happened, but the vampires must have washed the patchouli from her. That had been her only defense. Now there was nothing to stop her from being drained to death.

Once she knew the routine in this house, she'd looked for weaknesses in security. This home's version of Jan was a human housekeeper named Yolanda. She was a black Brazilian with great cooking skills, without using garlic. And she had a soft spot for the human captives. Sophie and two other prisoners were allowed some freedom of movement in the house during the day, though they couldn't go outside. An alarm system ensured that. Sophie never saw Maria, who was locked in the master suite with its own bathroom. There was no sign of Lise and Francine from the previous house. They were either still living there or were dead. Or possibly undead. Sophie shuddered at the thought.

She checked every window in the rooms she had access to. All of them were locked and had alarm sensors, as was every door. There was no way she could sneak out unnoticed. Even if she managed to race through a door when Yolanda was bringing in groceries, she wouldn't make it far before a guard caught her. Especially if she was on foot, or even swimming in the canal. She doubted she could steal Yolanda's car or one of the guard's. But she would have to try.

The key would be to create a diversion. A huge one.

One night, two black SUVs pulled up in front of the house at 7:00 p.m. sharp, instead of the usual single vehicle. Yolanda had said that they had moved many humans to Squid Tower to sustain Thogg's troops stationed there. But his army was growing with the new vampires he created, as well as the ones he had converted to his cause. Rather than risk police scrutiny by allowing them to hunt, he was providing their meals with more prisoners like Sophie.

As the SUV doors slammed outside, Sophie shuddered at the thought of more hungry mouths pressing upon her neck. And there was nothing she could do about it. The evenings were always the same: The vampires and humans hung out in the living room watching TV, acting like it was an informal get together. Then she would awake the next morning with no memory of how they had mesmerized her and which of them had fed upon her. She felt profoundly violated.

Carl's voice echoed down the hall. Not him, again. She was sick of his affectations: the world-weary sophisticate who was ever so jaded. She realized he had the right to sound world weary, being tens of thousands of years old and all. But he could cut the pretentious crap. After all, he was just a vampire caveman. Get over yourself, Carl.

Yolanda unlocked the bedroom door.

"They want to chat with you in the living room," she said, a strained look on her face. She knew what "chat" really meant.

Sophie applied to her neck and forearms the last drops of patchouli from the vial she had hidden. Not that it protected her anymore. She quickly brushed her hair with the brush they had given her and went to the living room.

Carl and six other vampires, two of them female, lounged on the sofa and chairs. Three new prisoners Sophie hadn't seen before sat uncomfortably on the rug. They were a young black guy and a white guy who was older, maybe early thirties. The third prisoner was an Asian woman in her twenties. They pretended to watch a cooking reality show and ignore their captors staring at them. As newbies, they wouldn't know yet their captors were vampires. And that vampires don't watch cooking shows. They wouldn't have an inkling that they themselves were on tonight's menu.

"Ah, Sophie, so kind of you to join us," Carl said. "You look ravishing in that T-shirt. Just like you did last night and the night before."

"I don't get out to go shopping much," Sophie said.

"We must buy you some clothes while you're our guest."

"Something in dark red would be nice," she said. "Something that hides blood stains."

The new prisoners looked at her nervously.

"I thought we were doing therapy now," the woman said.

"We are," Carl said. "I believe it's important to chit chat before diving into all the tedious confessional stuff."

Sophie wished the vampires would hurry up with the mesmerizing and get this nightmare over with.

"Sophie can attest to how good our therapy methods are," Carl said. "Isn't that right, Sophie?"

"These sessions are mesmerizing," she said.

"I've got to grab something from the truck," one of the unfamiliar vampires said. "You can start with the 'therapy' without me."

He left his easy chair and walked to the foyer. As he passed through the front door, Sophie bolted.

She didn't know what impulse sparked her to do it. She just ran with all the energy in her through the foyer, at the door, before it was closed.

In Florida, because of hurricane building codes, all doors must open outwards. She flung her body at the closing door and pushed her way through. The exiting vampire didn't even realize what was going on until she was tearing around the corner of the house.

She knew that in order to escape she needed to create a distraction. And the one she'd cooked up during all her idle hours was a doozy. It was also potentially fatal for her. But she had no other choice.

When she had come up empty while searching the house during the daytime for escape routes, she found something interesting. A pegboard beneath the kitchen light switches held a set of padlock keys with the label "shed," one of which she pocketed. The shed was what she hoped to reach before the vampires caught her.

There it was, built against the back wall of the house near the pool. A very sturdy garden shed built with concrete block walls and a steel door.

She pulled the padlock key from her pocket with shaking hands that fumbled and dropped it in the grass.

The vampire rounded the far corner of the house and saw her. He walked briskly toward her.

It was so dark in the backyard that she had to feel in the grass for the fallen key.

"What are you doing out here?" the vampire asked. He was almost upon her.

Her fingers touched the key. She stood up, tried to will her hands to stop shaking, and got the key into the lock.

The key wouldn't turn.

"You think you can hide from us in the shed?" The vampire said from only ten feet away.

Her heart was in her throat as she jiggled the key.

It turned, and the padlock popped open. She pulled it from the hasp and yanked open the steel door, keeping it between her, the doorway, and the vampire.

The rumbling growl of a cave bear filled the night.

"Oh, hello there," the vampire said, his voice on edge. "Good bear, good bear. I'm a friend of your daddy. Good—"

The bear roared, and the vampire screamed.

Could a vampire bear kill a vampire human? Sophie wondered. Maybe not, but it could mess him up pretty seriously. And allow her to escape.

Based on the thudding of a body against the wall of the house, the bear roaring, and the vampire screaming, the fight was getting ugly. She heard more footsteps coming around the house, so she rushed toward the canal.

A look back revealed the vampire being tossed like a rag doll by the bear. Carl arrived in the backyard.

"Stop, Lucy! Down, girl!" he yelled.

Sophie slipped into the water without making a splash.

MATT HAD JUST ARRIVED home after covering a city council meeting when his police scanner came to life.

"Ten-twenty-two on Stork Street. All nearby units please respond."

That was code for a disturbance. But then there was more.

"All unassigned units report to Stork Street immediately to meet Fire Rescue. Several civilians injured."

This was a little odd, Matt thought. He turned his computer on and looked up Stork Street. It was just south of the northern boundary of Jellyfish Beach.

"The Stork Street incident now reports fatalities, in addition to a car going into the canal. Also, there is property damage at several homes. SWAT Team is responding to the scene."

Matt decided he would pay a visit to Stork Street. He texted the newspaper to request a photographer be sent. And then the scanner squawked yet again.

"Multiple reports of a giant wild animal attacking residents of Stork Street. Some reports mention a bear. Please exercise caution."

Matt immediately called Missy.

"Oh my," Missy said. "What street did you say that was?"

"Stork Street," Matt said over the phone. "On a canal off the Intracoastal. North side of town. I'm heading there now."

When they hung up, Missy looked up the address on her phone.

"And I have a rash on my butt," her patient said. "I never imagined vampires would get rashes."

"Sorry, Mrs. Hink. I have an emergency situation."

"My rash is an emergency?"

"No. There's one involving the Neanderthals. I have to check this out. Make sure the crypt you sleep in isn't moist inside. You might need to buy a dehumidifier."

"What about the rest of my appointment?"

"Let's reschedule for tomorrow, okay?" Missy asked as she gathered up her stethoscope and gear.

"Tomorrow is Bingo Night. If those Neanderthals don't cancel it."

"We'll do the following night, okay? Thanks, Mrs. Hink. See you then."

Missy slipped out of the condo and took the stairs so she didn't have to wait for the elevator.

When she had looked up Stork Street, then used the satellite view, she spotted the house from her vision where Sophie was. She must have missed it when she scanned the area the other day. There it was, barrel-tile roof, rectangular swimming pool, boat dock without a boat, large shed-like structure attached to the house.

She had to get there right away in the off chance she could use the chaos to free Sophie. There was no time to recruit vampires from Squid Tower to help. They were probably under surveillance anyway. It would be just Matt and her against an untold number of Neanderthals and a marauding vampire cave bear.

What could go wrong?

WHEN SHE ARRIVED at Stork Street, flashing red lights were everywhere. Police cars blocked the entrance to the street. She recognized Matt's old pickup truck pulled onto the sidewalk of the main road just before the police cars. She peered through the darkness to see if he was in it.

His truck shuddered. It tilted to its left, landed on the street on the driver's side, and then fell upside-down.

A gigantic cave bear stood beside it, seemingly pleased with itself.

Matt wasn't in the cab. Missy drove past Stork Street and pulled into the empty parking lot of a convenience store. The only weapon she had in the car was one of the flimsy wooden stakes she used in her vegetable garden. She hopped out and ran back to the street. The vampire cave bear was no longer around. So she slipped between the empty cop cars with the flashing lights and ran toward the house that matched her mental image. It was a few houses away on her left.

The scene before her was from an apocalyptic nightmare.

Overturned cars were scattered about. A coconut palm was toppled across the road. In the front of the house, a cheap suit like the Neanderthals wore lay on the grass buttoned-up, knotted necktie in place. All that was missing was the body that had worn it. Instead, ashes spilled from the sleeves and collar.

And, since tomorrow was garbage pickup day, every single trash container set out at the curb along the street had been knocked over, contents strewn over front yards. It seemed the prehistoric cave bear had the same instincts as its modern counterparts.

Where was Sophie? Was she in the house or had she fled?

Two black SUVs were parked in front of the house in question, and neither was damaged. She assumed the vampires were inside the house, minus the one who had been destroyed. Or, if Sophie had escaped, they were searching for her.

She didn't know what to do. How could she search for Sophie? She needed magick to help her.

There was no way to do the same kind of search for her using her spirit essence. But Missy could use a much simpler technique, not unlike some animals and many hunters used to find prey.

She would search for Sophie by looking for body heat, like an infrared sensor without the technology. For her, it was a simple spell. She knelt between the SUVs where she wouldn't be seen and began clearing her mind.

Until someone tapped on her shoulder.

17
OCCUPATION

She flinched from the hand that touched her shoulder. The odd thing was, the hand wasn't cold and lifeless. It was warm, as if alive.

It was Matt.

"This place is crawling with vampires," he said.

"I know. That's why we're here."

"I mean they're roaming about everywhere, like ants from a disturbed anthill. I think Sophie or other prisoners escaped and they're looking for them."

Other escaped humans would complicate her search for Sophie, but helping anyone escape the vampires was worth it.

"I saw some vampires searching down by the canal. Maybe she tried swimming away."

The problem with swimming is that vampires have extra-sensitive vision and hearing. Unless Sophie could swim great distances underwater, she could be spotted when she broke the surface.

A gunshot echoed nearby.

"Who's shooting whom?" Missy asked.

"Probably the cops shooting at the bear, or whatever it is. I saw it batting down mailboxes for fun. It almost came after me."

"It did come after your truck."

"Is my truck okay?"

"You don't want to know. Now, give me a moment for a quick spell."

Missy tried casting the spell again, drawing upon the elements of fire and spirit to identify body heat. She focused the spell toward the canal.

And then she felt the sensation: an invisible tugging at her consciousness, like an invisible kid trying to drag her to the toy aisle.

It came from down the street, toward the dead end on the Intracoastal. She hurried in that direction, Matt following her. The tugging sensation grew stronger, trying to pull her to the left.

"I think Sophie—or someone—is in the water behind this house," Missy said, pointing to a newer two-story home with a metal roof. "Let's hope the owners don't mind us trespassing."

They went up the driveway, went around the side of the garage. At the water was a covered dock with a boat suspended on davits. A single light on the dock shone into the water.

"Stop," Matt whispered.

Dark silhouettes of men passed across the light on the dock.

And suddenly the entire backyard filled with light.

"What are you doing on my property?" demanded a voice coming from the back porch of the house.

Missy and Matt froze.

"I see you down there by the dock. You stay away from my boat. I got a gun, and I ain't afraid to use it."

There was no answer from the men by the dock. Instead, the floodlight illuminated two bats flying high above, away from the water and over the house.

The homeowner, in a bathrobe, walked hesitantly toward the dock to investigate. Missy and Matt slipped back around the house to the street.

"Hopefully, she swam to another dock," Matt said.

Missy reactivated the spell and waited a moment. The tugging sensation returned. This time, it was from the other direction, back toward the vampire house.

"Good," Missy said, "she's trying to outsmart them. They're probably assuming she's making her way toward the Intra-coastal, away from their house."

She followed the tugging sensation and Matt followed her. Things were quieting down in the neighborhood. The vampire cave bear must have headed elsewhere or been captured. That last possibility was highly unlikely.

Missy was yanked by an unseen force to her right, to a home only two doors down from the vampire house. Only one black SUV remained parked in front of that house now.

They passed around the older ranch house. At the water's edge, there was no dock, only a stone seawall. And the arms of someone struggling to get out of the water.

Missy and Matt ran to the canal to help the woman. When they reached her, she looked at them with alarm, but saw they didn't look like Neanderthals. She allowed them to take her arms and pull her up onto the seawall.

"Are you Sophie?" Missy asked.

The woman nodded, her drenched hair swaying across a face that struggled not to cry.

"I'm Missy and this is Matt. We're here to take you home."

They helped her walk up the gently sloped lawn. She was shivering.

"I have towels in my car," Missy told her.

Sophie didn't answer. She was obviously traumatized.

The three went around the corner of the house and collided head-first with bats headed the opposite way.

Sophie screamed.

One of them hit Missy right in the forehead. She staggered backward, and the bat, too, was stunned. It dropped to the ground. All she could think was it would turn into a Neanderthal at any second and her only weapon was the wooden stake for tying up her tomato plants.

The bat fluttered weakly and attempted to get airborne again.

And she drop-kicked it with all her might. It sailed across the grass and into the swimming pool with a tiny splash and a tiny scream.

Then it exploded in a cloud of red vapor and tiny bat-fragments.

"What the—" Matt said. "Water destroys them? What if it rains?"

"No," Missy said. "I bet it's the chlorine that does it. There weren't any chlorinated swimming pools in the Paleolithic era."

Sophie was still screaming. The other bat was tangled in her hair. It tried to escape while she swatted it desperately.

"Ah, her hair is wet with saltwater," Matt said. "That seems to have no effect."

"She's traumatized already. We need to help her. But that bat could turn into a Neanderthal at any moment. Sorry, Sophie."

Missy pulled her toward the pool and pushed her in.

The bat exploded just like the other one had. Sophie tried to wash the bat fragments from her hair, but they were dissolving naturally, the way the staked vampires had turned to dust.

"Sorry about that," Missy said. "We weren't equipped to fight a Neanderthal vampire. Let me help you out."

"Don't touch me please," Sophie said, swimming to the pool ladder. "Let's just get out of here before any other vampires come after us. And, by the way, maybe chlorine kills them in bat form, but not as humans. I've seen them swimming in the pool at night. And the pool there definitely has chlorine."

Missy watched Oleg run a hand across his bald scalp. Since being in captivity without a razor, stubble had grown in a narrow ring around his lower head. Vampire hair grows much slower than that of alive humans. Which was for the best, because it was hard to find a decent vampire barber or hairdresser.

"When I was in the army, I saw men executed," Oleg said in his Russian accent. "Firing squad. Hanging. I've always thought the worst part of it would be the waiting for your final hour. Worse than dying in battle. When you enter an engagement, you know you might die, but you keep your mind on the fighting. Just sitting here like this is unbearable."

"We'll find a way to get you out," Agnes said. "I swear."

Oleg shook his head ruefully. He wasn't buying it.

Agnes and Missy were visiting the prisoner in the storeroom where he had been confined. It was part of the pool complex and it was packed with pool chemicals, cleaning supplies, and the floats used in the vampire water-aerobics classes.

Thogg had granted Agnes permission to visit the prisoner because she was still president of the HOA. After she dropped Sophie at her house, Missy had arrived claiming she was treating Oleg for an unnamed medical condition. Two Neanderthal guards armed with spears were waiting outside the room.

"What has Thogg been doing since he arrested me?" Oleg asked.

"You know the Steadman condo that hasn't sold? Thogg commandeered that for his living quarters," Agnes said. "Thogg didn't just live on the yacht. He owns several homes in town where his vampires live, but several of them have moved here to Squid Tower. Some of them are not Neanderthals. They were turned by Thogg and his crew, so they will remain loyal to him. But there are other pre-existing vampires he recruited to his cause. We might be able to win them over to our side."

"What is he doing with the other vampires in our area?" Oleg asked.

A large percentage of Jellyfish Beach's human population was retired. That was also the case for vampires, werewolves, and other supernaturals. While there were always some who preferred to be independent, most supernaturals formed communities where they lived together for safety and a common understanding. Missy knew there were some hives of younger vampires in town, but most vampire communities had residents that were turned as senior citizens and moved to

Florida for the active-adult retirement lifestyle that made the state famous.

"Thogg has been threatening Alligator Hammock, I hear," Agnes said, referring to a vampire community of single-family homes in the western suburbs. "There are rumors he's planning to attack them soon if they don't swear allegiance."

"Those vampires are soft," Oleg said. "They'll submit."

"Why is Thogg so intent on taking over senior communities?" Missy asked. "His soldiers are all younger."

Agnes laughed. "He doesn't want us to be his foot soldiers. He wants us for our money. His personal fortune isn't enough to pay for all his grandiose ambitions."

"I don't understand what his end goal is," Missy said.

"I think all he wants is power," Oleg said.

"When he has absolute control of all the vampires in this country," Agnes said, "he'll conquer the humans."

"Good luck," Missy said.

"Don't be so dismissive. It could happen," Oleg said. "More and more vampires are infiltrating human society. Think of all the night-shift workers who could secretly be vampires. Think of all the companies with employees who work from home. How many of those are actually vampires attending their video conferences in a room sealed off from sunlight? All it takes is for the military and the police agencies to be compromised, and the vampires could win. Humans would then be nothing more than our food source, our livestock."

He looked at Missy in a way that made her uncomfortable. She reflexively touched the vampire-repellant amulet worn under her blouse.

"You're sounding sympathetic to their cause," Agnes said.

"Nonsense," Oleg said, waving his hand dismissively. "As a

soldier, I always try to put myself in my enemy's mind. Thogg has a giant chip on his shoulder because he's a Neanderthal. He wants to prove that Neanderthals aren't inferior to modern homo sapiens."

"And he wants to get revenge for his subspecies being made extinct," Agnes said.

Oleg nodded. "While Thogg's ambitions are theoretically possible, most likely they'd result in all vampires being wiped out. The few remaining would live in hiding like cockroaches."

"That was what it was like during the Dark Ages," Agnes said. "It wasn't until the Renaissance that vampires could live normal lives again."

"Before my time," Oleg said. "I was born in 1734."

"You're such a youngster," Agnes said.

"And he's in great condition for a body age of sixty-six," Missy said.

"That won't do me any good come Friday at sunset," Oleg said.

Everyone was quiet as the thought of Oleg being staked hung in the air.

"We promise you we'll rescue you," Agnes said.

"Don't fill me with false hope," Oleg said. "I have to come to terms with my demise. Since I was turned, I have always imagined my existence continuing for eternity. I'm trying to grasp what the end would be like. Do vampires go to Heaven?"

Agnes looked away. She clearly didn't believe so. Missy wasn't sure. There had always been a question of whether vampires had souls. The kind and generous vampires Missy knew must surely have souls. But it was a contentious debate for vampire theologists.

"I believe you will," Missy said, patting Oleg's cold, white hand.

The door opened. A guard appeared, holding his spear at the ready.

"Your visiting time's up," he said.

Missy and Agnes said goodbye to Oleg, promising to visit him again. What was unsaid was that there was precious time left before sunset on Friday.

ANGRY SHOUTS CAME from the parking lot. Agnes hurried through the lobby as fast as her quad cane would allow. Missy opened the lobby door for her. The unrest came from the regular evening line at the Blood Bus.

The line was longer than usual. The reason for this was a large group of Thogg's troops had cut in front of the line. The Neanderthals, and their newly turned vampires with a high percentage of Neanderthal DNA, forced their way in front of the Squid Tower residents.

The folks who arrived an hour before the Blood Bus each night to be first in line—Ethel, Mort, Sylvia, and the like—were not the type to give up their places without a fight.

"You take your hands off me, you caveman brute!" Ethel shouted.

Sylvia smacked a particularly large Neanderthal in the head with her cane.

"I'm always second in line," she said. "You can't cut in front of me."

The Neanderthal whose head just got bonked by her cane was one of Thogg's top lieutenants. He picked up the elderly vampire and threw her forty feet across the parking lot into a ficus hedge.

Missy ran to her and helped her out of the hedge. Sylvia had cuts from the branches, but the wounds quickly healed in front of Missy's eyes.

"Are you okay, Sylvia?"

"I'm pissed off, is what I am."

Sylvia wrenched herself from Missy's hands and hobbled back to the blood food truck. She began hitting the Neanderthal again with her cane.

The furious Neanderthal didn't know what to do. He was about to punch her, but the other Neanderthals were laughing at him. Instead, he took Sylvia's cane and snapped it in half, tossing the pieces onto the property next door.

"You're going to buy me a new cane!" Sylvia yelled at him. "And not one of those cheap adjustable ones!"

The Neanderthal thugs laughed. The lieutenant picked Sylvia up and draped her over his shoulder, holding her by the ankles with one hand. He ignored her fists pounding on his butt as he took a bag of fresh whole blood from the server in the bus and sipped on it.

Once the Neanderthals had taken their blood and wandered off, the crowd was still restive.

"They better not run out of blood because of this," someone said.

"I bet they didn't even buy a meal plan," a liver-spotted man said. "They're drinking the blood we paid for."

Agnes walked away from the bus, trying to shake off a wrinkled woman with hair dyed jet-black who was voicing her anger.

"Every night is nothing but endless complaints," Agnes said

when she walked up to Missy. "These vampires complain about everything in normal times. They'll complain to me if their pickleball match is canceled because of rain. So imagine what it's like now with an occupying army in our home. 'The Neanderthals took my parking spot.' 'The Neanderthals left litter on the shuffleboard courts.' 'A Neanderthal peed in the pool.' I hear whining like that from dusk till dawn."

"I'm sorry I influenced your decision to submit to Thogg," Missy said.

"It was a foregone conclusion. We would have voted to submit anyway under all the pressure they were giving us."

"Will Thogg conquer any other communities?"

"No. Dear Leader isn't the Napoleon he thinks he is. We need him to continue his conquest elsewhere, leave our community, and return the hostages."

ALMOST AS IF Thogg had overheard his conqueror credentials mocked, a large caravan of black SUVs rolled out of Squid Tower later that night. Missy saw it when she went to her car to retrieve a blood pressure cuff for a patient exam. She texted Agnes about it.

"I heard they're going to Alligator Hammock to force them to submit," Agnes replied.

Word spread faster than a rumor about two-for-one coupons that the Neanderthal thugs were away, leaving only a few guards behind. Missy sensed that trouble was brewing.

And just like the pivotal rebellions and revolutions in human history, bloody and vicious as they were, the vampires of Squid Tower rose up.

Except this uprising wasn't actually bloody. Or vicious. Or much of an uprising at all. It was more like civil disobedience. The oppressors probably didn't even notice it. The fact was, the residents of Squid Tower were mild-mannered, as non-scary as vampires could be.

It began with Marvin. Still angry at his treatment by Thogg, he went big. He broke the ultimate taboo.

Marvin parked in a handicapped space without a permit. And not just any handicapped space, but the one right next to the boardwalk that crossed over the dunes to the beach. Even an obnoxious curmudgeon like Schwartz wouldn't have been so brazen.

Marvin parked in the blue-lined space and laughed defiantly. He got out of the car and leaned against the front grill, waiting for jack-booted thugs to beat him into submission.

He waited and waited until it got too close to dawn and he had to go inside. His car was in the spot for two more days before Agnes left a note on the windshield asking him politely to move.

Amy Held in unit 302 protested in her own fashion. In a condo HOA, nothing was more sacrilegious than improper and un-permitted decorations on the outside of your unit. She threw caution to the wind and hung an American flag and illustrations of Thomas Jefferson (whom she had known personally) all over her front door and windows.

"Let the Neanderthals fine me all they want, I won't pay," she vowed.

Nothing happened, except for disapproving looks from her next-door neighbor Sally.

Schwartz, of course, had to outdo everyone in obnoxiousness. Upset about his friend Oleg's death sentence, Schwartz went crazy. He dumped all the furniture from the pool deck into the pool. This was a major escalation, and when word spread of what he did, all the residents retired to their condos, double-locked their doors, and waited for the reprisals.

Nothing happened.

Even when Ethel refused to clean up after her dog, nothing happened. She allowed the poop to sit there right by the "pick up after your pets" sign at the front entrance, steaming in the moonlight. And nothing happened.

"I was giddy with excitement about our revolution, but I feel kind of empty now," Marvin said to a neighbor.

His neighbor, Maurice, who had actually almost died in the French Revolution, shook his head and walked away.

Schwartz knocked on Agnes' door a little too close to dawn for comfort. But he was too agitated to sleep.

"How do we get out of this, Agnes?" he asked.

"We don't. Unless we're all willing to be staked," she replied.

"I was afraid you were going to say that."

18
OLD MEMORIES

S ophie seemed to become ten years younger when she reunited with her mother. The hardened, traumatized young woman whom Missy had fished out of the canal had melted into her mother's arms, both of them sobbing. Any of the tension Missy suspected lay between them dissolved for the time being, and there was nothing but pure mother-daughter intimacy.

Missy had given them their space, as they talked in low tones in the guest bedroom. She went to Squid Tower to visit Oleg and witnessed the conflict at the Blood Bus. It was full dawn when Missy returned home and knocked on the door.

"Let me look at those puncture wounds, Sophie," she said.

Twin fang marks, tiny and red, were over the jugular veins on both sides of her neck. Another pair was on the inside of her right forearm, just below the elbow. She wiped them with cotton swaps soaked in rubbing alcohol, then smeared them with antibiotic ointment.

"Will she be okay?" Darla asked.

"I think so. I know more about vampires than about their victims, but vampire saliva has an enzyme that prevents infection. It would do vampires no good to get their food source sick. I'll write her a prescription for oral antibiotics, just in case. Then we'll check into a hotel."

"Why?" Sophie asked.

"In case they come after you. The vampires or their human servants. Thogg knows where I live."

"I was hoping to get on the road to San Marcos," Darla said.

"They could come after you. It's best we stick together until things settle down. You're safer with my magick."

Even though Acceptance Home Care accepted only supernatural creatures for patients, Missy still maintained her Nurse Practitioner license, allowing her to write prescriptions. Let's be clear, werewolves and vampires are helped by antibiotics, too.

While Darla and Sophie were out filling the prescription, Missy packed some clothes and food, then brought the cat carriers in from the garage. She went online and made reservations at an extended-stay hotel outside of Jellyfish Beach, but close enough so she could respond to evolving events.

Darla and Sophie took longer than Missy had expected to return. They'd done some shopping because Sophie had no clothing or personal items. The moment they arrived, Missy said they all had to head to the hotel.

"What's the rush?" Darla asked. "Sophie is exhausted."

"We need to protect her."

"She's right, Mom," Sophie said. "It freaks me out knowing the house where they kept me is so close by."

So Missy locked up the house, set the burglar alarm, and

cast two different protection spells to protect the property from supernatural incursion and alert her if it happened. Then their small caravan got on the road.

Less than an hour later, they were settling into their two rooms at a hotel next to the interstate. It wasn't the most charming place in the world, but it was nice and anonymous. And it had free breakfast.

Missy brought takeout dinners back to their rooms to avoid risk. Darla and Sophie had a mini-suite, so they all ate there. The conversation was light and trivial. No one wanted to ask Sophie what she had been through. It was too soon for that.

But after they finished eating, threw away the food cartons, and turned on the TV, Sophie pulled something from her back pocket and dropped it with a loud clang on the coffee table.

Missy picked it up and studied it. It was a folding knife, a jackknife of sorts. It looked ancient. No, not as old as a flint knife from the Neanderthal era, but from the sixteenth or seventeenth centuries.

Then she opened it. Instead of a typical knife blade, it was a cylindrical, sharp-pointed instrument like an ice pick. Not meant for cutting or slicing. Meant only for impaling.

"Where did you get that?" Darla asked.

"I stole it," Sophie said. "From the house. One of the vampires left it on a chair. It must have fallen out of his pocket. I took it because I needed something to protect myself when I escaped."

"That looks like it's meant for slipping through ribcages and skewering hearts," Missy said, handing the knife back to Sophie. "In other words, for killing vampires."

"I know," Sophie said. "These vampires kill vampires. That's how they conquer other clans."

"Did you see them kill anyone?" Darla asked.

"Yes. They have a lot of vampire hostages. I saw them kill two of them, two of the most rebellious hostages."

"Senior vampires?" Missy asked with alarm.

"No, they were younger. And I know they've killed many humans, draining them to death, though I didn't see it. They drained others to make them vampires. They always made me forget what I saw. But I do remember hearing their last dying breaths."

"Can I touch the knife?" Darla asked.

"That's why I brought it out, Mom. I thought you could read it and learn something to help us."

Sophie put the knife back on the table and slid it close to her mother.

"Sometimes this takes a while," Darla said to Missy. "And please don't stare at me. It doesn't help if I feel self-conscious."

Missy looked at the TV while Darla took a deep breath and picked up the knife, holding it in both hands in different positions, caressing it.

Then her eyes rolled back in her head and she slumped backwards against the sofa backrest. Missy looked at Sophie, who smiled reassuringly.

In Darla's vision, she was an undead creature. She had a man's body, strong and stocky, with coarse body hair. It was the body of a twenty-five-year-old, but this man had existed for tens of thousands of years. Her power of psychometry was reading the memory the man had left on the knife his hand had been touching in the front pocket of his pants. At this moment, the man was hunting.

In a shopping mall. Hunting for clothes. He had a burning desire for a new flannel shirt and a pair of jeans. Darla's mind intruded slightly, questioning why he'd want flannel during the warm months of Florida, but she pushed her own thoughts aside and let herself ride with the man's memory.

Even though his memory was very boring.

He found a shirt he liked and tried it on in the changing room. He needed a size large enough to accommodate his massive upper body. She saw him in the changing room mirror: huge, well-defined pectoral muscles and rippling abs, but they were all covered with coarse, dark hair which kind of ruined it for Darla. His face was Neanderthal-like, but handsome and could easily pass as a modern human's. He had a scar below his right eye.

The shirt was large enough to fit his chest, but hung long on his body, because it was made to fit a taller man. He would simply tuck it into his pants, he told himself.

Next, he tried on several pairs of jeans. His bulky thighs were an obstacle. This part of the memory was spotty, because he had little contact with the knife. Then, it was vivid again, as he left the mall wearing the jeans he had just bought and slipped the knife into his back pocket because his jeans were too tight to hold it comfortably in a front pocket.

The memory disappeared. Darla found herself staring at the ugly painting of a man riding a bike that hung on the wall of the hotel. The knife had fallen out of her hands onto the sofa.

"How'd it go?" Sophie asked.

"Boring," Darla said. "I'm going to need more time with the

knife." She described what she had experienced while Missy typed notes on a laptop.

"It sounds like Carl," Sophie said. "He's like Thogg's Number Two. I remember him wearing new jeans and sitting in the chair where I found the knife. It must have slipped out of his rear pocket."

"Can you access older memories?" Missy asked. "We need to know more about these vampires and their motives."

"I'll try," Darla said. "I can't control much. The memories control me. The most recent ones usually have the most potency. But older memories will come through if they are strong and impactful to the person who handled the object."

"Or the Neanderthal who handled it," Sophie said.

"Yes. I'll try again. I hope you guys are patient. I can tell this guy owned the knife for a long time. It will take a while for me to retrieve enough memories to be useful."

"No rush," Missy said. "Except that a vampire very dear to me is going to be staked on Friday at sundown. But no pressure."

"Thanks," Darla said sarcastically as she took calming breaths and cleared her mind of the present.

She handled the knife, opening the cylindrical blade with its needle-sharp tip. She folded the blade back into the brass handle that had intricate designs of unicorns, dragons, and sea monsters . . .

. . . and she was back in Carl's body in a small, dusty shop. The place looked like it was from another era. She saw, through the tiny panes of a window, a nearby body of water. She was surprised to recognize San Marcos Bay, except the opposite shore was not developed like it was today and all the boats were antique sailing vessels. Where today's fort stood was a construction site with the fort's coquina-stone walls incomplete.

My God, it must be the early seventeen hundreds.

The shopkeeper, wearing an apron and a powdered wig, asked Carl if he liked the knife he was examining.

Carl said yes, and retrieved five coins from a leather pouch, handing them to the shopkeeper.

"Where are you from, my lord?" the shopkeeper asked in Spanish, which Darla understood.

"Madrid," Carl said.

"What brings you from such a fair city to our little garrison town?"

"I am stopping here on my way back to Spain from Puerto Rico. I seek the magician known as Humberto of Aragon. Do you know where I can find him?"

"He comes to the market square every afternoon. You can ask for him there."

Carl thanked the shopkeeper and stepped out onto the narrow cobblestone street that lined the bay. It was winter, a cold, blustery day. The only kind of weather he could stand in this hot climate. He had lied to the shopkeeper; he hadn't come from Puerto Rico to Florida, the usual route of the treasure fleets heading back to Spain. He had come to San Marcos on a naval ship straight from Spain and would return on it as soon as he completed his mission.

He gripped his new knife in his hand. This land of Florida was so sparsely populated with humans and would be a great place for him and other Neanderthals to settle. He sensed that very few vampires existed here. They wouldn't be a threat to a new colony of Neanderthals, unlike the vampires of Europe and the Northeastern American colonies where the Neanderthals were oppressed and preyed upon just as they had been when his subspecies disappeared from the earth. Except for those, like himself, who were undead.

No, the local vampires of Florida would not be a threat to a large group of Neanderthals. But Carl on his own would be vulnerable as soon as the vampires realized he was here. That's why the knife, made for killing vampires, was a critical purchase.

His memories of fighting and killing other vampires came over him as he stood on the cobblestones, and, thus, they came over Darla. The memories were jumbled and danced across different historical eras. There was a battle with a vampire wearing chain mail and a steel helm. Another vampire who almost killed him wore sandals and a tunic. A group of vampires wearing animal skins were killing Neanderthals before Carl managed to flee.

Then, undecipherable, scattered images and sounds passed by until a powerful memory took over. It was of an event that took place tens of thousands of years before, but he relived it in vivid detail, standing there outside the shop. It was a memory soaked in fear and anger and self-loathing.

It was of Carl on guard duty outside the cave where his clan slept. He stood far from the small fire near the entrance to the cave so his eyes would adjust to the darkness. It was a frosty night, so he pulled his bearskin coat tightly shut. He stared at the stars, at the constellations their shaman would point out to them representing the wild horses, mammoths, bison, and other animals they hunted.

That's when he was knocked to the ground.

A man sat astride him, pushed his chin up, and bent down

toward him. Only the man was barely recognizable as a man. The creature was hairy and animal-like with a small head.

It growled and then sank its teeth into Carl's neck.

This was the night when Carl was turned by this vampire of a more primitive hominoid species. The night when Carl died and was brought back to a lifelike existence. And then abandoned by this creature.

Carl didn't know how to exist in his new reality. His clan, the only people he had ever known, expelled and almost killed him. He spent years as a lonely nomad, drinking the blood of animals he caught.

Finally, he stumbled upon Thogg's clan of vampires like him. And with them he stayed for millennia.

He would repay them all these years later by acquiring the magic that would allow them to thrive in the hot climate of this land of Florida. That is, if the wizard Humberto lived up to his reputation.

Darla dropped the knife and broke the link to Carl's memories. Here she was in a hotel off the interstate some three hundred years after the memory movie she had just experienced. It was disorienting.

Missy sat across from her, typing away at her laptop. She looked up and smiled at Darla.

"Keep going," she said.

"It's broken now. I'll explain what I experienced."

"You already did, Mom," Sophie said. "You were talking the entire time. Giving us a play-by-play of what you experienced."

"We need to find out who this Humberto was, and if he used a spell to help the Neanderthals," Missy said. "I wondered why they chose Florida. When they were alive, Europe was in ice ages and the Neanderthals were adapted to living in the cold. I could see why they'd be attracted to a place with so few modern humans. When they first came here after crossing the Bering Strait, it must have been during an ice age. But then it warmed up here and would have been very inhospitable to them. They would need magic to adapt to the climate."

"But what's the point of living here today? The state is crowded with humans," Darla said.

"Yes. Very primitive humans. I think Neanderthals would feel quite at home here."

"If we find out what magic they're using, can you fight it?" Sophie asked.

"That's exactly what I want to do," Missy said.

Knocking on the door made everyone tense up.

"Housekeeping," a female voice said.

19
LOCKED UP

Missy looked through the fisheye lens peephole. A woman stood close to the door wearing a maid's uniform. She looked legit. Missy opened the door.

And the woman fell into the room, landing on Missy's feet. Four male Neanderthals rushed in after her. They carried handguns and immediately swept through the room among the surprised women.

Sophie screamed and ran toward the bedroom, but only made it a few feet before a tall Neanderthal picked her up and dropped her on the couch. Missy tried to cast a protection spell, but a Neanderthal tackled her before she could utter a word and slammed her into the drywall. The spell wouldn't work with someone already in her personal space. Darla was so shocked by the attack that she didn't even move from the couch. The housekeeper had scrambled out of the room on her hands and knees.

In seconds, Missy, Darla, and Sophie were immobilized with vampire arms around their necks, guns pressed against their heads. The vampire that held Missy was strong, and the smell of mold in his clothing was even stronger.

The one vampire with his hands free appeared to be in charge. He had a scar under his right eye.

"My name is Carl," he said, nodding to Missy and Darla. "Sophie made a mistake thinking she could escape me. Once I have tasted your blood, my lovely, I will always be able to find you. You are mine forever until I drain you to the last drop. Too bad you don't have the genes of my people. I would have loved to make you my vampire child."

He seemed to notice Darla for the first time.

"Is this your mother?"

Sophie nodded.

"They say sweet blood runs in the family. Your mother will join you as a blood cow. And you," he looked at Missy with a predatory glare, "are the witch, yes? We've had enough of your interference. By the authority of our supreme leader Thogg, I sentence you to be executed on Friday at sundown."

He turned to his accomplices. "Mesmerize them. Have them gather all their belongings and check out of the hotel. Keep an eye on them to make sure their trances don't fade, but don't make the desk clerk suspicious. I'll wait for you in the SUV."

The moldy-smelling vampire looked Missy in the eyes. His lips were moving, but she heard nothing he said. He followed her to her room where she grabbed her suitcase and laptop bag. She hadn't even unpacked anything yet. She remembered passing through the lobby and a brief interaction with the desk clerk who kept repeating "nonrefundable." And then she was in the backseat of a black SUV.

THE MOLDY-SMELLING vampire snapped his fingers and Missy realized she was standing in the storeroom at Squid Tower where Oleg was being held. The vampire left the room and locked the door behind him. In the dim light from a single bulb hanging from the ceiling, Oleg stared at her from the pool lounger where he sat.

"So what are you in for?" he asked with a smile.

She blinked, still confused about how she got here from the hotel.

"They mesmerized you, dear," Oleg said.

"I've never been before. This was the first time."

"It's a lovely tool for preying on victims. Especially if you wipe out their memory. Then you can keep drinking from the same well night after night."

Missy shuddered and checked her neck. No puncture wounds, thank God.

"They're going to execute me because of my interference," Missy said. It still hadn't sunk in yet. "I'll be the first witch executed in America since the witch trials."

"The Neanderthals are desperate to spread fear throughout the vampires of Florida," Oleg said. "And they seem to be botching it. Agnes visited me earlier and said the Neanderthals didn't have any luck intimidating the HOA of the vampire community west of town, Alligator Hammock. They took some hostages in retaliation. We'll see how well that goes. Well, actually, you and I won't be around to see."

"Don't give up, Oleg. I'm going to use every bit of magick I have to try to save us."

The problem was, her heavy artillery, the Red Dragon talisman, was safely hidden at home along with the grimoire that contained Don Mateo's spells. She thought it would have been too risky to bring them to the hotel, and it turned out she was right.

"Oleg, while we're cellmates, please be patient with me. I'm going to be making a lot of noise casting spells and conjuring."

"In case you haven't noticed, there's nothing else to entertain me in here."

"I also need to summon a ghost that lives with me. He rarely comes when I call him. I'll warn you that the summoning will get on your nerves. If and when the ghost does show up, he's a whole new level of annoying."

"We Russians are patient people. Do what you have to do."

"I'm going to put a cone of silence over this room so the guards don't hear me. Unfortunately for you, I can't put it over just me. It seals off rooms and buildings."

Oleg shrugged.

Somewhat self-consciously under Oleg's gaze, she knelt on the floor. There was nothing to draw a magick circle with, so she traced an invisible one on the concrete with her finger. She gathered the energies within her and from the earth, then recited the Latin words. Once she sensed the cone was solid, she began the laborious process of getting the attention of the ghost of the wizard who'd been dead for 400 years.

First, she tried reaching him telepathically. She said his name over and over in her mind and sought a connection between our world and the spiritual world. Sometimes this worked with Don Mateo. This time it didn't.

Next, she tried magick. If she had the Red Dragon with her, that would have compelled the ghost to come. Instead, she tried a generic summoning spell that worked on various supernatural entities.

Her imaginary magick circle was unbroken, so she remained within it and chanted:

Fairy, pixie, ghostie, beastie,

Get your spectral butt here quickly.

Don Mateo, I summon you.

She released a flood of power that sent the words flying into the ether.

She waited. And waited.

Still no Don Mateo.

Now it was time for a cruder form of summoning. Witches and wizards had a name for the technique. It was called shouting at the top of your lungs.

"Don Mateo, I need you! Please come. They're going to execute me. I need you now!"

The cone of silence had better be working, Missy thought.

"Sorry about that, Oleg. Ghosts do what they wanna do. They're worse than cats when it comes to obeying."

Oleg removed his hands from his ears. "You know vampires have extra-sensitive hearing, correct?"

"Right now, the way I see it, Don Mateo is the only one who can save us all."

"At last, some kind words from you, my lady." Don Mateo appeared, sitting atop stacked boxes of toilet tissue. He was only semi-corporeal at the moment, so he could get away with not crushing the boxes.

"My kind words had the desired effect of getting your butt over here. Don Mateo of Grenada, this is Colonel Oleg Kazmirov."

"Who are you talking to?" Oleg asked.

"You don't see the ghost sitting on the boxes over there?"

"No."

"Can you hear him?"

"No. I thought you were talking to yourself."

"Forgive me then for being rude, but I need to continue this conversation. Don Mateo, we're in dire straits here. They're going to stake Oleg and behead me tomorrow. We seriously need your help."

"How exactly could I help you?" the ghost asked.

"With your incomparable knowledge and wisdom."

"You may continue with the compliments."

Instead, she told him the story of Carl that Darla had learned through her psychometry.

"Do you know of a wizard named Humberto in San Marcos? I don't know what year this was, but it was when the Spanish still ruled the city."

Don Mateo sighed a ghost's non-breathing equivalent of a sigh.

"I knew Humberto Rodrigo the same way I know you. He managed to get his hands on my grimoire after I died, and I was bound to him. He was a corrupt, venal old man who would do any kind of spell or hex for the right amount of gold."

Missy was excited.

"Tell me, what kind of spell would help Neanderthals thrive in a hot climate?"

"I don't know what Neanderthals are."

"That's right, they weren't discovered until centuries after your death. Neanderthals are a prehistoric ancestor of modern humans who lived hundreds of thousands of years ago. I think they went extinct about forty thousand years ago. At the time, Europe was much colder than it is today. The Neanderthals who are threatening us are vampires."

"Ugh." Don Mateo made a face. He didn't like vampires. Not that many people did.

"These vampires had to adapt a remarkable amount to the development of civilization, technology, and new languages," Missy continued. "But their bodies haven't changed. They're the same bodies they had when they were turned into vampires a hundred thousand years ago. Magic, though, could help them adapt to a very different climate."

"Unfortunately, I do not know if Humberto performed such a spell for vampires. But in my grimoire, there was a spell I developed with the shaman of the Timucuan people to help their weaker members endure cold spells. In North Florida, it can occasionally get below freezing at night during the winter. This spell wasn't specific to heat or cold, it simply allowed people to adjust their body temperature."

"That sounds promising," Missy said. "Maybe that was the one Humberto used. Could the spell really keep working for hundreds of years?"

"For as long as the person was alive."

"Or in the case of vampires, for as long as their bodies existed?"

"Yes," Don Mateo said.

"Do you know a spell to undo this one?"

"No, not a specific one. There are, of course, magic-nullification spells."

"I need something big," Missy said. "Some way I can turn the spell off in all the Neanderthals at once."

"You ask for a lot. We would have to design a nullification spell that works specifically like that."

"I have time on my hands right now," Missy said. "But I do have a deadline tomorrow evening."

"I wish you wouldn't joke like that," Oleg said. "I am not afraid to die. But wordplays like that are a fate worse than death."

"Vampires don't have a sense of humor," Don Mateo said. "That's one of the reasons I don't like them."

"Well, let's get to work," Missy said. "First, explain the body temperature spell, and we'll construct one to nullify it. We can't make potions or amulets because I have access to nothing other than the stuff stored in this room. It will have to rely on my powers and the earth energies."

"I give you no guarantee that we can nullify the spell among all the vampires at once," Don Mateo said.

"And they can't know they're victims of the nullification spell. It has to happen naturally."

"I can sense you don't have the Red Dragon with you. I beg your pardon, but are you crazy, my lady?"

"Ah, Don Mateo, you're worth your weight in gold to me," Missy said.

"I'm a ghost. I weigh nothing."

"Exactly."

Missy was trying so hard not to panic or sink into despair about the terrible predicament she was in. And the stupid ghost wasn't helping. There had to be a way to nullify the spell so the Neanderthals would be overcome by the heat. In their weakened state, they would be easier for the vampires of Squid Tower to defeat. And she had spells to assist them.

But none of this would work without the Neanderthals

being disabled in some way. But how? Just making them sweat wasn't enough.

While she was thinking, her eyes absently roved around the storeroom, its bathroom-cleaning supplies, the pool accessories.

The chlorine.

20
ASLEEP ON THE JOB

"Maybe we can use chlorine in some way," Missy said to the ghost.

"Chlorine?"

"It's a chemical element. I think it was known back in your day. A compound form of it is sodium chloride, which is salt."

"Are you speaking of alchemy?"

"No, it's just chemistry. For some reason, it destroys the vampires when they're in bat form, but not when they're in their humanoid bodies. Maybe we can draw upon it for the nullification spell."

"That would not be necessary," Don Mateo said. "But you could use it for a separate spell against the vampires."

"Good idea. Now tell me about the body heat spell."

Don Mateo went on at great length describing the Native American shaman's efforts to protect babies, the elderly, and other vulnerable people from the sudden, overnight freezes that occasionally caused suffering. Much of the shaman's work involved herbs and prayers to various animal spirits. Don Mateo, a skilled wizard in his day when he fled Spain two steps ahead of the Spanish Inquisition, added a complex invocation of the elemental energies combined with the electromagnetic power of the planet. He described a lot of quasi-spiritual stuff that, as a modern witch, Missy didn't understand or appreciate.

The fundamental premise of nullifying a spell is to undermine the structure of the magic that makes a spell work. It's like unraveling the weave of a fabric. Once you begin that, it only takes a few tugs on the thread for the entire thing to come apart.

Fortunately, Don Mateo knew the spell from memory. You can't always depend on a ghost to have a sharp memory, but Don Mateo was a spectral encyclopedia. Missy had him repeat the spell over and over without activating it. (The ghost wouldn't be able to cast it, anyway. He was just a ghost.) Missy listened carefully, absorbing every detail, noting the important structural aspects of the spell.

Then she calculated how to take apart each of those structures. She devised a spell that would do that, weakening Don Mateo's spell enough so that a simple tug would unravel it all.

"How am I going to get it to work among all the vampires?" she asked.

"You need to do it to one of them in person. If your spell is powerful enough, it will spread to all the vampires who are under the original spell, no matter where they are."

"How often do the guards come by to feed you?" she asked Oleg.

"They've only given me one blood bag since I've been in here," he said.

"What about bathroom breaks?"

Oleg laughed. "That hasn't been a problem. I can last days without having to go."

Missy banged on the storeroom door.

"Hey!" she shouted. "I need help in here."

After several minutes and much banging, a key rattled in the lock and the door opened a crack.

"What is all this noise for?" a Neanderthal asked.

"I have to go to the bathroom. I'm a human. I have needs."

"You will stay in here," he said. "I will get a bucket."

When he left, Missy knelt within her imaginary magic circle and quickly began the nullification spell. She didn't have the Red Dragon, but her regular power charm—a small leather pouch stuffed with herbs and precious metals—hadn't been taken from her. She held it in her pocket to amplify the power she summoned from the earth, the air, the fire of the sun, the nearby ocean, and the spirit within her. She recited the simple invocation she had written.

When the door opened, the guard was surprised to see her kneeling on the floor. As he reached through the door to drop the bucket inside, the spell was complete.

With only her mind, she flung the spell like a spear at the Neanderthal. He flinched as if something had hit him. He looked around, confused. His hands shook as he stood upright, fumbling with the keys as he shut the door. He took forever to fit the key back in the lock and turn the bolt.

Missy said a quick spell and the clinking of the keys landing on concrete came from just beyond the door.

Hopefully, he won't realize he dropped them, she thought.

"Now what?" she asked Don Mateo.

"Now you wait."

"How is your magick going to help us?" Oleg asked. "I heard

only your side of the conversation. This is supposed to make the Neanderthals be overcome by heat?"

"Yes. It won't kill them or anything, but they'll be lethargic and possibly even get heat stroke. Our vampires can then hopefully subdue them. And if I get out of here, I can cast sleeping and binding spells against them."

"We need someone to find those dropped keys and let us out of here," Oleg said. "Knowing my neighbors, they'd probably pick them up and put a sign in the lobby saying they found lost keys."

"Mac," a Neanderthal voice boomed from outside the door. "You dropped your keys, you moron. Here."

"Thank you, sir," Mac answered. "Does it seem a lot hotter tonight to you?"

"By the gods, it's never been this bad before. I can barely breathe. And it seems to be getting worse by the minute."

"Must be the humidity."

"No, it's not just the humidity. It's the heat. If vampires could sweat, I'd be soaking wet right now."

"I wish our great leader hadn't picked summer to conquer Florida."

"Watch your tone of voice. Now, I've got to go inside for the air conditioning."

"Okay, time for Plan B," Missy said.

"Can't you just blow up the door?" Oleg asked. "And blow up the Neanderthals while you're at it?"

"Oleg, I've explained to you guys before. I practice earth magick. I don't blow stuff up like in an action-adventure movie."

"You're boring."

Yes, she was. Missy could unlock simple locks using her

telekinesis. More complex tumbler locks required some magick as well. Bank vaults were out of the question. But she would have to wait until day when the vampires weren't around so she wouldn't be caught. But then all the vampires, good and bad, would be holed up asleep and there wouldn't be a climactic, action-adventure battle.

This was frustrating. But there was one thing Missy could do in the meantime.

She cast a spell to fry the building's air conditioning system. She heard condensers explode and smiled. The vampires of Squid Tower would be annoyed and would complain bitterly to the property manager about the lack of AC. But the Neanderthals would be miserable.

She smiled evilly.

Then she set about devising a spell that could combat the heat-enervated Neanderthals and drive them off the property and, hopefully, out of town. Maybe even destroy them. She made notes on her phone to help her remember it.

Then she retraced her magick circle on the floor, put herself into a meditative state, and did the energy harvesting she always did before casting a spell. But instead of drawing upon the power of the earth, this time she focused on one particular element: chlorine. The buckets of chlorine in the storeroom were her focus. After she drew the power from them, she tapped into that of the chlorine in the world around her, from swimming pools to the chloride of the earth's crust, to the salt in the ocean. Once she felt she had amassed enough of this power, she sealed it inside herself for later use.

As dawn approached, Oleg snored on his pool lounger while Missy tried to sleep in a chair with broken plastic straps. Vampire snores are just like human snores, only longer because of vampires' slower breathing rate. Long periods of silence in which she started to fall asleep were punctuated by buzz-saw breaths that seemed to go on forever. She still hadn't fallen asleep by the time morning light appeared in the cracks of the door.

When the sun set on this day, she and Oleg would be executed.

A key jiggled in the lock. The door inched open and a seam of light poured in.

"Stop!" Missy shouted. "Don't let the light in. There's a vampire in here."

"Sorry," said a voice outside. It was Matt. He closed the door.

"Matt! How did you find me?"

"A bit of reporting work," he said from behind the closed door. "I was making inquiries with the day-shift gate guard and he introduced me to the maintenance guy. He complained that he hasn't been able to clean the pool because he's forbidden to go into the pool storage room. There had to be a reason why, so I bribed him to let me borrow the key. Even though I thought you'd be able to unlock it yourself with your magick."

"Long story," she said.

"You need to get out of here," Oleg said. "I will hide in the back behind these boxes so you can open the door."

"Thank you, Oleg," Missy said. "I'll come get you out when it's dark."

"That's when I'm to be staked."

"I'll be back before that. I promise."

After Oleg had shielded himself behind the boxes, Missy opened the door just enough to squeeze through. The light hit the rear wall of the storeroom and part of Oleg's hiding place, but he was safe from its reach.

She left the door unlocked, just in case.

She was so happy to see Matt she gave him an enormous hug. This evidently surprised him before he wrapped his arms around her in return. She enjoyed the body contact more than she thought she would and prolonged it a few seconds more. Until a warm, tingling sensation told her this was not a good idea right now.

"We have a lot to do and we have to act fast," she said.

"I have no idea what you mean."

"Oleg and I are going to be executed tonight."

"My God!"

"You and I are the only people who can do something about it and end this occupation once and for all."

"Last I checked," Matt said, "we don't have Navy Seal training."

"We can't go around staking Neanderthals because they'll all be locked up in condos and other rooms. And we can't transport Oleg out of here without him getting sun-killed. And because of the human guards who work for the Neanderthals. We have to incapacitate them and there's no time for Paul Leclerc to round up his band of thugs."

"Your plan just keeps getting more impossible."

"We have surprise on our side," Missy said. "And I have sleeping and binding spells to use against them. First, I need some intel."

"You're even talking like a Seal."

Missy texted Agnes, who was usually reachable even during the day. She asked if Agnes knew how many human guards there were and where they were usually found.

Agnes texted back: "I don't know where they are during the day. Probably around the property perimeter, in the garage near their vehicles, and outside of the condo Thogg uses on the top floor. I don't know how many there are, but I've seen at least five or six."

Missy shared the information with Matt.

"Let's go from the outside and work our way in."

"So what am I supposed to do?" Matt asked.

"Distract them while I'm bewitching them. Or at least hold them off if they come after me."

"I don't have a gun."

"Matt, this is Jellyfish Beach in broad daylight. They're not going to shoot at you and draw the police here."

"I hope you're right."

The first guard they found was sitting on a bench on the end of the wooden dune crossover that led from the common area to the beach. The Caucasian with a military haircut was watching a group of women in bikinis walking at the edge of the surf. His back was to the condos because he was guarding against outsiders coming from the beach. Missy wanted to get as close as possible to him to make her spell most effective.

They went up the stairs and walked along the wooden walkway until the guard heard their footsteps and turned around, surprised to see them.

Matt gave a friendly wave. The guard didn't wave back. He just glared at them through dark shades and stood up threateningly.

Missy focused her energies and murmured the Latin words.

The man suddenly appeared massively drunk. He slumped down onto the bench and his chin dropped to his chest.

"He's asleep. Now I'll use the binding spell to keep him immobile, even if he wakes."

She went through a similar process, but this time the words

she intoned were in Old English. The man stiffened slightly, and that was that.

"Now let's find another one."

"That's it—he's incapacitated?" Matt asked.

"Yep."

"That was easier than I thought."

"They won't all be this easy, believe me."

The next guard was hanging out at the front gate, chatting with the Squid Tower attendant through the open window of the gatehouse. This employee of the Neanderthals was a tall, muscular Black who could snap Missy and Matt in half with one hand. He noticed them approaching him, clearly not expecting to see other humans wandering around the property.

"We're with the pest control company," Matt said.

The man stepped toward them and scowled. Missy finished reciting the Latin words of the sleeping spell, and the man staggered. He grabbed the gatehouse wall to steady himself and sat down heavily on the pavement. Soon after the binding spell, he froze in the fetal position beneath the guardhouse window.

"What did you do to him?" the gate guard asked. Missy recognized him as Manny.

"I suggest you stay in here and keep out of the way," Missy told him. "Your security company still works for the Squid Tower HOA. This guy," she pointed at the sleeping man with her foot, "works for an entity that was trying to take them over illegally."

"Gotcha," Manny said. "I'll keep busy in here."

Since the residents slept all day, the only people Manny opened the gate for were landscapers, delivery services, and repairmen. It was not a busy job.

Next, Missy and Matt prowled through the parking garage

in search of another of the Neanderthals' humans. They walked through each floor and up each ramp until they came upon a small fleet of black SUVs parked on the upper floor.

The human saw them coming. He got out of the front seat of one of the SUVs and straightened his suit jacket. The handle of a pistol protruded from his waistband.

"What are you doing here?" the man demanded. "You're trespassing."

"We're with the Census Bureau," Matt said. "How many of you are there?"

The Hispanic man with a shaved head glowered at them. He pulled out his pistol.

". . . *Somnum nunc*," Missy intoned.

The man sat heavily in the front seat.

After casting the binding spell, Missy took the gun he had dropped on the floor of the SUV. She handed it to Matt.

"Just in case," she said.

She searched the man. In his pants pockets, tight from his overly muscular thighs, were the key fobs for the SUVs. She retrieved two and closed the front door on him.

"Sweet dreams," she said.

"What are we going to do next?" Matt asked.

"We'll disable the guys guarding Thogg's condo later. That's going to be trickier if there's more than one, and I don't want to alert Thogg and his vampires. We need to rescue Darla and Sophie. I don't know where they're being held. If they're locked away in one of the condos here, we can't get to them. So let's try the sober homes. At least the two we know about. Follow me."

She tossed Matt one of the key fobs and they pressed their unlock buttons to see which SUVs they belonged to. They started them up and Missy led the way out of the garage and through the front gate. She waved at Manny as she drove past.

First, they stopped by Missy's house so she could feed Bubba and Brenda. They rubbed against her legs with affection and hunger. Actually, it was probably not in that order. While Matt waited in his vehicle, she retrieved the Red Dragon talisman from its hiding place in a bag beneath one of the cat litter boxes. She slipped the ancient carved-metal figurine into the left pocket of her jeans. She would need the extra power it gave to her spells.

Then she and Matt were off to the house in the north part of town from which Sophie had escaped. The neighborhood seemed mundane compared to the other night when the vampire cave bear was rampaging. Several broken mailboxes still lay in front lawns. A single BMW sat in the driveway of the vampires' house.

"Hopefully, someone will answer the door," Missy said. "I need visual contact with a person to make these spells work. Try to engage them so they don't slam the door in our faces."

"I can be very engaging," Matt said.

"When you're not obnoxious. Which is what you are most of the time."

He smiled at her and shook his head before marching to the front door, Missy slightly behind him.

A dark-skinned woman answered the door.

"Hello," Matt said. "We're with the State of Florida Department of Vampire Affairs."

"Wh-what?"

"We're here to ensure that your vampires are being well cared for and aren't being abused."

"But how did you—"

Her head dropped and she slowly sank to the floor where she lay on her side and snored. Missy stepped over her and Matt followed.

The home was large, but the two of them made quick work of searching it. No bedrooms were locked, and Darla and Sophie weren't here. In fact, no one was here, human or vampire. The garage contained nothing but yard tools. The shed behind it was unlocked and empty. It smelled heavily of unwashed cave bear.

"Okay, let's head to the other home," Missy said. She had an uneasy feeling.

They drove to the south part of town and found the larger estate on the cove beside the Intracoastal Waterway. Again, there was only one car in the driveway.

Matt's nonsense about the Department of Vampire Affairs confused the woman who answered the door long enough for Missy to put her out. They searched the home and it, too, was empty.

"Man, this is a sweet place. How can a vampire afford this?"

"He runs a private equity investing firm," Missy said.

"Of course. If a vampire can get rich that way, why did I go into journalism?"

A pair of eyeglasses sat on an otherwise empty coffee table. They looked familiar with their old-fashioned frames and thick lenses. One of the frames was repaired with electrical tape.

"Oh, my," she said. "These are Wilbur's glasses."

"Who?"

"One of my vampire patients. He was captured here on the night of our failed raid. He can't see anything without his glasses, even with his enhanced vampire vision."

"Why aren't they with him?"

"Because he was staked? Oh, my."

They were in one of the rooms with water views. The *Man Cave* was moored to the dock behind the house.

"We have to go to the yacht," Missy said.

"I can't believe they brought it back here."

"They thought their enemies were neutralized. We weren't."

Missy race-walked across the pool deck and onto the dock, gathering her energies, Matt right behind her. But as they neared the vessel, a man appeared on the flying bridge.

"Hey! This is private property."

Missy kept going, getting close enough to focus on his face. He had a dark, three-day-old beard and wore a generic, white marine officer's shirt.

"Stop right there!" he shouted.

She didn't.

And the man pointed a gun at her. She went numb.

A gun went off right behind her. It must have been from Matt. Lord knows where he was aiming, but it got the attention of the man on the yacht who swiveled his arm until he was aiming behind Missy.

The splash of a man jumping into the water came just seconds before the gun fired. Hopefully, Matt sank quickly before the bullet headed his way.

By now, Missy was reciting the Latin words of the sleep spell. The man fired a second shot at the water, and she released the energy toward him. Just as he returned his attention to her, he dropped the gun and fell onto the bridge deck.

Missy jogged the rest of the way to the yacht. The gangway wasn't there, so she grabbed a mooring line and pulled herself up onto the main deck. The flying bridge was two decks above her. She needed visual contact with the man to put the binding spell on him.

The nearest door to the interior was locked. So she circled the deck, looking for stairs or a ladder. She had to reach him soon in case he woke up prematurely. There was a ladder on the other side of the glassed interior. She climbed up to the next, smaller level, which had cabins and a sundeck to the aft. Another ladder led to the flying bridge. She jumped onto it and began climbing.

And a hand grabbed her ankle.

SHE KICKED BACKWARDS, and the tight grip didn't loosen. She turned her head to see another crew member in a white marine shirt. Only it wasn't a human. It was a troll. And not an internet troll. Trolls are human-like enough to fit in and lead normal lives among us. But, to be honest, they looked even stranger than Neanderthals. Tall, with massive tree-trunk-like limbs, bald heads, and exaggerated facial features, they excelled in professional wrestling. More than a few NFL linemen are secretly trolls.

Trolls are strong, as this guy's one-handed grip on her ankle proved. And they were much harder to bewitch.

"What are you doing on our vessel?" he asked in an Eastern Europe accent.

"I'm a friend of Thogg's," Missy lied. "He invited me here for drinks tonight. I'm a little early."

"I was not told," the troll said.

In one way, real trolls were like their internet counter-parts: They liked to argue and get a rise out of you. Missy needed to keep him busy while she cooked up her sleeping spell.

"I was told that you'd be told," she said.

The troll tightened his grip on her ankle. She was afraid she'd slip off the ladder.

"Who told you that?"

"Thogg told me he'd tell the crew to expect me."

"Thogg wouldn't tell us himself. One of his assistants would. I'm going to detain you until I get this cleared up."

"No, you're going to take a nap right now."

He yanked her ankle, and her other foot slipped off its rung. She slid down the ladder and bonked her head on it when she landed.

"I am not taking a nap."

She quickly recited the Latin spell and grasped the Red Dragon talisman in her pocket, its electric tingling running through her hand and up her arm.

Nothing happened.

"Come with me," he said.

He was resisting the spell through sheer stubbornness. She tried again, this time with more power.

After she invoked the words of the spell, she added, "By the power of the Red Dragon, I order you to obey me."

The troll's eyes rolled up in his head and he dropped like a tree to the deck. The one-hundred-foot yacht shuddered.

"Darn trolls," she muttered.

The day was quickly running out, and she had to finish her work here. She placed a binding spell on the troll, climbed the ladder, and bound the sleeping crew member on the bridge.

She explored the interior of the yacht and found no one inside. On the lowest passenger deck were several cabins. The door of every one of them was locked. She knocked on the closest one.

"Anyone in there? It's Missy."

"Missy? It's Gladys," replied a sleepy voice from inside. "Can you help us?"

"The two crew members aboard have been disabled. I'm going to unlock the doors so you can get out once the sun is down. I'm leaving a key fob outside your door for a black SUV that's parked in front of the house. Drive all the vampires back to Squid Tower as fast as you can. Good luck."

The locks on these doors were simple sliding latches. Using her telekinesis, she unlatched all six doors. Then she raced down the dock. Matt walked toward her, soaking wet.

"You weren't shot!" Missy said.

"No, but I lost the gun you gave me. I couldn't hit an elephant at point-blank range."

"You distracted him. That was enough. Now let's get back to Squid Tower before sunset."

21
DEATH AT DUSK

The sun was low in the sky as Missy drove the SUV back to Squid Tower.

"I hope Darla and Sophie are being kept in a condo. Thogg seems to be concentrating all his vampires and humans there," Missy said to Matt. "But if he's keeping them in another location, I don't know how we'll get access to them, even if I can locate them with magick."

"Oh no," Matt said.

"What?"

They headed east on Jellyfish Beach Boulevard, approaching the Intracoastal bridge. Matt pointed to a sailboat mast protruding above a building, moving slowly south toward the bridge.

A loud bell like an old-fashioned alarm clock began ringing.

"Darn!" Missy said, accelerating, trying to reach the draw-bridge before the gate lowered.

But she was too late. Two cars in front of her slowed, and the gate came down ahead of them.

"Oh, my," Missy said. "This is horrible timing."

The bell stopped ringing, and at the crest of the bridge ahead of them, the road appeared to split as if from an earthquake. Then the two halves of the drawbridge lifted.

Slowly.

"It's almost sunset," Matt said.

"Don't you think I can see with my own eyes?"

Drawbridges can be a real inconvenience for those living on the beach. Missy usually visited Squid Tower at night when the bridges rarely opened. Right now, it was maddening.

The span in front of them with its yellow line down the middle stood fully vertical.

Missy and Matt waited. And waited. The sailboat's mast still hadn't reached the bridge.

"Why did the tender have to open the bridge so early?" Missy asked, pounding the steering wheel.

"Yeah, these sailboats are slow as molasses when they're running on motors."

They waited. The sun sank lower in the sky.

Missy briefly considered swimming across the waterway. Not a good idea.

Finally, the sailboat appeared to their left and disappeared from view. Its mast appeared above the raised bridge span. It inched along the top of the span.

"Come on, move it!" Missy yelled.

Now the mast was past the bridge, and the sailboat appeared again, moving south.

The bell rang again. The bridge span jerked, then began its long journey down to the horizontal.

Slowly.

"Can't you speed it up with your magick?" Matt asked.

"No. I can't. I wish everyone would stop asking me why I don't have God-like powers."

Missy fantasized about pulling out of her lane, passing the stopped cars ahead of her, racing the car up the bridge, and flying across the opening like a stunt driver in an action movie. Then common sense kicked in.

The sky was awash with deep yellow mixed with oranges and purples. There was still a lot of light, but she was afraid sunset had come. Her watch confirmed it. In fact, it was after sunset.

Oleg was sentenced to be staked at sundown. That was actually poetic license, because last light was about twenty-five minutes later and vampires rarely ventured out before that.

By the time the bridge opened, traffic moved again, they got through the traffic light at A1A, and drove the three miles to Squid Tower, it might be too late.

The bridge span landed, then jiggled up and down slightly before coming to rest. The bell stopped ringing. The gate on the opposing traffic lane opened. Then their gate did.

Missy honked her horn.

"What, do you think we're in New York?" Matt asked.

Finally, the cars in front of her began moving. As soon as she crossed the bridge, Missy passed the two cars illegally. It didn't help her because she got stuck at a red light at the intersection of A1A, but it felt good anyway.

Soon they headed south on A1A. Missy passed a truck and almost had a head-on collision with a delivery van before getting back into her lane. This area was a speed trap, but she floored it anyway. And finally, they arrived at the entrance to Squid Tower.

Missy pulled in. The day guard was still on duty and opened the gate for her immediately. She drove past the unconscious and magickally bound human guard still lying next to the gatehouse.

She parked next to a fire hydrant and ran around the building to the pool area, Matt right behind her

Missy wished they had stakes with them to impale some Neanderthals, but all she had was her magick. And her magick was the only thing that could end this, anyway.

The pool deck was blessedly still empty. The vampires weren't out yet. The dying light made long shadows from the pool lounge chairs that looked like reptilian beasts. She ran to the storage room and opened the door.

Oleg was still inside. Her body slumped with relief.

"What took you so long?" Oleg asked.

"I had errands to run. Is it dark enough for you to go outside safely?"

Oleg looked past her out the door. "I think so. As long as the sun has set and there aren't any errant rays."

"Okay, I took care of the humans who were guarding the grounds. I want you to go to the beach and then walk as far away from here as you can go."

Oleg walked to the doorway and hesitantly stepped out. He glanced around, and, seeing no guards, left the pool area and walked along the dune crossover. He stepped over the sleeping guard at the end and descended the steps to the beach.

"Let's go take care of the guards outside Thogg's condo, and then I can use my magick against him when he comes out."

There was only one problem with her plan. Thogg had already come out.

Missy and Matt ducked behind the storage room just in

time. Missy peeked around the corner as the leader of the Neanderthal vampires staggered out of the back door of the building onto the pool deck with a retinue of a dozen of his vampires. The remaining human guards, four of them, followed the line of vampires.

After them, the members of the condo HOA board, minus Bill, came outside. Missy realized they were being forced to attend as witnesses to the execution. Behind them, even more Neanderthals and the small number of contemporary vampires that were in their thrall entered the pool area.

Thogg had somewhere around fifty Neanderthals, more than Missy had realized. Her vampire seniors never would have been able to defeat them in battle. Her gut clenched in fear as it sank in that she was her vampires' only hope. She began gathering energies.

It heartened her to notice that Thogg and his Neanderthals looked ill. They were slow and lethargic. The heat was really getting to them without the protection from the spell they had enjoyed for centuries.

But then Missy realized that while she had been successful in undoing the spell, the effort had been a failure. The Neanderthals weren't dead or disabled. They weren't riding their yacht up to Canada or someplace cool. No, they were still here in Jellyfish Beach, ruling Squid Tower and holding their prisoners.

Perhaps they would be more vulnerable to her attack spell. All she could do was hope.

The only raised area for Thogg to take a majestic pose was on a platform next to the hot tub. His vampires gathered in front of him, between the hot tub and the swimming pool. The human guards were behind him. Agnes and the HOA members stood off to the side.

The interior lights of the tub popped on automatically as the sunlight disappeared. The light from beneath the bubbling hit Thogg's face with a psychedelic effect.

"Bring out the condemned," Thogg said with an imperious wave of his hand.

Four Neanderthals shuffled sluggishly to the storage building. Two went inside and immediately came out.

"The prisoners are missing," one said in a nervous voice.

Thogg wasn't happy. He glowered in that special way that only a Neanderthal could. The audience inched away from him.

"That is unacceptable. I will stake whoever is responsible for this."

The four Neanderthals by the storage building pointed fingers at each other.

One of them made a break for it, running around the storage building.

Right into Missy.

The Neanderthal grabbed her and Matt by their necks and dragged them out into view.

"I knew I smelled living humans," the Neanderthal said.

Thogg's mood improved visibly. "Bring them here. We will search for the escaped vampire later. The witch will suffer her sentence to lose her head now. The human with the scruffy beard will join her."

"It's not scruffy," Matt said. "It's just natural."

Two Neanderthals each pushed Missy and Matt around the pool to the diving board. Missy couldn't recall ever seeing the vampires who lived here diving from this board.

They forced Missy to her knees upon the concrete, with her

upper body bent over the diving board. Rough hands pulled her arms behind her and bound them together at a painful angle.

Oh, my, she thought as her heart raced. This is for real.

SHE HAD to unleash her magic now. But she was panicking, her adrenaline making her mind jumpy and unable to concentrate. With her arms bound, she couldn't clutch the Red Dragon talisman, but she had been counting on it to amplify her power.

A Neanderthal walked out onto the pool deck carrying an enormous sword in a steel scabbard. It was a two-handed type from the Middle Ages.

Matt struggled to get to her, but he couldn't break free from the grips of the Neanderthals. As much as the heat was bothering them, they still had enough strength.

She felt like she was going to faint, and her blood pounded in her head as it hung over the edge of the diving board.

"Do not despair, my lady," Don Mateo's voice whispered in her ear.

So the slacker ghost didn't always require begging to show up.

"The talisman in your pocket is touching your leg," he said. "That is sufficient contact for you to draw upon its power. Visualize it now, touching your thigh, sending you strength."

She did what he said. And instantly, she felt the Red Dragon's power making her leg tingle. It spread through her body like fire. Her mind cleared and her focus became razor sharp. The panic and despair left her body.

"As commanded by me, Thogg, your supreme leader, the execution of the witch shall proceed."

The elderly vampires of the Squid Tower HOA grumbled in protest. But did any of them do anything to help her? Nope.

The Neanderthal with the sword withdrew it from its scabbard and held it aloft. It was long and heavy enough to decapitate a rhinoceros. He showed off with it in front of the Neanderthal audience, making practice slicing and chopping motions. The Neanderthals ooh-ed and ah-ed.

Missy collected her own energy with the elemental energies and combined them. She felt them magnify tenfold from the power of the Red Dragon. She obviously couldn't check the notes on her phone, but with her added mental clarity she had a vivid mental image of her phone's screen and the words of the spell she had written.

She silently recited the words and used her energies to connect with the spell's special ingredient, both taking power from it and activating it in the surrounding environment.

"It is time," Thogg said.

The Neanderthal with the sword nodded and looked at Missy. He walked around the pool toward her, the point of the giant blade just inches from the concrete. The Neanderthal crowd turned to look at her and the bloodshed to come.

She whispered the invocation.

The Neanderthal came up and stood behind her. She couldn't see him, but knew he was lifting the sword above his head.

She shouted: "By the power of the Red Dragon, I command all with Neanderthal genes to shift and seek the element that calls you!!"

The power flew out of her like a rocket from its launching pad.

The sword clanged heavily as it fell upon the pool deck. Chirping sounds came from behind her.

And then a bat flew over her head. It flew in a circle above her, as if confused, and rose in altitude.

Then it plunged headfirst into the swimming pool.

And exploded.

Loud, angry voices swept over the pool deck.

One by one, Neanderthals were transforming into bats. Each time, the transformation was instantaneous, accompanied by a popping sound. And each time, the bat would fly erratically up into the night sky, before making a suicidal dive into the swimming pool. Each and every one burst apart when it contacted the chlorinated water.

The remaining Neanderthals rushed toward the building, but now they were transforming in twos and threes. Several bats were in the air at once before making their swan dives into the pool and becoming bat confetti.

The chlorine was calling them. And the chlorine was killing them.

Thogg was still there, seething with rage. He clearly wanted to be doing something heroic, but had no thought of what that would be. He paced back and forth, ordering his vampires to stop transforming. As if that was going to do any good.

Finally, he bolted toward the building lobby.

But faster than a rattlesnake striking, Agnes raced in front and tripped him before he got far. He tumbled into the hot tub.

He shrieked in pain.

"It burns!"

He thrashed about in the water but didn't have to strength to pull himself out.

"Get me out of here, it's burning me!" he cried.

The human guards were still standing behind the hot tub, bewildered by the tumult. They snapped to attention and rushed to rescue their leader.

That was when the members of the Squid Tower Homeowners Association Board of Directors fell upon them. They didn't require a vote. They just let their vampirism do its thing.

The frail-looking seniors made short work of the beefy humans. Necks snapped, throats ripped open, blood sprayed from arteries like geysers. The HOA board mauled the four guards and made as much of a meal out of them as they could. No sense in wasting good blood.

In only a minute or two, the four guards lay dead. One of their heads bobbed about in the bubbles of the hot tub next to Thogg.

"You and your vampires are not welcome in our community, Mr. Thogg," Agnes said. She and her colleagues stood around the hot tub watching Thogg suffer.

"Shift," Missy said.

With a pop, Thogg turned into a bat. He didn't fly more than three feet before he crashed back into the churning hot tub. He exploded, splattering the HOA board with bat goo. Not that they minded, since they were already drenched in human blood.

It was quiet in the pool area. The pool, the furniture, and the deck were littered with bat fragments. Some Neanderthals had escaped into the building, but every few minutes a bat would find its way outside and fly to its death in the swimming pool.

Missy was certain the spell would destroy every Neanderthal on the property. She hoped it would do so to any others elsewhere in Jellyfish Beach.

"Are you okay?" Matt asked her.

"Why don't you untie me so I can find out?"

22
LOCKED OUT

"Thank you, Missy," Agnes said, hugging her. Agnes was so short it was like being hugged by a child.

The other board members patted her on the back and shoulders with their cold vampire hands. Even Schwartz seemed pleased with her.

"I always thought Acceptance Home Care was ripping me off," he said. "But a nurse who comes with magic spells? What a bargain!"

"We still have a lot of work to do," Missy said.

"Someone has to clean up all this bat splatter," Kim said.

"I mean, we have to make sure that all the hostages come home, and the human prisoners are freed," Missy said. "And there might be some Neanderthals still around."

"That would be nice," Matt said. "I still want to interview one for the anthropological insights."

Everyone looked at him like he was nuts. He was nuts.

"Your insights won't do you any good if you don't have any

blood left in your body," Schwartz said. Coming from a vampire, the point was hard to deny.

"Excuse me, folks," Missy said. "I have a cousin and a first cousin once removed I need to find."

Missy left the pool area and headed for her car. Matt trailed behind her.

"Are you going to use that spell to look for body heat? It should work well here since all the residents are undead."

"Possibly," she said, striding across the parking lot to the black SUV she had illegally parked. "First, I need to see if they're even on the property."

Inside the SUV was her purse. And inside that was Sophie's werewolf romance novel.

"Step back. I have magick to do."

She knelt on the asphalt and performed the same spell that had located both Gladys and Sophie before. Using Sophie's energy from the book, Missy conjured the young woman's life force, manifesting it as a glowing orb hovering just off the fender of the SUV. Then she sent it in search of its owner. Missy followed the vision that appeared in her head.

She and the orb didn't have to travel far. Sophie and her mother were at Squid Tower.

Unfortunately, she couldn't tell what floor they were on. Now was the time to use the infrared-like spell Matt was referring to, the one that had found Sophie in the canal near the vampires' second house.

"Okay, they're in the building," Missy said to Matt. "We're going to have to go floor by floor until we find which condo they're in."

They took the elevator to the top floor, where Thogg had been staying. The elevator bank was in the center of the building and the hallway stretched to their left and right, angling behind them as if they were at the point of a "V." This allowed more units to have an ocean view. The architect would never have imagined that vampires would end up living here, often ruining the view with hurricane shutters closed to block out the sun.

Missy and Matt first went down the left branch of the hallway. The end unit, where Thogg had stayed, had both eastern and western exposures. There was no human body heat in the units they passed. When they came up empty on the righthand branch, they rode the elevator to the floor below and repeated the process.

Missy stopped in front of Unit 909. The warm glow of body heat came from within.

She knocked on the door and rang the doorbell.

"Anyone in there?"

"Yes!" said Darla. Please help us. We're tied up."

The door was locked. Of course.

"Can't your magick open it?" Matt asked.

Missy was developing a complex over her struggle to open locks with her magick and telekinesis.

Simple latches and deadbolts she could do. More complex locks posed a problem. The basic idea of a lock was simple: A metal thingy goes into another metal thingy so you couldn't open a door or window. The tricky part was the locking mechanism that moved the metal thingy into the other thingy. There were often springs and tumblers involved, and it could get very complicated.

In theory, it should be easy. But unfortunately, she struggled with more complex locks.

But she gave it a good try. She put every ounce of mental

strength into her telekinesis, boosted by magick energies. She made the latch on the door handle move in and out, but the deadbolt was an expensive one and beyond her capabilities.

She blew a frustrated gust of air from her lips which made her bangs flutter. There had to be a way through this.

She ignored Matt, who stood beside her impatiently. She refused to think about her relatives who were anxious for her to free them. Instead, she let her mind go blank.

And suddenly she realized what the problem was.

Long ago when she was young, emphasis on long ago, Missy's telekinetic abilities felt like her superpowers. Years later, as she developed her skills in magick, her own form of magic, she developed powers beyond that basic paranormal ability she had been born with. But telekinesis was still *her* magick. Her growing witchy abilities were used to bolster her telekinesis.

But now, years later, she had enough magickal powers that she didn't need her telekinesis for every effort that involved moving physical objects.

Maybe her magick would be enough to open locks on its own. Maybe relying too much on her telekinesis was hampering her potential.

Like right now, with this complicated deadbolt.

"Give me a moment, folks," she said. "I want to try out a new kind of lock-picking."

Missy didn't have a lock-picking spell in her encyclopedia of knowledge. But she did know a spell that, for lack of a better term, was her "rewind" spell. She could reverse a limited, short-term series of recent physical events—to make them go backwards.

So a bottle of milk knocked over and spilled could be undone like video being rewound.

And the routine locking of a door could be reversed as well, as long as the locking had taken place recently.

She prepared her energies and imagined the bad guy leaving the condo, closing the door, slipping a key into the deadbolt keyhole, and turning it toward the doorjamb. The rattle of tumblers, the clunk of the bolt.

Then she intoned the brief spell and released her energies.

The bolt slid back into the lock. She opened the door.

Why hadn't she thought of trying this before?

Darla and Sophie were tied together back-to-back on the couch. They were bound with yellow nylon rope that was also wrapped around the legs of the couch. The knots, near one of the couch legs, and in between the two women, were large, complicated, and impregnable. They had been tied with vampire strength.

"We thought we were going to die," Darla said.

"I have to go to the bathroom," said Sophie.

"Where's the homeowner?" Missy asked.

"Carl threw him out," Sophie said.

The spartan furnishings and the minimal effort at decorating confirmed that a male lived here, probably widowed before he was turned. A photo of a man posing in front of a Model T automobile hung uncentered above the couch.

"Let me find something to cut the rope," Missy said, moving into the kitchen.

When you subsist on blood, you need little in the way of kitchen accessories. If a female vampire had lived here, she might have kept cutlery from her human days out of nostalgia or in case she had human guests. No such luck with this guy.

But he surely had cutting tools of some sort, she thought as she rummaged through a junk drawer.

There, a pair of heavy-duty scissors lay in the back of the drawer. This would be much easier than using her spell to untie those knots.

Missy brought it to the living room.

"And the bats exploded the second they hit the water," Matt was explaining. "Something to do with the chlorine."

"I saw it before, Mom," Sophie said. "It's true."

"So they're all gone?" Darla asked.

"Let's hope so," Missy said as she tried to cut the nylon cords. It required a gradual chewing action with the scissor blades to cut through. She severed the cord by the sofa legs and in between Darla and Sophie. She placed the scissors on the table while they unwrapped themselves and Matt assisted them to their feet. They stretched their sore limbs.

"I'm going to the bathroom," Sophie said, leaving the room.

"I'm worried about her," Darla whispered. "She's been badly traumatized. I can't imagine what it was like when she was their prisoner. And being bitten. . ."

"We'll get her the help she needs."

"Looks like my knot-tying abilities have deteriorated over the centuries."

Carl stood in the doorway. He recognized Missy and his eyes narrowed to slits.

"Murderer," he said.

In movements so fast they were a blur, he knocked Matt across the room onto a dining table and gripped Missy by the throat, holding her in the air.

Darla screamed.

Why hadn't the shifting spell worked on him? Missy wondered.

She grasped the Red Dragon in her pocket and tried to reactivate the spell. There was no time to cast it all over again, but it was still out there in the ether. Maybe it hadn't reached Carl. A little extra juice might do the trick.

"Shift!" she said.

"Do you always spout random words at people?"

It looked like her juice wasn't enough. He tightened his grip on her throat, and gray spots swam across her eyes as her brain starved for oxygen.

She kicked him hard in the stomach. His abs were so hard her toe felt like she broke it.

Darla was freaking out, but at least she was carefully making her way around Carl toward the open door so she could escape. Where was Sophie?

The answer came with a throaty war cry from Sophie charging out of the bathroom. She grabbed the scissors on the coffee table.

And plunged one of the steel blades into Carl's back.

His eyes widened with surprise.

Sophie screamed and pushed the scissors deeper through his rib cage.

Blood began pouring from Carl's mouth, nose, eyes, and ears.

"Keep the steel in his heart," Missy said.

Carl dropped Missy to the floor and reached over his shoulder to grab the scissors. Sophie pushed them in even deeper.

A low moan came from the vampire, a sound that was older than humanity, older than time, born of the horror of prehuman primates facing the dark deaths that surrounded them at all times and defeated them in the end.

"Bummer," he said.

He disintegrated into gray ash littering the wood-veneer floor.

"He so deserved that," Sophie said.

THE BLACK SUV pulled into Squid Tower and parked behind the vehicle Missy had left in front of the lobby entrance. Then the driver thought better of it and moved to the visitor lot. Fears of fines from the HOA run deep in the souls of residents.

The doors opened and Gladys crawled from the driver's seat. Bill got out of the passenger seat and they both helped Henrietta from the middle seat. Residents who had been hiding during execution time came flocking out to greet them.

Missy was happy to see them safe and glad that no Neanderthals had returned to the yacht to stop them.

Agnes hobbled over with her quad cane and hugged the three freed hostages. Someone found a wheelchair and brought it to Henrietta, easing her gently into it.

Missy kissed each of them on their cold, pasty cheeks, even Bill.

"Was there anyone at the house or on the yacht when you left?" Missy asked.

"Just two crew members and the housekeeper, all unconscious," Bill said.

"Do you know what happened to the human prisoners?"

"No. And we haven't fed for three nights."

"I did," Gladys said. "I fed on a sleeping crew member before we left the yacht. That's how I got my strength back."

"Good. And the Blood Bus should be here any moment now," Agnes said.

"They must have moved the prisoners from the yacht somewhere," Missy said.

"Or they had run their course." Bill's euphemism was horrifying.

23
CAN'T WAIT TO LEAVE

issy spent most of the next night giving physical exams to senior vampires. First, she saw the former hostages. They had been malnourished while in captivity.

"They didn't feed us regularly," Henrietta complained. "Not a single bag of whole blood. They brought us humans who were already half-drained and anemic. And with these dentures, it's hard for me to bite necks."

Bill wouldn't speak about his ordeal. He was embarrassed and humiliated by having been so easily mesmerized. Locked in a cabin with nothing to do and no chance to make the heroic gunfire-filled escape he fantasized about, he had nothing to think about besides his powerlessness.

Gladys had lost the will to go on existing. Missy asked her why after the vampire had downed a full pint of O-positive.

"Thogg lied to me," she said. "He didn't like my stories after all. He hadn't even read any of them. I believed I had finally moved someone with my writing, that my words had made a difference. But it was all a lie."

"Don't feel badly. I enjoy your writing," Missy lied. "But the important thing is how your writing makes you feel. Aside from the few classics we study in school, all arts and culture are ephemeral and disposable. Keep on creating more of it and enjoy it for the moment. Unlike vampires, it doesn't live forever."

"I want someone to enjoy it besides me."

"Despite what they say, the class enjoys your writing," Missy lied again. "And the more you write, the better at it you get. Just move on to the next story."

Gladys seemed somewhat mollified. The pint of fresh blood hadn't hurt, either.

When Missy left the condo, she came upon Agnes in the hallway. The HOA president was going from door to door checking on the residents.

"All the ones I've talked to so far are relieved that Thogg is gone," Agnes said, walking with her quad cane to the elevator with Missy. "They're most concerned with getting refunds on the special assessment and seeing their monthly HOA fee returning to what it was before. The money bothered them more than Thogg's authoritarian ways."

"I guess a lot of them have been around long enough to know that every regime goes down, eventually."

"Just as mine did," Agnes said mordantly as they stepped into the elevator.

"You didn't have a regime."

"Perhaps I should have. Being a weak leader allowed Thogg to take over so easily."

"Agnes, you're not weak at all."

"Vampires need rules and structure. We need certainty. Since we defy the laws of nature, we need some other form of laws to comfort us as the world changes around us from century to century."

"I thought that's what the condo bylaws were for," Missy said.

"They're not enough. I'm going to reach out to the HOA of Alligator Hammock and discuss creating a federation between us. And any other groups of vampires in the area, too. We need strength in numbers. There are also the younger vampires out there who form informal hives. We need to ally with them, as well. And all the new vampires that the Neanderthals created. We can't just set them loose into the world with no one to guide them."

"Wow, Agnes. It sounds like you have the makings of a great leader. Greater than Thogg would have been."

"I have no desire to rule anyone. I just want to strengthen our community so another Thogg doesn't come along and destroy the comfortable existence we've built."

Missy knew Agnes was right. The vampires at Squid Tower enjoyed a safe existence of beach-going, bingo, and the Blood Bus. But they needed to work hard to protect it.

After they exited the elevator in the lobby, Agnes stopped in the middle of the floor and looked up at Missy. For a half second, Missy was afraid she was going to get mesmerized.

"I'm grateful to you for saving us," Agnes said. "Few vampires here want to admit how much we depend on a human, but we owe you an incalculable debt."

Missy felt herself blushing. "I'm not a normal human. I'm a witch."

"And not just any witch. You have some of the supernatural inside you, just like us. Maybe that's why I love you so much."

Agnes cackled gleefully and clopped across the tile floor to the property manager's office, bending over to wipe some bat guts off the floor with a handkerchief.

MATT'S EXPOSE appeared in *The Jellyfish Beach Journal* two weeks later. It was an in-depth piece on the fraud and illegal activities of Better Daze Recovery Center. He'd written stories before about corrupt sober homes and recovery services. But never had he encountered one that sold patients to vampires. It was his solemn promise to Missy not to reveal the secrets of the supernaturals who existed in Florida. It was also a wise career move if he wanted to be taken seriously as a journalist.

But how could he write about patients being sold to vampires without writing about vampires? Through intentional vagueness.

"Recovering Drug Addicts Sold to Human Traffickers by Rehab Center," read his headline. He had to fight with the copy-editor to get that one right. He wrote the long article without ever having mentioned exactly what the "human traffickers" did to the patients. But he implied that it was something illegal and not suitable for discussing in front of the kids.

The few patients he found who had survived being Thogg's livestock, who had escaped before being drained to death or turned, stayed anonymous. Matt didn't include any of their quotes about being fed upon. The police would eventually find out when they interviewed the survivors, but there was nothing he could do about that.

"What do you think?" he asked Missy at the cafe after she finished the article. They were having breakfast together, a familiar ritual for the pair. It was the closest thing to a date that Matt could get from Missy.

"Well-written, thoroughly reported, and scary as heck."

"Scary?" he asked.

"From how close you came to revealing the existence of vampires."

"But I didn't. And those survivors are going to talk whether I did the story or not. At least I used human trafficking as a cover story."

"True. And thanks to you, those scumbags at Better Daze will get shut down."

"And eventually go to jail."

Something made Missy's face grow sad. She looked down at her untouched bagel.

"What's the matter?" he asked.

"I worry about all the victims turned into vampires to join Thogg's clan," she said. "They're out there somewhere without their makers to guide them. They could be suffering. Or create problems that attract the police."

"Should someone try to find them?"

"Thanks for volunteering!" she said with a big smile. "You're a great guy."

"Wait a minute. I didn't say—"

Missy leaned over the table and kissed him on the lips for the first time. This kiss was barely more than a peck. But he picked up the scent of her shampoo and her sweet breath.

And he suddenly forgot the objections he was about to make.

ON THE LAST night before Sophie and Darla would drive back to San Marcos, Sophie slept on the couch in the living room. Her mother was in the guest bedroom. One of Missy's cats slept on an armchair, keeping Sophie company.

Sophie had awakened for some reason. It was 2:30 a.m. Suddenly, the cat stood up in alarm and ran to Missy's bedroom.

So much for being a guard cat, Sophie thought.

She felt watched. The hair on the back of her neck stood on end. After so many nights of being vampire prey, her self-preservation instincts were on high alert.

A faint whisper crept into her ear; from where, she couldn't tell.

Sophie.

Maybe she was imagining it. It was in her head, not her ear.

Sophie, I've missed you.

It sounded like Maria's voice.

"Maria?" Sophie whispered. Her voice was tiny in the large room, not intimate and close like the one calling her name.

Sophie let me in. I've missed you.

She glanced at the sliding glass doors to the back porch.

Maria stood on the other side of the glass.

I've been so lonely, Sophie. They've left me to fend for myself. My maker, Mona, is gone. You're my only friend.

Sophie left the couch and went to the doors. Her long T-shirt hung to her lower thighs. She stood close to the glass and studied Maria who stood opposite her.

Her former therapy colleague wore the same tank top and

shorts she had worn the last time Sophie had seen her at the second home on the canal. The clothes were dirty and had random spots of blood upon them. Maria's hair was unkempt, her face deadly pale. Her eyes peered from the depths of nothingness.

Maria was a full-on vampire now. She had been turned.

Sophie remembered that Missy's spell that destroyed the Neanderthals was supposed to affect any vampire with their genes. They had chosen Maria to become a vampire because she had more Neanderthal DNA than the other humans in the group. They meant her to be part of their project to increase the Neanderthals' numbers.

The project looked to be a failure. Maria didn't have enough Neanderthal in her to be affected by Missy's spell. It saved her undead existence. But it also meant that the Neanderthal race wouldn't return via vampire genetic cousins.

Let me in, Sophie, the vampire said on the other side of the glass. *I've missed you so much.*

In truth, Sophie missed her, too. They'd never been close, but they'd gone through therapy together and through the insanity of being livestock to feed the vampires.

Maria put her white palm against the glass. Sophie placed hers opposite.

"I've missed you too, Maria."

But Maria was lost to her now.

"I can't let you in," Sophie whispered. "It's time for us to say goodbye. You have to go now."

Don't make me go. I have no one.

"We have to go our separate ways," Sophie said. "You're a vampire and I'm your prey. It's not safe for me. You need to go."

I have nowhere to go.

"You'll find your way. Listen to your instincts. They'll tell you what to do."

Let me in so I can say goodbye properly.

"No. Go, please."

Sophie removed her hand from the glass.

"Are you talking to someone?"

Her mother, wearing a robe, stood in the archway to the dining room.

Maria was gone.

"No, Mom. I was just having a dream."

ACTUALLY, Maria wasn't completely alone. She had her new pet, the vampire cave bear named Lucy. It was waiting for her outside the screened-in porch. Maria wiped a bloody tear from her cheek and rejoined her pet.

"It's just you and me now. Let's go find something or someone to eat."

The undead bear gave a grunt of agreement and followed her out of the yard.

Loud thumping bass approached, and a muscle car rolled down the street. Probably someone returning from a night of partying or a late shift of work.

The bass and the fluorescent running-board lighting proved irresistible to Lucy. She began galloping through the front yard toward the car.

"No, Lucy," Maria commanded uselessly. The cave bear loved to play with cars and extract the tasty morsels of food that drove them, but it made too much noise. And when cars were destroyed, cops were called. Maria had hoped that they would come across a pre-dawn dog walker who, with their pet, would have provided a nice meal for the two of them. Now there was going to be mayhem instead.

The driver must have seen the gigantic dark creature thundering across the lawn on a trajectory to meet his car. He quickly reversed down the street. It was too late.

Grizzly bears can sprint faster than most creatures can run. Cave bears, as it turns out, are even faster. It came in handy to catch prehistoric prey like wild horses and antelope. As well as tricked-out Honda lowriders.

Lucy sprinted after the car and jumped onto its hood. The lowrider was now a no-rider, grinding its undercarriage on the asphalt until it could move no more. The bear's giant paw pushed through the windshield like it was toilet paper.

The driver somehow managed to wiggle away, so Lucy poked her other paw through the glass. The car's stereo was still playing, and with the windshield missing, the noise was flooding the neighborhood.

Maria ran up to the car and tried to distract the bear. Lucy would not listen to her. She was focused on one thing: the tasty tidbit that had scrambled into the back seat to avoid the probing bear claws.

Lucy responded by tearing the roof off the car. The shrieks of shredded steel along with the thumping bass beats were going to trigger calls to 9-1-1 any moment now.

A front bucket seat went flying into the air, landing on Missy's driveway.

Inside her home, Missy, her two cats, and their houseguests watched the mayhem on the street.

"What on earth is that?" Darla asked.

"It's a vampire cave bear," Sophie said. "It was the Neanderthals' pet."

"Should we call 9-1-1?"

"I already did," Missy said. "Hopefully, the cops will get here before the bear gets to the driver."

A male screamed in agony.

"Too late," Sophie said.

"You don't want to watch this," Missy said. "Come to the kitchen and I'll make you some herbal tea."

"No offense to your town," Sophie said, perching on a stool at the kitchen island, "but I can't wait to get away from Jellyfish Beach. For good."

"We don't have to wait until morning, honey. We can leave now," Darla said.

"Well, you need to wait until the bear has left the area," Missy said. "I'll make you some breakfast."

Something wet splattered the living room window with substantial force.

"I just lost my appetite," Darla said.

Missy didn't blame Darla and Sophie for wanting to get the heck out of Jellyfish Beach. Ruthless Neanderthals and vampire cave bears aren't helpful to your town's reputation. But Jellyfish Beach did have nice parks and decent shopping, at least.

Flashing lights flooded the windows as first responders showed up to clean up the cave bear's disaster. This took a while. Missy worried that a police officer might show up to ask if she had witnessed the mauling, but she was spared having to lie.

In the meantime, she fixed breakfast burritos for her guests to take on the road. By the time the police had left, and a wrecker took away the peeled-apart Honda, Darla and Sophie practically ran to their car.

As Missy hugged them and said goodbye, she whispered into Darla's ear.

"I want to talk to you more sometime soon about what my mother did to my father."

Darla looked at her with concern. "I don't know any more than what I told you."

Missy didn't believe her. But there was nothing she could say right now, except wish them a safe trip.

"Thank you for your help in getting Sophie back," Darla said.

Sophie hugged Missy a second time.

"Yes, thank you," Sophie said. "And I forgive you for pushing me into the swimming pool."

"You had a Neanderthal vampire in your hair. What else was I supposed to do?"

Sophie laughed as she got into the car. Darla went well above the speed limit as she escaped the neighborhood, Missy waving goodbye from her front porch.

THREE HOUSES down from Missy was the unoccupied home of Old Man Vansetti, who had recently departed the material world. In his backyard was a large shed where he had housed his riding lawn mower. The mini-tractor currently lay upside down in the grass that was in dire need of cutting.

The shed had a new occupant now. A 1,500-pound vampire cave bear slept here during the daylight. And occasionally a recently turned vampire woman who had nowhere else to go would join her.

Both of them were smart enough not to hunt in the immediate vicinity. And Missy's neighbors slept well in blissful ignorance.

Nowadays, it seemed that only through ignorance could you find bliss.

THE END

PLEASE LEAVE A REVIEW

Dear reader, thank you in advance:
Please give my book a better chance.
Success and sales depend on you,
So kindly post a book review.

WHAT'S NEXT

GET A FREE E-BOOK

Sign up for my newsletter and get a novella for free. It's available exclusively for members of my mailing list. If you join, you'll get news, fun articles, and lots of free book promotions, delivered only a couple of times a month. No spam at all, and you can unsubscribe at any time. Sign up at wardparker.com

COMING NEXT IN FREAKY FLORIDA

Book 6, *Dirty Old Manatee*

Midlife manatee insanity

Who's behind the plot to kill off Florida's sea cows? While midlife witch Missy Mindle tries to solve this mystery, she must nurse a rescued manatee back to health. The problem is, he's actually a human shifter, Seymour, who wants to celebrate manatee mating season with her.

Missy and her reporter friend Matt face corporate villains and team up with the ruthless Mothers4Manatees. Throw in a vengeful vampire who wants to kill her, and Missy's magick is pushed to the limit. Meanwhile, she discovers what life would have been like if she hadn't divorced years ago: living with a flabby, middle-aged guy who leaves the toilet seat up.

The Freaky Florida Horror Comedy Mysteries is a completed, clean, paranormal series filled with magic, monsters, and mystery; sarcasm and satire; and, of course, Florida Man. If you like paranormal mysteries with thrills, frights, and laughs, this series is for you. Grab this book and take the plunge into Jellyfish Beach today.

Find *Dirty Old Manatee* at your favorite online bookstore or at wardparker.com

ABOUT THE AUTHOR

Ward is the author of the Memory Guild midlife paranormal mystery thrillers and its urban fantasy sequel series, The Goddess's Daughter, as well as the Freaky Florida series, set in the same world as Monsters of Jellyfish Beach, with Missy, Matt, Agnes, and many other familiar characters.

Ward lives in Florida with his wife, several cats, and a demon who wishes to remain anonymous.

Connect with him on social media: Bluesky, Facebook (wardparkerauthor), BookBub, Goodreads, and Pinterest, or check out his books at wardparker.com.

PARANORMAL BOOKS BY WARD PARKER

Freaky Florida Humorous Paranormal Novels
Snowbirds of Prey
Invasive Species
Fate Is a Witch
Gnome Coming
Going Batty
Dirty Old Manatee

Gazillions of Reptilians
Hangry as Hell (novella)
Books 1-3 Box Set

The Memory Guild Midlife Paranormal Mystery Thrillers

A Magic Touch (also available in audio)
The Psychic Touch (also available in audio)
A Wicked Touch (also available in audio)
A Haunting Touch
The Wizard's Touch
A Witchy Touch
A Faerie's Touch
The Goddess's Touch
The Vampire's Touch
An Angel's Touch
A Ghostly Touch (novella)
Books 1-3 Box Set (also available in audio)
Books 1-10 Compete Series Box Set

The Goddess's Daughter Urban Fantasy Trilogy

(Sequel to the Memory Guild Series.)
Of Envy and Empaths
Of Fear and Fae
Of Vampires and Valor

Monsters of Jellyfish Beach Paranormal Mystery Adventures

(Sequels to Freaky Florida)
The Golden Ghouls
Fiends With Benefits

Get Ogre Yourself
My Funny Frankenstein
Werewolf Art Thou?
In Sprite of Herself
Worms of Endearment